She knew he would do anything to help her, but she also knew it could cost him his life...

The single light in the room came to life, startling her. Her pulse spiked.

Max.

Embarrassment heated her face. He must've heard her scream. Great! He must think she was nothing but a sissy.

He stood at the door, wearing satin shorts with a suggestive caption that read *Down Under*. The sight would have made her smile. But then she looked up, met his perceptive green gaze. He looked so tense, muscles coiled tight, the skin on his face so taut as if it was being sucked against the bone. He didn't say a word, just strode forward and gathered her into his arms.

"Was it another nightmare, sweetheart?" His voice was dangerously quiet as he stroked back her hair and peered into her eyes.

Elena pressed her lips together as her words died down in her mouth. A hundred retorts flooded her brain, but she wanted none to make it past her lips. As much as she wanted to prove to him she wasn't a scared sissy, she knew *he* was in an even worse mood than her. She didn't dare push him. Besides, the perverted part of her was enjoying the skin-on-skin closeness of him. His warmth, the spicy Davidoff scent. She raised her arm to twine around his shoulders then stopped just in time before she made contact.

What the hell was she doing? This was wrong, on so many levels.

For Elizabeth Campbell, disguised as Elena Martin, life isn't about walking away from the man who had imprisoned her for half a decade. Not anymore. Now it's about running. It's about searching. It's about escape. When threats lurk around every corner, and all leads are dead ends, she turns to the one man she knows will help her.

Max Logan has loved Elizabeth all his life and had gone as far as committing a murder for her. Then she disappeared from his life. Now she's back. Not as Eli, his childhood friend, but as Elena Martin, his karate student. He knows she's in trouble and thinks he's prepared to do anything to help her. But when a string of weird accidents and mishaps begin to occur, Max can't help but wonder. Is Eli responsible for what's happening, or is she as innocent as she claims? How can he be sure? And how far is he prepared to go to find out?

KUDOS for *Redeem Me*

In *Redeem Me* by Elvi Joy, Elena lives in fear that her old life will find her. On the run from an abusive relationship, she begins taking self-defense martial arts lesson at a local dojo, run by her childhood sweetheart, Max. She knows he would help her, but she can't bring herself to trust him enough to tell him her problem. The monster she is running from is relentless, and she fears that, if he finds her, he will turn Max against her as he has everyone else. But the time is fast approaching when she may have no choice. The story is both moving and intense, a true romantic suspense, with emphasis on the suspense. If you are looking for a romance with a little more meat to it, this is the one for you. ~ *Taylor Jones, The Review Team of Taylor Jones & Regan Murphy*

Redeem Me by Elvi Joy is the story of a woman on the run. Elena Martin has changed her name, disguised herself, and built walls to keep anyone from getting too close. She is also taking martial arts, in hopes she can defend herself the next time her past catches up with her. But she hadn't counted on Max, the man who runs the dojo where she trains in martial arts. Max knew Elena when her name was Elizabeth, and he has loved her since he was a teenager. Now that she is back in life, he is determined to keep her. But Max has no idea what he is up against, and Elena is too afraid to tell him. This can only lead to disaster. *Redeem Me* is a first-class romantic thriller. Well written, intense, and poignant, the story highlights the much-too-common situation of women trapped in abusive relationships with no escape. A chilling tale that is all too real. Very well done. ~ *Regan Murphy, The Review Team of Taylor Jones & Regan Murphy*

REDEEM ME

Elvi Joy

A Black Opal Books Publication

Black Opal Books

BECAUSE SOME STORIES JUST HAVE TO BE TOLD

GENRE: ROMANTIC THRILLER/ROMANTIC SUSPENSE

REDEEM ME
Copyright © 2017 by Elvi Joy
Cover Design by Jackson Cover Designs
All cover art copyright © 2017
All Rights Reserved
Print ISBN: 978-1-626948-11-2

First Publication: NOVEMBER 2017

Published by Black Opal Books **http://www.blackopalbooks.com**

PROLOGUE

*I*n death, Jerry Sanders did not look so cocky. I knelt over him, searching his cornflower blue eyes for a veil of puzzlement. A small spark of recognition. Perplexity. But he disappointed me. There was nothing but frozen fear in his unblinking gaze.

I allowed myself a few moments to watch the blood congeal over the long gash at his right temple. Saw the flushed pink skin of his baby smooth face wax over. As my gaze traveled down his torso, his hands amused me. Curled into semi-rigid claws, they reminded me of Frankenstein.

I could have spent hours, if not days, watching the fascinating pool of blood under Jerry's neck and around the area where his penis had once hung proudly from his body. Boy, hacking off that particular bit of anatomy had given me the chills. But in the end, it was all worth it.

Down the hall, Shannon's house party was progressing at full throttle. The band he hired was doing a swell job of letting loose their ear-splitting Rock. If I were to step outside now, the air would be ripe with the sickly stench of cheap perfumes, booze, and sweat from undulating bodies. Heat would be intense on the small dance floor, the noise level bordering on insane. Jerry should have been there too, playing drums, flashing his surfer boy grin, making moves on unsuspecting girls. Too bad. The only moves he would be making now would be into my heavy-duty rubble sack, and from there to the woods behind the old cemetery.

I hadn't planned on killing him tonight. Next week, maybe. Or a month from now. He knew what was coming for him, and he had made no effort whatsoever to avoid me. A part of me grieved for Jerry. Even at this moment of death, he was still the most handsome man I'd ever seen. If it wasn't for his idle hope and bad fucking judgment, I would have left him alone. But the other part, the part which had enjoyed his panicked stare, kind of convinced me I did the right thing by him.

Why prolong the inevitable? He'd messed with the wrong woman. He touched something he wasn't supposed to. Obviously, he had to die.

CHAPTER 1

Fear was a strange entity. It could live and breathe inside you like an oily, insidious monster, overtaking each and every cell in your body until you were robbed of your ability to breathe, to think, to move. The fact that she was ensconced in her own bathroom, enjoying the warm water pelt against her skin, with no one around to interrupt her moments of peace hadn't mattered to her mind. It had to go into freeze-mode, allowing the dormant fear to take over, debilitate her until she was forced to slump down onto the wet tiles and pant.

Panic attack. That's all it was, a freaking panic attack. As if the complications in her life weren't enough, now her body was failing her.

No. She refused to be useless.

Frozen to the spot as she was, she tried to force her mind to work properly. She forced air through her lungs, grateful no one was around to witness these moments of weakness. She went to the martial arts lessons every other day. She made it a point to work out like crazy in the safety of her home, where no one was around to hear her swear at her nemesis. She was good at self-defense moves. And had plans to take up shooting lessons as soon as she could save up some pennies. She was doing all the right things. Then why couldn't she shake off this fear that crept up on her at the most inconvenient times?

You're where you wanted to be, she reminded herself. She now lived in the normal she'd always craved. She didn't know how long it would last, this reprieve, so every second of every day mattered. *There are no moments you aren't ready for.* Nothing was going to surprise her or shock her. She had no friends left, no family, no one close that could be hurt because of her stubbornness. She was free, and secure, something she should not take for granted.

Reaching out, she grabbed onto the shower knob and got to her feet. Once she turned off the shower, toweled, and bundled herself into the bulky bathrobe she had picked up from the op shop, she did her last round of checks, then curled on the single recliner in her living room. A car horn sounded outside the house. It was raining, beautiful rain that pelted down in fat droplets, drenching her minuscule garden, turning the small patch of turned earth to muddy slush. All sounds were softened. In the faint streetlight, that slithered in through the half-open curtain, her home with its meager furnishings looked serene and peaceful.

She occupied one of the duplex units, something she wouldn't have done if the other one hadn't been empty. This corner of Highgate wasn't highly populated, thanks to the row of abandoned warehouses that occupied one side of the street. The area gave off some intense creepy vibes. But it suited her just fine. She had wanted no nosy neighbors, no interruptions to her routine. The old man who lived two houses away from hers seemed to be a tougher recluse than her. Him and the crazy cat lady, at the corner block, made her look like a social butterfly. Safety was important to her, so she had seen to the security herself. Top of the range, police grade locks from Bunnings. Entry door alerts, and window chimes, she had ordered through eBay. A Wi-Fi baby monitor installed above the front door. She had done everything she could.

Still, the doubt lingered. Had she locked the doors properly? What if she'd unlocked them again, without realizing?

No. She had checked it. They were locked.

Are you sure?

Again. She had to start all over again.

Cursing, she started at the front door. Her body was freezing. Still, she made herself concentrate. *Just once more*, she told herself.

By the time she crawled back to the recliner, it was closer to three in the morning. Closing her eyes, she felt the ebb and flow of thoughts running through her brain, the rhythm of her breathing, the gradually diminishing weight on her chest. She willed her heart to slow down, her thoughts to grind to a halt. To channel them away from the source of her nightmares, she thought about Max. Sexy, hard-ass, Max Logan. A far cry from the seventeen-year-old kid with shoulder-length hair parted in the middle. She thought about how she was going to train herself not to be so jumpy around this rough, stubble-cheeked version of him. Because sooner or later, he was going to notice. She liked the dojo, loved that he was her trainer. It had taken weeks of research and hard work before she could find a place that she felt suited her needs. To change now would be a big inconvenience.

Having Max around was a pleasant bonus. When he trained her, his capable hands touched her to correct her posture or moves, all the thoughts inside her head just melted away. Every time she trained with him beside her, that jolt of surprise stayed with her for hours, like a happy buzz that refused to dissipate. She didn't dare investigate too deeply into that particular thought pattern. Doing so would be futile.

Max Logan was a distraction she couldn't afford at this point in her life. He was all authority, capability. And he had this annoying habit of looking at her, that made her feel as if he was looking right through to the back of her brain. Those pretty green eyes saw too much. She knew she looked different these days, walked different. Still, there was a slight chance of him recognizing her as the girl from his past. So far, he hadn't acknowledged her. He dealt with her as he dealt with all his other students—with utter calm. Occasionally, he'd become cranky, if they didn't deliver what he expected from them. So, she'd left it at that. Since she didn't have any intention of mixing and mingling with him outside the safety of the dojo, she decided she shouldn't worry much about him. She wouldn't let past familiarity impair her judgment. She'd done that once, and look where that landed her?

'Don't make me do this to you, Elena.'

A voice popped into her head—cultured, smooth, refined. It was the one she had worked her ass off to block, yet there it was, forcing the air to rush out of her lungs. Stupid meditation and deep breathing techniques. What good was that crap if it couldn't help her mind to compute beyond her past?

"Fuck you."

Nothing had changed, she realized. Nothing would. Sleep was out of the question now. The queasy thoughts were back—oily, insidious. She bolted upright, but a wave of dizziness forced her to sit, head between her knees. Guess she'd skipped her dinner again.

Breathe in.

Breathe out.

Minutes dragged on. Finally, she pushed herself out of the recliner and marched toward her small kitchenette, took out a carton of milk from the bar fridge, and gulped down the cold liquid without bothering to look for a glass. All the while, her mind seethed, her nerve endings sizzled with anger. Her next stop was the corner where she had set up her equipment. Riding on the residual fury, she grabbed her padded gloves.

"Fuck you, bastard," she said quietly then threw a knockout right hook.

☙ↄ☙ↄ

For the love of God, woman, just leave me alone.

Max Logan leaned against the backrest of the chair and half-heartedly listened to the blonde sitting across from him drone on about her precious offspring. He didn't want to do this, not today, not tomorrow. But it was not as if he had a choice. He couldn't just up and go. He was stuck. It was his job to listen to parental concerns, no matter how trivial they sounded, and come up with solutions. Some days, being the boss sucked.

"Max," the blonde whined, bringing his attention back to her. He knew she was attempting for marginal sophistication with her phony English accent, but all he could hear was a petulant voice going *blah-blah-blah...*

Mrs. Coleman, or Letitia as she preferred him to call her, leaned forward, the deep V of her dress allowing him more than a glimpse of her ample cleavage. Even with the square wooden table separating them, he could scent the Chanel cloud clinging to her as she went on and on about how, she thought, her little darling had the potential to be a wannabe-Bruce Lee.

"He's got skills. You know he does," she declared, batting her fake eyelashes at him.

Christ, take me now. Max had an insane urge to roll his eyes and snort at the rich bitch, possibly both at once. He didn't. Of course, he couldn't. This was his livelihood, for heaven's sake. He was not about to waste his breath telling this woman that he had seen drunken frat boys with better hand-foot coordination than her darling champ. The kid didn't have it in him. And Max could bet his ass that this weekly circus was not the kid's idea of fun.

"Eleven months, Max. My Rohan has been in the beginner level for eleven months. Surely you agree that he is ready for the next belt."

"We'll see during the next grading, Mrs. Coleman," he agreed almost absently, his eyes searching out the nearest exit. *Don't need this drama.*

Ignoring her hadn't worked so far. Pretending to be busy hadn't worked out well either. The woman was determined to wear him out. For almost a year now, she had been trying earnestly, week after week, month after month. Still, he had to give her points for her determination to get him into her bed. Under any other circumstances, he would have been flattered. But not this. Call him crazy, but he had a few standards when it came to women. Not many, but a few. And number one on that list: he didn't do married women. Period.

"Have you thought about the private lessons I mentioned last week, Max?" Her tone slipped from determined to sultry.

Did I just yawn? I probably did.

"Max?"

Huh? Ah, yes. The lessons. "We have an adult beginners class starting next week. Maybe—"

"Max, you know that won't work for me." Her hand with red painted fingernails reached across the space between them and covered his forearm, just as her pump-covered foot nudged his left inner thigh, making her point clear. *Crap!*

Max surged to his feet as if his ass was on fire and

stared at the woman's unapologetic gaze. He lost his last shred of patience in a hurry, waves of anger slithering through his armor, coating his mind. His hands balled into fists. "Mrs. Coleman, let's—let's talk about this later. The classes are about to start, and I've to go." *Before I do or say something really stupid.*

Letitia gave him a knowing smile. Then slowly unfolded her body from the chair and sashayed away, giving him a very fine view of her ass in a tight pink sheath. Jesus Christ. This was not the first time she had hit on him, and it wouldn't be the last. But this was the first time she had made such a bold move. What was with this woman? When would she get it through her thick head that he was not interested?

"Problem?" Jake, his second-in-command, said with a chuckle from behind as Max contemplated his options.

Exasperated, Max shrugged. "Nothing I can't handle."

Jake snorted. This thing with Mrs. Coleman was a standing joke between them. "What is it this week?"

Swiping a hand across the back of his neck, Max forced out a grin. "Private lessons."

Jake cocked a brow. "For the kid?"

"Nope. For the mom."

Jake looked over his shoulder at Letitia's retreating backside before turning back to face Max. "You know, if it ever gets too much, you can always send her my way. I don't mind giving her some private lessons."

No shit. Max shook his head. "Not happening, mate. Company policy number one: Don't mess around with the client."

"But—"

Max cut in before Jake could finish his sentence. "Or in this case, the client's mom."

Jake sighed as he dragged a hand through his messy

blond hair. "Man, we must have been drunk as skunks when we made that stupid-ass policy."

Now it was Max's turn to chuckle. "That's entirely possible, considering how we were at Paddy's Place."

Jake wasn't too far off the mark with his "'drunk as skunks"' crack. They had been drunk. Plastered. They had been out celebrating St. Patrick's Day in a small pub out in Northbridge, owned by a mutual friend. It was there—with the crazy crowd milling around the converted church's floor space, wearing green top hats and glittery green T-shirts, with the smell of Guinness thick in the air—that they made the decision to buy the old warehouse out in the burbs and turn it into a dojo. Man, for two guys who'd started off their friendship at the Outreach shelter in the inner-city neighborhood, that had been some kick-ass move on their parts.

Max whipped his phone out from where he had tucked it inside his gi jacket and checked the time. Another minute and they were good to go. He turned to Jake. "Do you want to take this one? I will do the next two sessions. I got some paperwork to catch up."

Jake nodded, although his expression told Max he would rather be anywhere else in the world than at the dojo. Now was not the time, but Max couldn't help but wonder if Jake was ever going to change. He loved Jake like a bro. *Scratch that.* Jake was his family. But the guy had no sense of responsibility. He was one of those guys who always came up with brilliant plans but fell short when it came to execution. If it was left up to Jake, the dojo would have shut down a month after they opened for business. Max could, if he wanted to, dump all the fault for Jake's behavior at Sarah's feet, Jake's ex-wife. A bad break-up often did that to a person. But that was not all of it. Max knew this. And Jake knew it too. But unless Jake was ready to see the error of his ways and pull his head out of the fucking sand, Max knew he would have to step in and pick up the slack.

"It's the accent, right? It has to be," Jake said as they walked toward the group of six-year-olds gathered at the center of the rectangular room, all clad in their white uniforms, their expressions ranging from curious to hopeful to downright bored. "I mean—we are both black belts. Same height. Same blond hair. Hell, I've been told I'm way hotter than you. Still, when you're around, the chicks dig you more than me. It has to be that damned Irish accent of yours."

Max laughed at his logic, turned to greet the kids, then froze.

A woman hurried in from the entrance to his left. Not any woman, the bane of his existence: Elena Martin. Max noticed she was wearing her signature black sweatpants and an oversized white gi top with the dojo emblem hand embroidered against her left shoulder, and then he looked up at her face. He wasn't sure if she stopped first, or it was him. All he knew was his feet were suddenly rooted to the floor. He felt Jake walk past him, heard him clap his hands twice to get the routine warm-ups started. Max couldn't move. It felt like an eternity, but it was probably only a few seconds. Six seconds tops. A gnawing, hungry feeling started off as a flicker and grew to a roaring blaze in his stomach.

Jake yelled out again, ordering the group to do ten ab crunches. Elena's eyes, he couldn't help but notice, again, were a startling gray. He'd always had a thing for gray eyes, especially those that had witnessed the worst the world had to offer. Okay, yes, it wasn't just her eyes that always screwed up the control of his emotions. If he were to step closer to her, she would smell good too. Sweet and spicy.

Hauntingly beautiful. Unbelievably sexy.

Case to the point: Totally off-limits.

The moment the point registered, he cursed. *Keep walking, moron.*

He started walking across the room again, and so did she. And as they passed each other, inches away, their gazes locked. The urge to touch her bombarded him, and he had to grit his teeth against it. He hated that she was the one to sever the connection first. It should have been him. He should have had the guts to look her straight into her eyes and dismiss her as if she was a fucking nobody. When he reached the small table where he had left the attendance register, he took a glance back. She was gone. Probably settled into one of the plastic chairs they had set up for parents who preferred to stay and watch the session. He didn't check.

His fingers were trembling as he reached for the register and flipped the pages one after the another. He hated that his breath was coming in ragged little gasps, and he couldn't fucking do anything about it.

Find your calming center. Feel nothing. Want nothing.

One of these days, he said to himself. One of these days he would convince himself that she meant nothing to him.

❧❦❧

Elena stood outside the dojo, waiting for the six-year-olds to stream out after their session. She liked watching them. Their expressions and boundless energy fascinated her. She had sketched them a few times, stampeding out in their white uniforms, their smiles bright. The work had always been quick, as she didn't want the parents to notice what she was doing and cause trouble.

"Hey, Elena."

She froze, her smile fading.

Jonathan!

Pasting a fake smile, she turned to greet Jonathan, with his Pantene ad glossy black hair and uptilted dark eyes. His gaze slid down her. "You look good. As always." He had a faint accent—Asian, she assumed. His expression, as usual, was openly gawking.

"Hi, Jonathan."

"Want to get a quick bite after lessons? I know a place next door," he said, touching her elbow.

This was his regular MO. No matter how many times she had turned him down in the past, he just kept on trying. She had to give him points for his determination. But she had no intention of taking him up on his offer.

"I can't. I'm busy." It sounded lame to her own ears.

"Come on, Elena." Jonathan flashed his brilliant smile at her again. He moved closer to her, his fingertips now covering her elbow. "One quick drink. That's all I'm asking."

Scowling, she moved her arm away from his touch. Sadly, the guy wasn't astute enough to know he was making her uncomfortable. He touched her again, her waist to be precise. Her thin layer of tolerance, for Jonathan, was worn through. But before she could knee him in the junk, over her head, a deep voice said, "Ms. Martin, could you please step into my office?"

Startled, both she and Jonathan turned. A tall body was suddenly right next to her, and white-clad arm shot out to herd her away from Jonathan the Casanova. To be honest, it wasn't just Max's sudden appearance that startled her, but his touch. All those damned butterflies she had read about, they took flight inside her stomach. She forced herself to nod at Jonathan out of politeness.

Max let the door close behind them. His office, she noticed, wasn't really an office. Just a cramped space with a wooden desk and two mismatched chairs. The lighting was poor and the red carpet underfoot threadbare. Ensconced in the silence of the small space, she didn't know what to say. Then he stepped around her, his movement bringing him so close that the quiet scent she had always associated with him drifted to her nose. She rubbed a fisted hand over her heart. Why now?

Max stood with his hip propped against his desk. Elena held his gaze, noting that his eyes were really the color of moss, not the sea green she had imagined. He was beautiful, in a totally masculine way. And intense. Maybe too intense.

This wouldn't do. She had to get out of here. She reached for the door handle and froze when his hand settled over hers. A shiver of awareness slid down her spine. Her insides started a slow waltz. He was hot. Literally. And when he stepped closer, his heat seeped into her pores. The boy she had known and teased were long gone. This was a man. Max Logan was a sleek weapon honed to perfection by years of training. And he would never be hers.

"Elizabeth, wait."

Desire shattering as if it had been hit with a sledgehammer, she angled her face up to stare at him. He knew. Goddammit. He knew.

She managed to extricate her hand. "You never said anything before."

He shrugged and stepped back, taking his heat with him. "What's the point? I figured you didn't want anyone to know."

She saw from his expression that he meant it, as if he really understood why she refused to acknowledge their connection. "I—it's difficult for me, Max." He didn't know how difficult. He would never know how happy she had been to find him here. After so many years of dreaming about him. But he wouldn't know.

"Hey, it's no big deal." Max's voice sliced through the nightmare of her memories. She looked up and saw a flicker of regret in eyes that never expressed much of anything. "I would probably have done the same thing in your situation."

Elena paused. She saw it on his face. The pain. The disappointment. It was at that moment she realized just how much his opinion mattered. And yet, she couldn't offer him an explanation. She met Max's gaze, tried to make him understand. But words were necessary for an explanation, and she didn't have any. So, she settled for what she had.

"Sorry," she said into the heavy silence.

His face softened for a second. Then the mask fell back in place. His eyes scanned her face. "Should I talk to Jonathan? I know he's bothering you. Mostly, he's harmless. But if—"

"What? No." She blinked away the burning in her eyes. "Thank you. But I can handle him."

His lips curved in a wry smile. "Oh, I know you can. I've seen you move. It's him I'm worried about."

She rolled her eyes.

"Well, we don't call you Pocket Xena for no reason."

There it was—a glimpse of her old Max. Playful, funny, Max.

"Hey, I'm not that small."

His gaze skimmed over her. "You're not very big either."

"I—" She stopped and snapped her mouth shut.

A sad expression, one that seemed totally at odds with his confident personality, flickered on his face.

They stared at each other for the longest time.

Back away. Leave, her conscience sat up and screamed. She stayed exactly where she was, her body a carnival of hormone rides, her head tilted up to meet him in the eyes.

He dragged a hand through his hair. "All right, then. I'll…I'll see you around?"

Something twisted in her heart. Pain? Regret? "It was good to…you know…talk to you," she murmured. Honestly, what else could she say?

A nod. "Likewise."

The words were chosen with care, as if he'd weighed them very carefully. The expression on his face damn near destroyed her, they carried such regret.

Elena stared at him, wishing she had the ability to read him. Deep in the back of her mind, she had a feeling that she had hurt him. Again. But it was better off this way. Her eyes dropped to the tip of the scar peeking out from under her sleeve. That was an outward reminder of who she was.

Once again, she glanced up. The sound of her resigned sigh made his eyes lock on hers, and she swallowed hard before she could help herself. For a painfully intense moment, he didn't move. Then his hand reached out as if to touch her face. She stared up at him, at the raw intensity of his eyes. Fingers hovered, not making contact. The world reduced to just the two of them: the chatter of kids, the whir of the air conditioner, the burden of her past—it all disappeared, along with her common sense.

Touch me, Max, just this once. Touch me as if I matter.

For once, she wanted the heat and strength of him. Dark embers low down in her gut flared to life as he shifted closer. She had no idea what they were doing, enclosed in his office, with his staff and students one wall away. But her body was coming alive in ways unknown to her. But she didn't rush him, she just waited. She was, she realized with a burst of shame, hoping he would do much more than just touch her. Her brain flipped into fifth gear at the heel of that thought, ordering her not to be stupid. Her hormones, however, had other ideas.

"Max?"

He lowered his eyelids and shook his head a fraction. A moment later, he dropped his arm.

Stepping away from her so suddenly that she gasped, he wrenched open the door and walked away from her.

Oh, this was bad.

CHAPTER 2

Paddy and Max were already at the pub when Jake walked in. He waved at Sean, the barman, for his regular vodka on rocks, before joining his friends. He liked what Paddy had done with his place. It was a good set up. Striped floorboards, dark beams, solid tables and killer waitresses in short black skirts. The big screen mounted on the wall was showing the rerun of AFL finals, and the place was filled up like ants in a sugar bowl. As usual, Paddy had reserved them the "best" seats, four tub chairs stuffed into a corner right next to the loo. There were a couple of black leather settings by a log-effect fire. But would the asshole reserve those for his best mates? Hell no!

"You look like shit," Paddy said as Jake dropped into a chair opposite to Max. "Still hung over?"

"Fuck off. I haven't had a drop all day," Jake said cautiously. He avoided looking at Max. The jerk would know. He always knew.

Paddy snorted. "Yeah, right! And my name is Rumpelstiltskin." He turned to Max. "So, as I was saying, I'm gonna ask her out."

"Who is the unlucky chick?"

"Gail. She's his new chef," Max offered helpfully.

Jake grinned. "Fucking the help. Nice one, mate.

You do realize she must be good with knives." He mimicked cutting his throat.

Paddy shrugged and cracked his knuckles, showing off the impressive dragon tattoo curled around his left elbow. "Ha, ha, very funny. Gail's nothing like Kendra."

"Kendra..." Max sighed as he took a sip of his lager. "Oh, man. She was something, wasn't she? Those legs—wow."

Paddy leaned back in his chair and locked his fingers behind his head. His gray eyes twinkled with mischief. "Oh, yeah. Legs, ass, hair. She had the full package. I'd really thought she was the one."

Jake snorted and reached for the bowl of nachos. "Yup. Right until the point where she tried to chop off your junk with the kitchen scissors."

"Hey. How was I supposed to know when she said threesome, she meant me, her, and her little battery-operated friend? So, I made a small mistake. Boo-fucking-hoo. It's not as if I paid some hooker to break up my marriage, like someone here did." He aimed a sly look at Jake.

Embrace the awkward silence, folks!

It took his brain a few seconds to catch on. When it did, Jake noticed his voice had gone thick, and his hands were trembling like an old lady. "Low blow, bro. Really low."

Paddy shrugged and looked away.

"Dude, what the hell is wrong with you?" Max gave Paddy a stern look. Sarah was a subject they never discussed, at least not in Jake's presence.

Paddy gave Max an innocent look. "What?"

Max shook his head, giving him another evil eye. Jake heard the subtext: *What the fuck are you doing, bro?*

Paddy's face turned ruddy, as his temper rose. "What did I say? Why am I the bad guy here? He was the one who threw away a perfectly good woman for sidewalk Sally."

Jake had no clue what got his feet moving, but before he knew it, he was on Paddy, forearm pressed against the son of bitch's neck. "You've no idea. You hear me, you bastard. You've no idea why I did what I did."

Shock had Paddy freezing for a moment, then his hands were on Jake's forearm, trying to loosen the iron clamp.

The heel of a hand plowed down, connecting hard with Jake's elbow. Max! Jake's hands were still trembling when he crumpled and folded back into his seat, and his breath was coming fast and short. But, by God, he did not regret what he almost did.

"What the fuck, bro?" Paddy's face was pale as wax as he straightened the collar of his silk shirt. His eyes weren't molten but worried as he stared at Jake. "What the fuck?"

Max reached for his shoulder. "Jake, buddy."

But Jake shook him off. He had to get out of there.

He was aware of the weight of stares as he rushed out of the pub, onto the busy Lake street. For a moment, he just stood there, looking up and down the road. Rubbing his chest, he wanted another drink so badly, he was shaking from it.

He had fucked up. Big time.

He owed Paddy an apology.

He looked back at the pub, saw Max at the entrance, his expression pensive.

Sorry would have to wait.

Jake started walking toward the car park. He was about halfway to his car, just past the parking meter, and then realized someone was behind him on the path. It was so dark, he couldn't see properly, but he could feel eyes on him. He looked around but saw no one. Instincts, honed by years of training, told him his follower was hiding behind the large soup kitchen truck at the far right end. He pulled out his cell phone, tapped in 000, and had his thumb hovering above the call button. Just in case hell decided to break loose.

He waited, then waited some more. But there was no movement. Shrugging, he turned and walked three steps, then whirled around quickly.

At first, all he saw a dark figure, dressed in all black, sprinting across the carpark. It nearly gave him a heart attack. What the hell? A mugger? Some weirdo? Or someone he had pissed off in the past.

Against all caution, he took off after the fast-moving figure.

Something fell at his feet. A hat.

And then he saw her. It had to be a *her*, because you didn't often see that kind of long blonde hair on dudes. Something told him he knew this particular blonde. But his brain refused to connect the dots for him.

Then she was gone. Vanished like mist under the morning sun.

Was he tripping? Maybe Max had a point about his little drinking problem.

Horns blasted irritably, jerking him out of his thoughts. He saw he was blocking the pay-point machine. Lifting both hands in apology, he dragged his feet forward. He found his car, yanked open his door and slumped into the driver seat.

"Who the hell are you, blondie?" he murmured, and simply sat staring at the graffiti-covered wall before him.

જ્જ્જ

When Elena finished her work at Leederville and headed back to the shelter where she had parked her bike, there was not much traffic around. Granted, it was a little after twelve o'clock at midnight and Loftus street didn't have many places open at this time of the night. There was an Asian restaurant, a pizza joint, and a seedy bar named Screamers. Usually, there were people crowding the sidewalk near Screamers and cop cars roaming the area looking for drunk and disorderly jerks. Tonight, there was nothing but a few homeless guys sleeping under the Remembrance statue, and a lone taxi parked a few yards away from the bar.

Dammit. She shouldn't have stayed this late. But that was what happened when you let your creativity run forth crazy. The wall mural she had been commissioned to finish was one for a remodeled children's park—all gliding fairies, dreamy-eyed unicorns, and bright rainbows. She enjoyed the work, the solitude, and the hardships that came with it. Guy, the artist who had hired her to be his sidekick in this project, wasn't much into conversation. He just needed to get the job done before the Parks Manager from the city council came yapping about missing deadlines. She was grateful Guy hadn't asked for a reference. Or things could have gotten iffy. The money he gave her wasn't all that great, but he paid in cash and that mattered. She supposed she could have taken a job as a check-out chick or a bar waitress. But both required people skills and a tax file number. And those were the areas where Elena desperately failed.

As she reached the shelter, without warning, the overhead LED light winked out. Seriously? The government was cutting corners by rationing streetlights these days?

Feeling uneasy, she unlocked her bike, jammed her backpack into the carrier at front and began riding toward the busy Oxford Street. Unfortunately, the roads in this suburb were narrower than standard width and vehicles in all sizes occupied the road shoulders. She stuck to the main road as much as possible, grateful her hybrid bike was much forgiving when it came to little rocks, unsteady gravel, or sudden potholes.

As she crossed into Thomas Road, she felt a little paranoid. The silence was only broken by the wind rustling through the acacia trees lining the road, racket of crickets chirping, an occasional dog barking. She was jolted out of her thoughts when a car joined her on the road, it's head lights illuminating the street ahead of her. Elena frowned and looked over her shoulder. A dark red sedan had eased into the road only about ten yards behind her, the pace of the vehicle too sedate for her comfort. Something about the outline of the driver struck her odd, sparking her survival instincts.

Without warning, the driver behind her increased his speed. Not wanting to give the guy a chance to run her off the road, Elena quickly released her pedals, swerved onto the sidewalk, and took a sharp left to Lincoln Street.

Her heart began beating faster when the car followed her. Elena picked up her pace, panic surging like a wave inside her as the car sped up too. Glancing around, she realized there was no one in the vicinity, and considering the time, there wasn't going to be anyone around for a while. Her best bet was to try and lose herself among a crowd.

Just as she came up to the end of Thomas Road and took a left to Blythe Avenue, she saw the flashing lights of Astor Theater standing tall and proud to her right. If there was a show in progress, she was in luck. She could ditch her bike, barge into the theater, and cry for help. As if reading her intention, the driver of the sedan sped up and drove onto the otherwise empty verge. They were now moving parallel, she on the sidewalk, and the car close enough to ram her into the seven-foot concrete wall.

The wind slapped her face, nearly shaving her hair off in its power. Her eyes shot to her right and zeroed in on the driver. No, at the rate she was speeding, she couldn't see much. Only a flash of a figure clad in black. But what she saw was enough to confirm that she had run out of luck. Time slowed to a crawl, and images of her past flickered through her brain. Once again, she was being hunted. Anger that had been reeled in with months of practice burst forth, giving her a jolt of much-needed adrenaline.

"No—no—*no*—" she gasped.

With mounting terror, she realized that her hands and calves were cramping up, her heart trying to break out of her ribcage. If the attacker didn't get her first, an angina attack would probably take her down.

She heard a heavy crunch on gravel to her right and saw that her attacker had pulled sudden brakes to avoid hitting a sidewalk gumtree. *Oh, thank you, city council for planting trees at the most inconvenient spots.* A few moments, but that was all she needed. Wheels spinning, sending up a shower of grit, she did a quick U-turn and raced in the direction of the theater. With a grating of gears, the car roared backward, the tail hitting a skip bin behind. With a sickening thud, the skip bin fell over, spilling white goods and panels of cracked gyprock onto the sidewalk.

Click. Click. Click.

Lights came on in the nearby row of Victorian Terrace houses. A few doors opened. A dog raced through the opened door and began barking.

Shit.

Her attacker pulled onto the road and raced in the opposite direction. Applying pressure on her legs, Elena brought the bike to a standstill in one of the few empty spots left in Astor carpark. As she got down off her bike and slumped onto the warm asphalt, her thighs were burning. She told her shaking hands to be still, but they refused to listen to reason as she wrapped her arms around her knees. Fear of returning to her previous life screamed at her conscience: get up and run. She was so close to the finish line.

Full panic mode subsided with time. Tears came, as she knew they would. But instead of feeling relief, all she felt was anger.

CHAPTER 3

Elena gazed after Max with exasperation. The damned man had bested her again. Granted, she wasn't in top shape today. Because most of the past week she'd spent either hunting for a place to live off the grid, chatting to adoption agents who had no intention of helping her, or in the libraries where she'd utilized the free net to browse around for a job that paid in cash. Today, thank the Gods she didn't believe in anymore, she finished two out of her three quests. She was now the proud tenant of a small unit in Balga, a suburb best described as dodgy. And, as of eight this morning, she had a job at the twenty-four-hour veggie shop, cling wrapping vegetables.

"You're not paying attention, Elena." Green eyes watched her without blinking.

She angled her head. "I downed you twice today."

"Pure luck. Won't happen again."

She snorted and brought her hand down in a quick chopping motion. He dodged. They darted around each other, eyes locked in full on battle. Max must be one hundred or one twenty pounds heavier than her. It meant he had a massive advantage. The only way she would get the upper hand was if she caught him off guard. She attempted to go for his neck, while he swept his feet out and brought her down. Her ass hit the mat, her pride bruised, along with her tailbone.

Max looked down at her from his greater height. "Your head is not in the game."

She winced when she tried to get vertical on her own. *Jesus, take me now.*

He grinned, reaching out to haul her up. "That must have hurt."

"Shut up." She slowly climbed to her feet. Without his help, thank you very much.

Christ, that hurt.

Grinning, he turned to watch Jake sparring with an older man, both experienced. They were both quick on their feet. It was a thing of beauty to watch them move and spar. She should really take down some notes. Max turned back to her, lips twitching with the beginning of a teasing grin. "Hey, better luck next time."

Elena ignored the comment. She leaned in and dropped her voice. "I'll get you, you know."

"You think so?" Max's eyes twinkled. He cocked his head to one side. "Another round?"

Stepping out to the side of the mat, she grabbed her bottle of water and took a large gulp. All the while she pretended to consider his words. Then she struck. Before he could move into position, she dived and rolled, kicking his feet out from under him.

Boom! He went down.

Holy hell, it really worked.

"Shit," he sputtered, shoving his palm into the mats for traction.

Everyone in the dojo turned to look at them as she stood over him and cocked her brow. Max seemed as surprised as everyone else. But he recovered fast. Elena's heart was in her throat within ten seconds when Max uncoiled and rolled, bringing her with him. It was like being in a movie clip that ran fast forward. One minute she was enjoying her win, the next she was getting squashed like a bug. His breathing was labored as he fought for air. "I don't believe I've ever taught you that move."

She narrowed her gaze. "I'm improvising as I go."

"Are you now?"

Max's face shimmered gold as the sheen of sweat glimmered under the halogen lights. Her fingers itched to stroke his cheek, run them through his neatly clipped hair. Unnerved by that thought, she shifted. That was when she felt his not-so-little something digging into her thigh. Instantly, her body responded. Lust, razor-sharp, forked through her veins like lightning bolts. As he took a deep, sawing breath, it was clear that he had caught her reaction.

What the hell are you doing? Get up, she told herself, *get up and run.*

He didn't move. She doubted if he was even breathing. A trembling began in her legs, and arms, ending in her chest. They stared then stared some more, until someone coughed, breaking their connection.

Looking around, she found that the entire class had gone silent, no sounds of combat or inane chatter.

She really should get up and hightail it out of here.

Except she didn't want to move. For a moment, all sorts of fantasies winged through her head: Max kissing her, surging into her. Ropes. Cuffs. Blinds.

Dammit. No.

This couldn't be happening to her. She refused to associate Max with the tainted shit in her brain. He was pure, clean. She was—

Regret had her pushing against Max's chest.

There was an awkward moment when Max looked into her eyes—as if he expected her to scream and make a show, some female histrionics, at least a few indignant

F-bombs. All she did was blink. The hand that wasn't cupping her shoulder slammed into the mat beside her hip, and he lifted his upper body off of her. "Sorry about that. Are you okay?"

The concern, combined with his delicious proximity, threatened the dam that was holding back her yo-yo emotions. But she kept that wall, along with a small modicum of dignity, in place for fear of losing it in front of the peanut gallery.

"I'm fine."

Jake put his face in her line of sight. "You need a hand, buddy?"

Max grunted, took the hand his friend offered and got to his feet. Putting on her best blank face, she followed his suit. *See, all good.* It's not as if she was turned on or anything. Noooo…No way. She was good. Everything was great. Fucking great.

Dammit.

"I think you need to take a break," she heard Jake tell Max.

"What? No."

"I mean it."

Max swung his gaze to the clock on the left wall. "We still have ten minutes to go."

Jake moved closer to Max. "I'm not worried about the session time, and you know it." At that, his gaze dropped down.

Max followed Jake's gaze then swore just as quick. "Excuse me," he murmured to her, adjusting his gi jacket.

Then he was marching across the hall for the exit. He hit the door so hard it flew open and struck the wall with a loud jar.

Jake swung his head around and fixed her with a pointed look. She thought he was trying to tell her something. But what? What was his problem?

He glared at the gathered crowd and barked, "The show's over. Get back to your positions."

ᘛᘚ

Enjoying the warm, early March weather, Max decided to go for a run in Hyde Park instead of hitting the gym. Jake insisted on tagging along, which in itself was a miracle. The guy looked like something the cat had dragged out of the trashcan. His hair was messy, his eyes bloodshot. Dark stubble covered his cheeks.

They ran for about two' miles, then took a breather when they reached the hour-glass-shaped lake at the far end of the park. Right on cue, two women from their self-defense classes approached them, in an effort to get their phone numbers. Max, not having the patience to deal with those giggling airheads, gave them a polite smile and asked them to redirect any queries to the email provided on their website. Jake, on the other hand, had no intention to pass up the opportunity. Flipping on his default-man-whore settings switch, he flirted with them. Eye gleaming with feminine calculation, they flirted right back.

Gag me, please.

At first, Max had thought that Jake flirted because he couldn't help himself, like it was an ingrained trait. But these days, Max knew the truth. Jake didn't enjoy the flirting, he fucking hated the whole mating dance routine. Still, he did it, without fail. To prove a point to his lovely ex. At the end of the day, he was determined not to let her feelings matter.

Throaty feminine laughter brought Max back to the present. Max observed the scene before him with a frown. From the looks of it, Jake was in his element. The women stood close to him, hands glued on their hips, giv-

ing him appropriate *hmmmss* and *aaaahhhs,* their attention fully focused on Jake as he told them some funny
story about a guy from the dojo. As Max watched, one
went as far as rubbing Jake's biceps like a cat in heat.

*Must control myself. Shouldn't push these idiots into
the pond.*

"Dude, we're running late," Max pointed out.

Blue eyes grim, his friend shot him a disgusted look.
"Come on, mate, we're in the middle of something here."

"Sorry, bro. Gotta go." He flashed the women a polite smile then started jogging back the direction they
came.

Jake caught up with him a few minutes later.

Max flashed his friend a sideways glance. "Flirting
with students? Classy."

"Feeling jelly, bro?"

Max slowed to a halt. "Jelly?"

"It's the latest cool term for jealous. You should look
it up."

Max snorted. "Do me a favor and stay away from the
clients. Or we'll have to close shop."

As he pulled out the cooler bottle from his backpack
and gulped down the water, Jake dropped the bomb.

"So…speaking of clients…What's with you and that
Martin chick?"

Just act normal, Max told himself as he took another
chug. *Like nothing's going on.* He had to find his vocab
fast. "I don't know what you mean," he choked out wea-
rily, irritated his usually lax best mate was questioning
him.

"Yesterday at the dojo—"

"That was an accident, Jake. Accidents happen."

Jake shrugged. "If you say so."

"Nothing's going on. She's our client. Other than
that, I don't know much about the woman." That much

was true. Sort of. He didn't know adult Elizabeth. Or Elena, as she called herself these days. As for the rest— that would remain in his head.

Jake shook his head. "Something's going on between you two. I just know it. You're acting too weird when she's around."

Max swallowed, Jake's words surprising the hell out of him. He didn't know what to tell Jake. Until he figured out what the hell was going on, it was better to keep all the fucking thoughts locked up deep inside him.

It was his own goddamn fault, though. Why couldn't he just mess around with the women who didn't seem to have any compunction at throwing themselves at him, and just forget the one he could never have in this life-time?

Because she intrigued you from the beginning and you're still crazy about her.

She was a respectable woman, widowed-from what he'd heard through the grapevine, and he was a not-so-regular Joe with a sketchy past. And yet, according to his cock and gray matter, she was still his fucking true love. There was a recipe for disaster. Right there.

Jake cocked his head, staring at Max. "You—" He stopped, his mouth falling open. "Fuck me, Max, you want her."

Max tried to keep his expression neutral, bracing himself for the inevitable. Silence stretched between them, harsher than a scream. Jake just gaped at Max with his fish-out-of-water expression for God knew how long.

"Nothing's going on okay? She's is our client. That is all there is to it."

Jake dragged one hand through hair and pointed the other accusingly. "You said no messing around with cli-ents."

Hearing that, Max took a deep breath, anger burning

like a hot poker in his gut. He leveled a diamond-hard glare at his mate. "Would you just shut the hell up? I am not messing around with anyone."

Jake looked skeptical. "You sure about that? Because I'm telling you, man, I have seen you stare at that woman. And I have seen her stare at you when she thinks no one's looking. You know I'm not the brightest tool in the toolbox on most days. So, if I have noticed then…We need to keep up the good reputation, man." He left his words hanging.

Yes, Jake, you're a good one to talk.

Max let his fingers tighten to fist against his thigh. "Jake, I'm not messing around with her. I swear. Sure, she's easy to look at. Hell, I admit I have looked at her once or twice. But that's all there is to it. The dojo means so much to me. You know I won't do anything to jeopardize that. You just have to trust me on this."

Even as he said the words, he felt a pang of something sharp in his chest. But he shoved that feeling deep down, to a place where he could pretend it never existed.

CHAPTER 4

*M*ax Logan's iPad gave me a lot of information. Scrolling through, I figured out the names of his dentist, his best mates, the kind of music he liked, take out joints he preferred, even the last woman he had taken out on a date—which by the calendar entry, happened seven months ago.

Hmmm...it fascinated me to think how everyone turned over their lives to modern gizmos these days. Dinner dates, birthdays, shopping lists—even freaking laundry days—it was all in there. Whatever happened to spontaneity and creativity? How could one let a palm-sized machine direct their whole life for them? As if using brain power wasn't cool enough for this funk-rock generation.

Christ, I was one of them. Yet, most days I felt so ancient. So far removed from the life milling around me. Like an island in the—

I caught myself before I waded into philosophical territory. Some days it was hard for me to contain my thoughts. It was better to let them run free like a loose-snow avalanche. Today was not that day. I had things to do, plans to make, and people to see. Swallowing my regret, I replaced the cell phone on the charger cradle next to his bed. One mission accomplished, onto my next.

I wandered around his house, all the while touching something here, sniffing something there, and taking perverse pleasure in the fact that he had no idea of my whereabouts. He would return home tonight, drink from the bottle I had drunk, wash with the soap I had used, and he wouldn't ever know I had encroached into his private space. How freaking cool was that?

One thing ticked me off, though: For a guy, Max Logan was exceptionally neat. Unlike the normal members of his species, he didn't leave his dirty socks on his bedroom floor, or half empty pizza boxes on his coffee table. They were no science experiment projects going on with the milk cartons in his fridge. Everything expired had been thrown out. Freshly done laundry was folded and put away in the small linen cupboard in his postage-stamp-sized laundry. His kitchen sink—spotless. Bathroom—a claustrophobic's worst nightmare, but otherwise neat.

Oh, well. At least there was an X-box and a giant-ass recliner placed smack dab in the middle of his living area. Or I would have had serious doubts about him.

I wandered through to the second bedroom he used as an office and ran my finger on the cheap Ikea desk that occupied the maximum space. Again. Dust free. A few of the photos left on the desk caught my interest. Random photos of him with a few other dudes, snapped in Bali or some other holiday hotspots. But none with a girl. The one with him in his karate uniform, his face impassive and gaze hard, sent a chill down my spine. I would have to be careful if I decided to mess around with this guy. For one, I doubted he would be as easy as the others to take out. Two, my gut said that he was trouble.

Feeling rather pissed at the sudden onset of doubt in my powers, I reached for the laptop he had left open. An old Dell one. Again—no password protection. I shook my *head at his stupidity. Either the guy was living in la-la land, or he was giving far too much credit in his skills to look after himself. Look how easy it was for me to break into his house and paw through his stuff? And I was no pro at this game. I did what I had to from time to time, but I didn't make it a habit of breaking and entering into stranger's homes.*

I browsed through the different files, most based on karate, some on healthy eating. A lot of spreadsheets centered on the dojo. A yawn was working its way through my throat when I clicked on the file named "personal."

Scanned copies of his certificates, soft copies of his mortgage contracts, and—TA-DA.

I didn't know if I felt happy or sad when a photo came up and filled the screen. The face that stared back at me was one I held very dear to my heart. I slumped, closed my eyes, let my head fall back, and tried to take it all in.

"You're not one to forget, are you, Max?"

Disappointed, I sighed, closed the browser, and slammed the laptop shut.

So, it was decided.

Max Logan had to die.

ᏋᎶᏋᎶ

Someone had been in his house, Max was sure of it. Something felt off the moment he stepped inside, through his garage, and threw his car keys into the small leaf-shaped plastic tray on the kitchen bench. For one, the tray wasn't where he had left it. It had been moved—far enough for him to take notice. The gnawing feeling only got worse when he saw that someone had gone through his unopened mail and other junk he had left in there to deal with later.

The possibility that intruder might still be in the house made him hold his breath, listen for the faintest signs of life. Nothing but the hum of his refrigerator. Still, he grabbed a knife out of his butcher block and padded quietly into his living room. Moonlight streamed through the floor-to-ceiling windows and spilled across the floor in elongated rectangles. He groped for the wall, to his left, and flipped on light switches as he went. As far as he could tell, everything was in place—TV, laptop, loose cash in the beer mug above the microwave.

He edged toward the bedroom, keeping an eye on the half-open laundry door. After a preparatory deep breath, he flung open his bedroom door, adrenaline rushing, his body poised to attack whoever might jump out of the darkness.

"Dammit." He was starting to suspect he was crazy. There was nobody out here but him. The bedroom was empty, bed made, drapes half-open, fly screen in place.

Still, the window at the far-left corner conflicted him. Had he left that window open when he left this morning? He often did that. But it had been raining last night, and he remembered pulling open the curtains to check if any of the windows were open.

He did a quick one-eighty and stalked back to the living room, scanning his possessions as he went. X-box, Sony music system, trophies...What about that book he left on the couch last night? He had been too lazy to hunt down a bookmark, so he had left the book face down on the armrest before he went to bed. How did it end up on his coffee table?

Nothing made sense.

He took a deep breath, rolled his shoulders, told himself to relax. Maybe he was getting paranoid.

Then he walked into his office and proved himself wrong.

His laptop—he never shut his laptop, something Jake had pointed out like a million times. '*You're going to wreck it if you leave the lid up, you idiot.*' Now his laptop lay on his desk, shut, angled slightly to the left. And the pictures on his desk—why the fuck would a thief touch his goddamn pictures? Unless the jerk was planning a trip to Thailand and needed some pointers.

Tingling in anticipation and trepidation, Max pulled out his desk chair and fired up his laptop. On the first glance, everything seemed untouched. He wasn't exactly a pro when it came to computers. He knew the basics to get by. Had picked up enough Excel skills out of necessity. So, he wasn't exactly sure what he was looking for. In the end, more to satisfy his curiosity than anything else, he clicked a few keys and brought up his history.

"Fuck." He lifted a hand, dragged it through his hair.

There it was, the damned evidence that someone had accessed his documents that morning.

"Fuck. Fuck."

The possibilities drove him near-crazy. He quickly logged into his bank account and checked the account balance. If somebody had hacked into his laptop in the morning, they would have had plenty of time to pull out the money by now. He expected the worst—a complete wipeout—then sighed in relief when he saw that hacker hadn't bothered with his nest egg.

That did, however, leave a question: What the hell did the son of a bitch want from him? If not his money, if not his valuables, then what?

ᶜᵔᵓᶜᵔᵓ

After weeks of gray overcast skies, the rain finally decided to show up. As Jake drove back from the barbeque at Paddy's place, the houses lining the streets wavered in the downpour, their windows warm with lights. Thoughts spun around his head as he drove with automatic precision.

Going to the get together this afternoon had been a stupid mistake. He had forgotten how viciously loyal some women can be. He had taken great pains to avoid talking to Annabel, Sarah's twin. His plan had been to show up and say a "hi" to everyone, then quickly melt away, go upstairs to Paddy's man cave, and have a beer or two. But the small garden had been too crowded with people talking animatedly one over the other. His plans didn't work out quite as well as he'd hoped. Before he knew it, he was facing Annabel. She was wearing a baggy black top and tight jeans, and she looked the way Sarah always did: happy, bubbly. His first mistake was that he had tried to overcome the potential awkwardness by starting a friendly chat with her. His second was letting her acid-coated words seep into his skin and worm its way into his brain.

Fuck!

He went home with a head crowded with thoughts about Sarah. Her smile, her scent, her taste. He had done the right thing by letting her go, hadn't he?

He thought about her as he changed into his sweatpants and a ratty green jumper. Then he thought some more as he went to the kitchen and slapped together a tuna sandwich.

As he methodically chewed his way through his dinner, Jake felt everything around him was disjointed, skewed. His home didn't feel like his home anymore. He kept seeing Sarah's face when they were happy together, and love seemed to pour out of her, making him feel secure.

Growing up on the streets had taught him that he had to throw the first punch and throw it quickly. He had applied the same motto to his marriage. He'd thrown Sarah out before she did the honors.

At that moment, he so badly wanted not to have to blame himself for the mess that was his life. He just wanted someone to reassure him that he had done the right thing.

Pushing his plate away, Jake stood and walked to his bedroom. He opened the built-in wardrobe, questions going through his head like a loop. He began pushing aside the clothes and suit bags and quilt covers. By the time he had half emptied his wardrobe, he began cursing.

When Sarah walked out with her stuff, she had left behind a red leather bag. There were items in there which were too painful for him, so he had shoved them deep into the wardrobe to deal with later. Items that included their wedding CD, a collection of their honeymoon photos, a white Valentine's Day gift bear, and the satin nightie she had worn on their wedding night. Most precious of all, there was a small velvet box holding her engagement ring.

The bag was missing.

Jake shoved aside the clothes, lifted shoe boxes, yanked out the coat hangers, and threw out the cardboard boxes with his books. Then frantic with worry, he pulled everything out, dumping them on the floor, and on his bed.

It really was gone.

He dropped his ass onto the carpet and sat staring at the empty space inside the wardrobe. Was he losing his mind? Had he misplaced the bag somewhere? Alcohol was dulling his edges, making his mind all fuzzy. But he had never thought he would be losing his marbles in the process. Was that what was happening here?

He slammed a palm on the floor and lifted himself up. As he moved, his eye caught on something. A lock of long, blonde hair wedged in the crack between the open wardrobe door and the lower hinge.

Had someone been in his house? Over and over, the question whirled through his brain, in useless circles. Desperately, he tried to collect his thoughts. Then for no particular reason, the image of Elena Martin slammed into his head.

There was something about that woman that got on his nerves.

Nah, he was just being paranoid. More to the immediate point, what was he going to do now?

He walked to the dining room and grabbed the phone he had left charging on the table.

"Max?"

"Jake? What's up?" There was loud music in the background, and Paddy's voice calling something. It made Jake feel left out, alone. He had told Max he was leaving because he had a headache, and instead he was hyperventilating in his home, thinking his blonde stalker had broken into his house. Pathetic.

"Jake? You there?"

"I—ah—have you seen my wedding CD?"

There was silence. "Wedding CD?"

"Yeah. I had it in this red bag in my room. Now it's gone."

"Hang on a sec." There was a soft whoosh then silence, as if Max had moved out of the party to someplace quiet. "I haven't seen your CD. Is everything all right?"

Sweat ran down from Jake's forehead. "Yes. No. I mean, everything's all right. Kind of. But—There is this long blonde hair."

"Mate, you're not making any sense. What blonde hair? Have you been drinking again?"

"No. I think I am being—I mean, maybe not. But—"

He gave up trying to explain everything. The possibility of him going crazy was starting to seem real even to him. And anyway, it was bloody tiring.

There was a pause at the other end. "I'll come over. Just give me twenty minutes."

Jake took a deep breath. Then he clutched his phone. "No. Forget I called. I—I'm going to bed. See you tomorrow."

He hung up.

CHAPTER 5

*A*nger burned in my chest as Max cocked his head and smiled at the woman in her pricey suit across the road. The man whore. He didn't know how valuable the item he held in his possession was, or he didn't care. Not like me.

I ached to go to him, plant my fist in his perfect nose, rearrange that handsome face and ridiculously straight white teeth. But doing so would be a mistake. The stakes were high. I couldn't afford mistakes.

Max glanced my way, his green eyes scanning, assessing. Smart, I had to give him that. I worked to keep my face full of false boredom, fought not to yank away the wig jammed on my head. Appearances were important. Details and meticulous planning were important. To any casual onlooker, I should appear as nothing more than a bored parent waiting to pick up their child after the lessons.

The woman in the pricey suit, a born flirt, grinned and walked away to her snazzy little Audi. Max waited for a beat, did a swift about turn, and went back the way he came.

His fighter's body and killer smile tempted me to go after him like a hound after a blood trail. I could already imagine him in my bed, his limbs tied up, his lips begging for mercy. And that one moment when his fear would morph into utter defeat.

My face trembled with the urge to grin, but I knew it would look out of place. So, I drummed my fingers on the steering wheel. And waited.

When the time came, Max Logan wouldn't know what hit him.

⌘⌘⌘

Elena slipped out of the dojo fifteen minutes before the lesson was over. She could have waited till the end, but that meant giving Jonathan the dumbass, another chance to ask her out on a date. The guy was nothing but persistent. He just didn't seem the kind to take no for an answer. And he had, for some reason, determined he was going to date her. *As if!*

Stepping out into the carpark, she did a quick three-sixty, scanned the parking lot, the rain-washed glow of security lights. Nothing seemed out of place. An early March wind wound its way down, freshening the air. The evening sky was a dark blue smattered with purple-orange clouds. The night-blooming jasmine, lining wall behind her, was in full bloom. She saw the beauty of stark white against black. But the sight did not melt the cold icing encasing her heart. Her mind was full of thoughts, plans.

She lurked at the side of the building, odd caution keeping her from crossing the parking lot to her bike. At some point, she would have to get a car. Bikes were handy for quick getaways. She could easily slip into thick crowds if it came to that, but they had serious limitations.

She looked to her left, then right, before worming her way around a green trash can. Her gaze scanned her sur-roundings, always looking for trouble. Something moved in the shadows to her right. She froze then quickly crouched behind a salvation army collection bin. After fifteen minutes of waiting in the dark, she decided to take her chances.

Nobody was watching her, for God's sake! It was her paranoid bitchy self making her twitchy. She should—

It happened so fast.

"Give me your purse, dollface."

A man materialized in front of her, jumping out of dark so fast, she just froze. He was tall, way taller than her. His figure all rangy and lean in the black sweatshirt and sweatpants he wore. Add the black ski mask to the picture, things weren't looking up for her.

"You don' wanna mess with me, darlin'," he rasped, down under accent rolling off his tongue like thick tar.

Swallowing hard, she opened the side zip of her backpack, took out her purse. It had all but seventy dollars in it. The guy grabbed the purse, jammed it into his back pocket.

"Gimme your bag," he demanded.

"Th—those are my certificates. Pl—please. Let me keep them."

The guy seemed to ponder this for a moment, then he shrugged. "Fine. Keep it. Now come with me."

What. The. Hell? "Wh—what?"

He flashed a gap-toothed smile. "My boss got plans for you, honeybun."

Fuck! This must be the guy who had followed her the other night.

Without warning, the guy whipped out a knife, the blade glinting silver in the streetlight as he waved it under her nose. Nausea rose hotly in her mouth. Where the hell was he taking her? She shot a quick look at the dojo. The classes should be done any minute now. All she had to do was stall him a bit.

As if reading her intentions, the guy grabbed her wrist and tugged her forward. "Come on, bitch. Walk," he repeated, tipping his chin toward a battered up red sedan parked at the far end. The car park was separated from a decrepit laundromat by a graffiti-covered concrete wall. If he got her there, he could drag her into his car, or even into the laundromat through one of its shattered side windows, and no one would hear a peep.

Anxiety crowded her head. But as usual, the fog lifted quickly, leaving a spark of anger behind. The still functioning part of her brain urged her to run back to the dojo, cry out for help. Maybe she should scratch the jerk's eyes out, kick him where it counted. *Do something, Elena. Anything.* She should switch off, shape a plan. Move. Attack.

"Walk. I don't have all day." He was getting impatient. His beady eyes scanned the door to the dojo once then zeroed in back on her face.

Plans. She needed plans to get out of this.

To make certain that she knew he meant business, the human trash grabbed her hand and twisted her forefinger back. At the first crunch, she gasped, the pain catapulting her from confusion to fury. *The son of a bitch will pay for this.* As her system rebooted, she shut off the part of her brain that wanted to whine, "it's not fair," and "not again." It was happening, and she had to deal with it.

She dug in her heels. The bastard who held her was quick on reflexes. He spun her around and clapped a meaty palm on her mouth, silencing her screams as he dragged her to his car. Acting on instincts honed by months of hiding, she grabbed on to his forearm, brought her right arm up, and used the heel of her hand to smash against his nose. Startled, he jerked back. The knife slipped out of his grip and fell to the ground with a clatter. Then he cursed, grabbed her hair, and threw her face first onto the asphalt. Sharp, loose gravel pierced into her palms and cheek. He was on her within two seconds, sitting astride her buttocks, his heavyweight nearly crushing her innards.

"Come quietly, bitch, or I'll snap your neck," he rasped into her ear, his palm closing around her throat, cutting off her air supply.

Fury surged through her veins like a flood, her chest burned with impotent rage. Against the asphalt, her hands balled into fists. In her mind, she rewound and fast forwarded through Max and Jake's lessons. She saw the moves in her head, calculated, then reacted. She flopped her face back onto the asphalt as if she had had a sudden dizzy spell, not caring about the gravel biting into her skin.

That's right, you jerk. I'm playing possum.

Her stillness seemed to have startled her assailant. He got off her. Rising to his full height, he hooked a booted foot under her and flipped her over onto her back.

Her body reacted all on its own. She kicked up, her left foot catching the guy on his kneecap. The force sent him tumbling backward, completely off balance, his arms grabbing thin air.

His head met the asphalt with a satisfying crunch. Elena scrambled to her feet and kicked a cracking blow to her attacker's groin. He screamed. There, that must have hurt.

The door to the dojo opened ahead. Jonathan stepped out first, laughing at something Max said. They were quickly followed by rest of the class. She felt more than saw Max's gaze zeroing in on her like a sniper's target.

Her attacker staggered to his feet. He looked at the open door of dojo then mumbled something like, "Stupid bitch," before breaking into a jerky jog toward his car.

Her heartbeat drummed inside her chest as she

watched the bastard pull his door shut, move the gear-shift, and punch the gas. Gray smoke boiled from his tires as they left rubber on the asphalt.

She saw dimly that people were gathering, running toward her, asking each other what had happened.

"Damn, damn, damn," she whispered.

She passed a palm over her face, and it came away wet. Blood. No wonder her face stung like a bitch. She knew she must look a sight. She had to get out of there. The last thing she wanted was to bring attention to her-self. She did a crisp about turn and took three steps for-ward before she felt a heavy hand clamp on her shoulder, arresting her movement. *Dammit.*

She turned, saw Max's face—stony, sans expression. Without a word, he picked up her backpack from the ground, turned to her, and took her face in both his hands. Every cell on alert, she stood frozen as he studied her face.

"You're hurt."

She nodded.

Jonathan asked something, so did Jake. But she couldn't hear anything beyond the blood thundering in her ears. Max paid no attention to them either. His atten-tion was fully focused on her. This was a nightmare, a dream come true, hell on earth.

The feelings, what they meant, they scared the hell out of her.

"Who was he?"

"I—I don't know. A mugger, I guess."

Someone inhaled sharply. The fine muscles under the surface tensed as Max clenched his jaw.

"Mate, should I call the police?" It was Jake.

The question had the effect of a cattle prod. She jumped back, forcing Max to drop his arms. "No. No po-lice. I just—I just want to go home."

"But, Elena—"

"Please, Jake. I don't want any more drama tonight. I'm tired. I'll file a report tomorrow."

"She's bleeding. She needs a doctor." It was Jonathan.

Thanks, Sherlock!

"No. No doctor. Seriously, I'm okay. I think it looks worse than it feels."

She smoothed back her hair, ignoring the pain coursing down her hand. With a little clarity that came after the pain, she knew something. The stupid finger was either broken or dislocated. So much for her training. Look how easily a guy had overpowered her. He had slipped right under her radar. She would have to up her training. Change tactics. Allocate money she didn't have to buy pain meds.

Max stepped forward. "You need a doctor, Elena. Just to be on the safe side."

"It's after hours, Max. Royal Perth hospital will be your best bet," someone chipped in.

Max turned to her. "RPH, it is. I'll drive you to the doctor and take you to your home. Where you parked?"

Most of her nerves tangled up. "I—I didn't bring my car today. I—I came on my bike."

When he gave her a look that said he was seriously pissed by her choice of transport, she quickly added, "I'll be okay. I'll leave my bike here and catch a bus. I really don't need a doctor."

"Yes, you do. Your face is a mess."

"There is no reason to make a fuss ab—"

"Then don't talk. Just listen to what I say."

"You're making a big deal out of nothing."

"I'll let the doctors decide that."

"I said I don't need a doctor and that's it, *Mr. Logan.*"

His eyes bored into hers. When he spoke, his words were measured. "I said I'll drive you, *Ms. Martin*. This happened while you were leaving *my* dojo. We've got a duty of care to our clients. So—" Max snapped his mouth shut.

In the ensuing silence, she realized everybody around was staring at them with identical amused looks on their faces.

Crap.

For someone dead set on laying low, she was doing a fantastic job, wasn't she? She opened her mouth, but found no suitable excuses lined up on her tongue. "Ah…okay." The fingers of her good hand curled and uncurled over the strap of her backpack as her thoughts raced. She would have to convince Max to drop her off at her house, somehow, because no way could she let him take her to a hospital. Hospital meant records, Medicare card check, insurance check. No way.

In casual dismissal, he turned to Jake. "Jake, can you lock up, mate?"

Jake stared at Elena's face then into Max's face. Something—a silent communication—passed between them. Then Jake shrugged. "Yeah. Okay."

Max turned to Jonathan. "Stay with her. I'm going to bring my car around," he said and sprinted off to employee's car park at the side of the building.

Jonathan looked at her oddly. "*Sensei* Max looks pissed, doesn't he?"

She attempted a joke. "Must be worried about compensation claims."

Jonathan shook his head. "He likes you, Elena."

Far out!

She flushed. He watched her struggle to say the right words. Struggle and fail spectacularly. "Uh…I'm not sure…"

Jonathan smiled in the cold moonlight. "Never had a chance, did I?"

For a split second, Elena was tempted to feel sorry for him, say the right words to soothe his wounded ego. She'd never actually hated Jonathan. She just never appreciated his not-so-subtle advances. Opening her mouth, Elena—

Remembered the monster in her life.

It was better this way.

芝芝

As Elena sat in the relatively comfortable leather seat of his three-year-old Nissan pickup, she was so quiet Max suspected she had fallen asleep. Part of it was his own fault. He was so damn mad at her. After he'd brought the car around and deposited her inside, she had refused to play nice. He had asked her, with as much politeness as he could muster, how she was feeling.

Her answer: "Fine."

Her ice-queen response had grated on his nerves, but he'd ruthlessly controlled his fury, telling himself that she was probably in shock. Had to give her some slack.

He had then proceeded to ask her if she wanted a drink of water, and her response: "Cut the concerned routine, Max, and just drop me off at the nearest bus stop. Jeez, I'm not going to sue your dojo if that's what you're worried about."

At that point, he had pretty much lost all of his good manners. *Fuck that*, he had thought. If she wanted a fight, he would give her one. So, he did what any man with an ounce of red blood running through his system would have done. He'd steered the car to the shoulder and kicked the fucking brake so hard, she almost went through the windshield. Thank heavens for seatbelts.

"What the hell is your problem?" He resented like hell that his blood pressure was high and every time he looked at her battered face, his heart just jumped up and lodged in his throat. Her lips were swollen, and there was a purple bruise, the size of a fifty-cent coin on her left cheek. It had nearly killed him when he saw her in that parking lot tonight, her face a bloodied mess. To top it all off, her prissy attitude—he wasn't having any of it.

"You. You're my problem."

His molars sure got a workout. "Don't push me, Eli. Not now," he muttered when she started to argue with him.

"You were the one who pushed me into going with you. Did I ask for your help? I didn't."

"You just don't know when to quit, do you?"

"Hey, if you're hellbent on playing the white knight, just do me a favor and drop me off at my place. Or if you got a problem with my attitude, then just dump me here, and I'll find a way back home."

He hadn't meant to reach out and touch her. He really hadn't. But somehow his arm snaked forward, and he grabbed her right wrist.

With as much control as he could spare, he gave her arm a shake. "I know what you're doing, Eli. But it's not going to work. You always got mouthy when you're scared. I can see it hasn't changed much. But trust me, sweetheart. There's nothing to worry about. The doctors will take good care of you. And I'll be right there with you."

Her gray stare made a trip around the interior of his car and ended up on his face. She hardly breathed. "I won't go to a hospital." He heard the determination, wondered about it for a split second, but anger surged to the forefront, erasing other thoughts like waves lapping the shore.

"The hell, you won't."

For a long moment, she didn't respond. Then she shot him a single look. Her stare blank. He really wanted to shake her.

"What?" he snapped, allowing her to see his fear and anger.

"Let go of me," she whispered. She didn't look scared anymore. She looked broken and vulnerable. God, he hated that look on her.

He dropped his hold and placed both his hands on the steering wheel. He didn't understand her fear. He knew there was something there that needed some digging. However, his first concern was to get her to the hospital. Later, he would worry about all those little details that didn't add up about Elizabeth Campbell *aka* Elena Martin.

Muttering a few choice words, he started the ignition. She reacted so fast, all he could do was say, *Holy shit.* With one hand, she disengaged her seat belt, while the other shoved open the car door. Max hadn't been smart enough to gauge her reaction. Or he would have thought about putting the child lock on before depositing her ass into the passenger seat. By the time he switched off the ignition, drove the gearstick into Park, and rushed after her, she had gained at least twenty feet on him. But he got her, at the cost of a mini heart attack and burning leg muscles.

She struggled, as he had known she would. But what he hadn't anticipated was her pearly whites taking a chunk out of his arm. Goddammit, that hurt like a bitch, but he kept dragging her backward.

Thank Christ, there weren't any patrol cars nearby. Or he would have to explain what he was doing on the roadside, manhandling a woman, and trying to bundle her up into his car in the middle of the night. Maybe his dream about getting a police mugshot taken at the precinct was finally coming true.

"Elizabeth," he whisper-yelled. "Stop making a scene and get your ass in the car. We're going to the doctor, whether you like it or not."

She tried kicking him on his shin and scored once. Hell, if she could do that, maybe she really didn't need a doctor.

"Let go. You can't make me."

Yes, he spun her around and shook her. Shook her until her small frame jerked like a puppet on a string. And he wasn't all too proud of it. "Wanna bet?"

Her eyes popped wide then narrowed with aggression. Max felt an old surge of adrenaline through his veins, the tightening anticipation he got whenever he sparred with Elizabeth. He missed their banter more than he'd realized.

"Take your hands off me."

"I will, if you shut up and get into the car."

She went curiously still. *Oh, please.* He knew she was up to something. When all was said and done, this crazy girl hadn't changed much. Maybe morphed from crazy to super crazy, and yeah, he shouldn't forget about her killer curves. But—

She swallowed hard. "Max, I think I'm going to throw up."

"Nice try, darling. You're still going."

She paled like a sheet of paper, and he saw her throat work hard to keep something down. "What, seriously?"

She elbowed him in his guts and leaned over the curved concrete barrier. "Yes, you ass. Seriously."

She started weaving on her feet, and that was when Max decided he had enough of her bullshit. He wrapped his arms around her small waist and lifted her off the ground. His intention was to take her to the safety of his car and hightail it to the nearest available clinic. Probably not the brightest idea he'd had in his life.

Thanks to his Heimlich grip around her belly, his Nike caught the worst of the stream of her upchuck.

Fan-fucking-fantastic.

When it was over, she groaned and curled over his forearm. His own stomach rolled in sympathy. But he managed to gently lower her feet onto the ground and slightly bend her at a forward angle before the second bout began. Thankfully they were just dry-heaves. He held her through it all, rubbing her back, crooning non-sense that he wasn't even sure she was listening to. He sucked at the nursing shit, but he held up because he was all she had at the moment.

He stroked back her hair from her face, taking care not to bother her swollen left cheek. "Better?"

She nodded. "Thanks. I feel much better now."

She swatted at his arm, and he got the hint. He let go of her waist and watched her drop to her knees. He squat-ted down beside her, in all his vomit-covered glory.

"Sorry about your..." She waved in the direction of his feet.

"Don't worry about it."

"Sorry anyway."

"Baby, you really need a doctor."

She shook her head vehemently. "No, I don't. I can't go to a hospital, Max. Please don't push me on this mat-ter."

"But—"

She looked him directly in the eye. "I've got my rea-sons. Please, I'm begging you."

Whatever he saw in the depths of her gray gaze con-vinced him not to push the matter any further. So, he just nodded. "Fine. No doctors. Have it your way."

She gave him a weak smile. "Oh, I will. You know I always do."

Exasperated, he scanned the area around them. The highway was mostly empty. Still, the roadside shoulder wasn't the best place for her right now. She needed a bed, pain meds, a shower. Besides, the wind was picking up. The forecast earlier had predicted rain in the evening. "Will you let me take you to your place?"

Her weak smile vanished as if he'd flipped a switch on her circuit breaker. Apprehension clouded her gray eyes. Still, when she put her hand up for him to grasp and haul her up, her features were composed into a blank mask. "Thanks, *Sensei*. Appreciate it."

CHAPTER 6

Max stood in the light rain and stared at the small, shabby unit that was Elena Martin's home. The yellow paint was peeling, the roof over the front porch needed a desperate facelift. Her garden consisted of a weed-choked yard and a few pots of scraggly roses. The fly screen on her door sported several large holes. Someone, possibly Elena, had tried to patch up the holes with duct tape. On the plus side, the place looked so dilapidated, any self-respecting thief would think twice before he attempted a break-in.

"This is it," said Eli, as she dug into her backpack for her keys.

He saw her wince and knew her hand was giving her far more trouble than she had led him to believe.

"It's small, and nothing fancy," she warned, and Max had to bite back the retort at the tip of his tongue. She was embarrassed, he could see it now. The Eli he knew had always been proud. *The Campbells are too proud for their own good,* his father used to say. Which brought him back to his initial worry. What was she doing here, living in a house like this, in a suburb as creepy as Highgate? And what's with the double padlocks and door alarms? He could understand the security angle, but what if there was more to it?

The house was neat, rooms small. The living area was separated from the kitchen with a half wall. The floors were cracked terracotta tiles, clean, but in need of regrouting. Silently, he scanned the rooms, trying to imagine Eli living in such a cramped space. The utilities were basic—a rolled up sleeping bag, and butt-ugly recliner, which he felt must have come with the house. She had set up a small gym corner—a couple of two-kilo weights, four water bottles filled with sand, and an overstuffed European pillowcase. He gathered it must be her punching bag.

First, her change of name and looks, then her unreasonable fear of hospitals, and now this. She was in trouble—that much he knew. Just how fucked up was her situation? His stomach clenched in anger at the thought.

Almost before he knew what he was about to say, he blurted. "What's the fuck's going on, Eli?"

To her credit, she didn't falter. Slowly, she folded her arms. "What makes you think something's wrong, Mr. Logan?"

Mr. Logan? He would get to that shortly.

"For starters, why are you living in this shithole?" He waved his hand in a dismissive gesture across her gym corner.

It took her a minute. "Are you insulting my home?" she finally growled.

"Yes, I am. And I've been meaning to ask you. What's with your stupid hair? You look like a beach bunny."

She rounded on him. "Fuck you. I'll color my hair however I want," she said explosively then froze as if an invisible hand had struck her. She took two steps backward. Her breath began to come out short and fast. "I'm sorry. I'm sorry. I shouldn't have said that. I—you make me feel and say things that I—"

She stopped, then stared at the tightly clasped fingers on her good hand. It would have been easier if she had finished her sentence. The cliff-hanger she left hanging between them allowed him time to hope, to think, to remember.

He went and stood over her. Common sense warned him not to concentrate on the spicy scent of the woman before him. Think about the pile of paperwork waiting for him back home, the thriller he was planning to watch with Paddy, even the stink of the vomit now covering his two hundred dollar runners.

Instead, slowly, deliberately, he inhaled. When that wasn't enough, he let his knuckles drag down the soft skin of her swollen cheek. "What do I make you feel, Eli?"

She took a hurried step back. Since he had expected that move from her, he didn't feel particularly disappointed. "Please," she said. "It's been a long day. I'm not really thinking. What I meant to say was…ah…Thank you for everything you did tonight." There was an edge of panic in her voice.

Interesting. That was a brush off if he'd ever heard one. He took a step forward, and forced himself to be patient when she took one back. "Elizabeth, look at me."

He saw her struggle to regain her composure. Her hands trembled as she wiped the moisture off the divot above her swollen upper lip. "I…ah…guess I'll see you next week at the dojo."

He smiled and laid a hand over hers. "Are you asking me to get the hell out?"

She pulled away. "I was trying to be polite," she gritted out. "Take the hint."

To hell with it! He took a step forward. "Eli, baby, I know you're in trouble."

For a moment, she froze. Fear flickered in her eyes.

Then she blinked, and all expression leached from her face. "I don't know what you're saying, Max." Words fell like lead bullets from her mouth.

Oh, hell. She was in *trouble*. "Honey—"

She held up her left hand to cut him off as he approached. "Goodnight, Max, Thank you for the ride home."

He switched his tone to sound more coaxing. "Eli, baby, I can help you. Whatever it is, you can count on me. You know that, right?"

She swallowed and turned even whiter. Max started to reach for her again, but she pulled away and busied herself by walking to the small kitchen and filling the old kettle with water from the sink tap. That done, she put the kettle on to boil then got a loaf of bread and a jar of vegemite from a cupboard above the sink. "I've got an early start tomorrow."

She was dismissing him.

Max looked around, then back at her face. He wouldn't get anything out of her, not tonight anyway.

"I…ah…I'll see you on Tuesday?"

"Sure," she said, her voice steady.

But Max had done his fair share of running to know that she was about to do a runner on him. She probably wouldn't ever set her foot in the dojo again.

Nothing he said would make a difference to her. He saw that in the stubborn thrust of her chin. The way she held herself up.

Eli was determined to run and to take her demons with her. And he would be right on her heels.

ꙮꙮ

"Haven't seen her for a few days," the crusty old biddy said, taking another puff from her cancer stick.

"Pretty thing like her, living in that dingy street, I always worried about her, you know?"

Yeah, right. Totally believable.

"So Ele—I mean, Grace didn't tell you where she was going?" That was another monkey wrench in the works. She was Gracy Hampton to this lady. It meant, she had either forged papers for getting a rental or the landlady hadn't been very particular about her reference checks. He bet it was the latter.

"Nah. Just dropped her house keys and this month's rent money in my post-box. Not even a post-it note."

Gone. She was just gone. Vanished like smoke. The thought repeated in Max's mind, like a skipping CD, as he thanked the lady and walked to his car.

He had known she would run, and he'd been prepared to follow her, but he had underestimated her speed. His idea had been to give her some space, then come back in the morning and talk her into opening up to him. That failed, he'd been prepared to stake out. But she'd slipped right through his fingers. If she had returned her keys, it meant that Eli wasn't planning on returning. She was hiding, staying completely off the grid, and making sure no one knew her whereabouts.

What was she up to? Where was she?

∽∾∽

Maria Alvaro lived in a beige and gray weatherboard house with a peeling front door and neatly trimmed front lawn. There was an old swing set placed on one edge of the lawn, a faded red slide next to it. A kid-friendly wind chime, with Pooh bears and Tiggers all tangled up, hung from the porch. A small walker blocked the wooden side gate.

Still, the detail that Elena found almost strangely

comforting was the pair of scuffed baby shoes left on the welcome mat.

Elena hadn't let herself think what she was doing, and, more importantly, she had imagined Maria Alvaro would not be home. Her source had led her to believe that Maria and her husband worked day shifts at the local Coles Supermarket while Maria's elderly mother held the fort. So, she almost let out a gasp when the door opened, and a plump young woman in black leggings and a green T-shirt with an orange streak of dried up tomato sauce along her left shoulder filled the entrance.

"Yes?" Her voice had a slight lilt, confirming her Italian ancestry.

"Maria?"

Wariness flickered in those pretty eyes. "That would be me."

Elena didn't allow fear into her words, but it was there, just under the surface. With each passing moment, it was becoming clearer that kidnapping wasn't her forte. "I'm sorry to bother you. But could I have a quick word with you?"

Maria's expression didn't change, but Elena could hear a new apprehension in her voice. "What is this about?"

A child wailed from somewhere inside the house. Nausea swept over Elena.

"I...ah...it's about your baby."

"Baby?" Maria frowned, fingering the small cross that hung from a thin silver chain around her neck. "What about my baby?"

Elena hadn't thought about what she could say that would actually convince the woman she was legit and not a head case. Yet, the lies rolled off her tongue easily enough. "I'm Serena. I run the Kinder Joy Montessori school on Tara Street. You must have seen it, the yellow building with Sesame street picture on the walls?"

Maria frowned. "I...I'm not sure..."

The baby wailed harder, his desperate cries growing louder. Elena took a small step forward. "This won't take long. I would like to talk to you about our new school and how it would benefit little kids like your son."

Maria looked torn. Clearly, she didn't trust the stranger. But she was too polite to slam the door shut in a neatly dressed woman's face.

The screams turned up another notch. Decision made, Maria gave her a small apologetic smile. "Ah...maybe some other time. I need to check on my son."

She started to push the door shut, but Elena put her hand against it. "This won't take long."

Maria's eyes rounded with unmasked fear. "Please leave," she said curtly, her hand trying to grope the security chain.

Oh, crap. This wasn't going very well. She hated that she had to do this, but Elena knew she really had no other choice.

She reached into the large tote she hung on her left shoulder and pulled out the hunting knife she had sharpened that morning for this very purpose. She pointed the business end at the woman, praying the woman would behave. Helplessness made people throw rational thoughts out the window. Survival mode, combined with strong maternal instincts, the woman would resort to just about anything. Elena knew she would have to be extremely cautious.

"Step back," she growled, injecting enough threat into her voice. She pushed against the door, and Maria pushed back.

But Elena was stronger, so the door swung inward. Gulping, her eyes darting around like a butterfly caught in a net, Maria stumbled back. "Please. Don't hurt me. I'll give you all the money I got."

Elena shut the door behind her. "Where's your mother? The one that looks after the child while you're at work?"

Maria froze. Elena could almost see the wheels turning inside the poor woman's head, trying to fit all the pieces together. "Church—She's gone to church."

Elena had no clue if the woman was telling the truth or bluffing, but it was too late to worry about that. "Walk." She pressed the tip of the blade at the woman's nape, letting her feel the cold of the metal against her flushed skin.

It was bright in the cluttered living room. The television was on, where Wiggles danced around merrily to some song about a big red car. There was a playpen set up in one corner, but there was no baby in it. A white plastic high chair, with a messy bib and an orange smeared sippy cup on its tray, stood close to the four-seater dining table. The air was ripe with the scents of baby lotion and dirty nappies.

"Go pick up your baby," Elena told the woman.

The woman half turned and looked over her shoulder, her expression pleading. Tears fell freely from her pretty green eyes. "Please. Don't hurt my child. I'll give you all my money."

"Get the baby," Elena said again, staring at the woman with mild contempt.

Sobbing, the woman walked to what Elena presumed was a nursery. *A few more minutes*, Elena told herself, *then it will be all over*.

Maria stopped and swung her gaze around the room, as if mentally trying on various objects as weapons: the telephone, a vase, remote for the TV, pedestal fan.

"Don't get any ideas. You won't like the results."

Elena emphasized the point by dragging the blade along her open palm, letting the woman see how creative she could get if things got out of hand.

A small sob escaped Maria's throat as she resumed walking. Elena followed, trying not to stare at her reflection in the three, identical ceiling-to-floor mirrors on the wall to her left.

God, when had she turned into this a cold, ruthless bitch?

The room Maria entered was dark, sun block curtains drawn. Elena stood at the threshold, not wanting to violate such a sacred space with her tainted presence. "Bring the baby to me."

She watched Maria hurry to the child and lift the screaming baby out of the baby cot. She pressed his face against her chest and sobbed. Her words were quiet, soothing. "Hush...Mama's here, sweetie. Mama's here."

That was all it took. The baby quietened. He reached out with one pudgy hand and grabbed Maria's breast. Elena watched fascinated when Maria disengaged the baby's hold and shifted him to the swell of her right hip.

Keeping the blade pointed toward Maria, Elena blindly searched for the light switch. She found it on her second swipe.

The lights came on, illuminating Maria and her baby.

Elena stared at the baby.

The baby with the shock of dark, almost black hair. The baby with uptilted brown eyes that told her in no-nonsense terms of his wonderful Asian heritage. The baby whom she was now positive did not belong to her.

Disappointment came as a giant tsunami wave. But she did not waste time to reflect on it. She did a crisp about turn and ran. She ran until her lungs burned and her thighs quivered with exhaustion. She ran until her heart jolted around inside her ribcage like a loose stone. She ran until tears clogged her eyes and she couldn't see where she was going. Finally, she collapsed face first on the damp earth covered with soggy gum leaves.

CHAPTER 7

The sky was pearl gray when Max walked to the Leederville children's park and wandered around the semi-deserted paths in the light sprinkle of rain. He didn't really know where else to look for Eli. Really, she could be anywhere. So far, he'd checked out the local libraries, coffee shops in HighGate, food courts in major shopping malls. There was no sign of her. He would have had better luck catching smoke. Then he remembered what he had once overheard Jonathan say, something about Eli painting a wall mural for a park. So here he was, subtly checking out hobos sitting on parking benches, their worldly possessions stuffed into Coles shopping trolleys, and women jogging in their tight sportswear, wearing matching fitbands and iPods. He felt like a peeping Tom.

The thing, he realized fifteen minutes into his sleuthing, was when you're looking for someone, you kind of see them everywhere. He thought he saw a woman in black T-shirt out of the corner of one eye, but when he turned around, it was a young Mum running for shelter with her baby in a buggy.

He saw someone in the distance and was sure it was Elena on her bike. But when he got closer, it was an old man in a waterproof black Parka. He looked up and gave

Max an open-mouthed smile, showing off a silver capped tooth.

Three weeks! It had been three damn weeks since he had any decent sleep. Three weeks were more than enough time for a woman to get into unimaginable trouble. There were so many sick fucks out there, and there were so many ways to destroy a woman. Max fought to control his regret, his fear, his rage. He needed to keep a level head if he was going to find her.

You've earned street smarts the hard way, Logan. Start putting them to good use.

He walked for another hour, telling himself he needn't worry. She was a big girl. She had been taking care of herself long before he came into the picture. Then he remembered her big gray eyes from fourteen years ago, staring up at him in unblinking horror.

I don't know what to do, Max. Help me. He was trying to rape me. Please…please…

She had felt small in his arms, fragile and soft. Holding her close, he had felt her heart pound, smelt her fear, almost tasted her panic.

Dammit. Where the hell was she?

In the end, wet and mad, he went back to collect his car from the parking lot of Screamers. He reversed and drove out of the parking lot then had to wait at the exit to merge with the traffic. Up ahead, the bus stop was crowded with school kids in red jumpers and green uniforms. As he watched, the Transperth bus arrived, hissing as the wheels went through a huge puddle, splashing water right on a woman hurrying up the sidewalk.

Eli!

Chin low, backpack slung over one shoulder, a woolly cap over her long wet curls, she couldn't look more vulnerable and desolate if she tried. A part of him wanted to gather her close, the rest of him simply wanted to strangle her. He didn't know how he did what he did, but between the one second that it took for his heart to beat and next, he was winding down the window, craning his head out, and screaming her name.

Through the rain that pounded on the pavement like arrows, he saw her freeze. Then she was lifting her chin, rain pouring down her face, and looking up. He saw the moment when recognition flashed. Then she was shaking her head.

People filed their way in, tagging their smart cards as they went. A tall, gangly boy moved across to block her view from him. Trying to rein in his temper, Max jerked out his seatbelt, pushed open his door, and stepped out, all the while ignoring the honks from irate drivers behind him. In the few minutes it took his gaze to focus, she got on the bus, and sat, one seat from the rear door of the bus.

"Eli," he screamed again as the doors closed and the bus slid away, taking Eli with it, leaving him in the rain.

But she stayed with him every second of every day.

ᴄ⁄ᴈᴄ⁄ᴈ

Elena walked home slowly. Above her, the dark clouds were segregating again, like an army regrouping before the battle. She could feel the cold seeping into her bones, hear her booted feet splashing in the puddles. People moved past her, rushing in their hurry to get home, their bodies a blur through her tear-filled eyes. She had a sudden impulse to drop onto her knees and scream until her throat was scraped raw.

Max! It was all right when she didn't have to see him, smell him, or touch him. Out of sight, out of mind. But now…She remembered the anguish on his face as he stood in the rain, the utter disbelief as the bus pulled away. She had hurt him—again.

Max. She nearly said that aloud, but then the image disappeared as quickly as it appeared, and she shook her head, letting tears fall, feeling grateful. It was for the best.

Or was it?

Of course, it wasn't. But she had no other choice. Some women were cut out for white picket fences and two-point-five kids. She was destined for fake IDs, seedy motels, dark alleys, and a life on the run.

Hell of a life, Eli.

She was at the end of her list. Just three more to cross off. Then…she didn't know what she would do if both the leads turned out to be dead ends. Tomorrow she would check out the townhouse in Kensington. The agent who tipped her off told her that the family who adopted the baby boy was a couple in their late forties. The husband worked for an IT company, and wife was a music teacher for the local girls-only college. They were lovely people, with a solid ten-year marriage behind them. The only thing missing from their perfect life had been a child. Sammy—that's what they had named him—now filled that gap. All that would be lost in a split second if she got her hands on that child.

Inside her home, she looked at the post-it note in her hand and peered at the address marked with red felt-tip pen, she felt the surge of hope that had kept her going for the past few months. It had taken her weeks to track down the agent, cajole her into giving up confidential information, and the strain was getting to her. Elena looked around her, for a moment, seeing things as if viewing them through the eyes of a stranger. She lived in a hovel, her living space littered with post-it notes, blobs of blu-tac, city maps, and hastily scribbled words written on pages torn from a notebook. She looked, lived, and walked like a hobo—her mind brimming with thoughts that made her feel like an obsessive stalker. She didn't eat well, didn't sleep well. If she slept, her dreams were abstract to her, filled with shadows and light, of kind green eyes—of ropes hanging from ceilings.

She made tea, took it to the small scarred table by the window that looked out on to the street. She had regrets, plenty of them. But the name that topped the list these days was Max Logan.

Max, with his beautiful smile and gentle touch. He didn't have to spell it out for her to know that he wanted her. Sex, she heard, if done properly could be pleasant. And sex with Max, she knew it would be phenomenal. Because she wanted him. Despite all the ugliness, all the filth, she still wanted him. Which was precisely why she was going to have to be more cautious where he was concerned. He was sort of her Achilles heel. She hated that she had put him in a spot where he now felt obliged to look out for her. She missed him, yet she couldn't imagine being with him. It occurred to her, like a blow to her gut, that perhaps she might never see him again. A pity. Or a blessing. Depended on the way one chose to look. If things worked out the way she planned, she would be on her way to Adelaide by tomorrow evening.

She lifted her cup to her lips. She started to take a sip but then stopped. She had heard something. A small scuttling sound. A faint scrape. She stayed completely still, threw a quick look around her room. The scraping sound came again. Her mouth went dry, adrenaline kicking her racing pulse up a notch. There was no time to pack. She would be leaving evidence behind. But she had far worse things to worry about.

She thought about the laundry door, with its double bolt and safety chain. How long would it last against someone determined to get in? Once again, she thought about Max, but what good would that do?

Making herself breathe slowly, she padded to the

kitchen and picked up the backpack she had left in the cabinet under the sink and a knife from the draining tray. The scraping now grew louder, and something else, a dull thud. She didn't wait around to listen. Her mind had taken on a steel clarity, hard-edged, knife-sharp. She tiptoed to the large window beside the dining table, slid the well-lubricated window aside. There was no flyscreen, she had seen to it the night she moved in.

As she emerged out through the window into the thumb-sized front garden, there was a splintering sound from somewhere inside the house. She knew if she hung around, she would see a familiar figure take shape in the semi-darkness of her laundry. Instead, she ran. And only stopped when she reached the end of the long street and heard shouts. It took her a moment to backtrack her thoughts and center them on her flight mode. When they did, the scene became clearer, and she saw the house she had occupied for all but one week was now a mass of writhing flames, pitching skyward in a mad frenzy.

She started to walk.

CHAPTER 8

Two weeks later…

Elena just stood there, on the street, before Max's home, staring at the latch on his laser cut gate, as if the answer to all her problems lay there, not sure if she wanted to do this. She had come this far, yet she couldn't make up her mind now. Still, she had to face the facts. Her accommodation situation was screwed up, and that meant, royally fucked. The whole I-sleep-in-bus-station-benches-these-days kind of sucked.

Days were okay. She either roamed around shopping malls or spent hours trawling through public library computers. But there was only so much research you could do in public before some nosy do-gooder noticed. Nights were the worst. She didn't want to be picked up as a homeless vagrant, so she had to keep moving from bus stations to parks and vice versa. Most nights she just curled up behind a dumpster or park bench and stayed awake, listening to every little sound. Thrice she had to hide in the stinky toilets to escape from the patrolling cops. She couldn't keep going like this. A few days of reprieve. Time to regroup and plan. Plus, an easy access to free Wi-Fi and a computer. That's all she needed.

A young girl on a pink bike with a wicker basket out

front swept up from behind, nearly pushing her onto the gate. Elena lurched, stumbled. If it wasn't for her hold on the top rail, she would have fallen face first onto the metal latch. The woman who followed the girl, mother presumably, jumped off her bike and rushed to Elena.

"Are you okay?"

"Yeah. I am."

The woman apologized, all the while covertly eyeing her backpack, unkempt hair, torn jeans, and threadbare jumper. Elena watched the woman, not liking her intrusive look or her not-so-subtle grilling. How long had she known Mr. Logan? Were they friends? Relatives? Entirely inappropriate questions. Next, she would want to know the shoe size and her religious affiliation. God, Elena hated small talk, and people who thought they had gotten inquisition down to an art form. So, she gave the woman and the child a vague smile, opened the gate to Max's home, and stepped inside.

Decision made. There was no going back now.

She raised her hand to knock on the door and nearly hit Max in his eye.

"Oh!" Startled, she stared at Max, who now stood with an open expression of shock, one hand on the doorknob. He blinked, and she lifted her hand in what she thought was a friendly wave. "Uhmm…hi."

He didn't move, more like she had waved a magic wand to freeze him rather than a polite hello. If looks were anything to go by, his would have burned a hole right through her brain. Was he mad? Was he happy to see her?

Then he moved—more like exploded into action. He grabbed her wrist, yanked her forward, wrapped the other arm around her waist, and lifted her feet off the ground. She had a moment of disorientation, a split-second thought that maybe she was making a mistake, then she was getting pressed against a very hard male chest, and all her thoughts died a quick death.

"Son of a bitch," he murmured into her hair. "Son of a bitch. There you are."

Unsure what to do with her hands, she placed them on his chest, just above the round discs of his light brown nipples and pressed. His arms tightened around her once more, nearly squeezing the air out of her lungs, then he was setting her back on her feet.

She looked up at him and offered him a cautious smile. "I—"

"All these weeks," he murmured, staring at her face. "All these weeks, and there you are."

He shook his head and continued staring at her, as if too stupefied to make up his mind about her. His stare made her feel supremely self-conscious, nervous like a trapped cat. All the doubts came hurtling back like a train without brakes. Maybe this wasn't such a great idea. She racked her brain for an alternative and came up empty. So much had happened in the past two weeks.

"Can—can we talk? Is this a good time?"

He blinked. "Christ, where are my manners? Sure. Please, come in." He moved aside to let her through and headed straight down an open corridor, toward his living area, expecting her to follow.

"Thanks." Her mind and feet both seemed to be moving a little slowly. But then, it was pretty obvious her brain cells had exploded like bubble wrap at the sight of the shower-fresh version of Max Logan. His hair was mussed and wet, his feet bare, and his chest was too. She couldn't help noticing the three-inch scar crossing his tanned abdomen, just above the waistline of his low hung jeans. It made her wonder what kind of life he had led after leaving Sunset Bay.

"Um, you want coffee?"

Now would be a good time to stop gawking. Stop it, you idiot. "Uh—no, I don't drink coffee."

Elena stepped inside the house, checking out the place as she followed Max into his kitchen. The place had an open plan, but the living and dining areas had been partitioned off with ceiling-to-floor shelves filled with a mixture of books, clocks, and sculptures. Interesting odds and ends that made a house a home. The living space had leather recliners and a giant TV. A sliding door from the dining area led out onto the alfresco with a neat outdoor setting in wood. Dining space, she noticed, had a scarred oak table and three matching chairs. She wondered momentarily about the missing fourth chair. He followed her gaze and smiled. "I found the table at a thrift shop. The fourth chair was broken beyond repair. So I got it for a steal."

She smiled a cautious smile then cleared her throat, pointing to the framed photograph on the mantle. "Is that your dad?"

Absentmindedly, he ran a hand through his wet hair as he studied the picture, giving his locks a finger-combed look. "Yeah."

"How is he?"

He turned away from her and moved to the fridge. He yanked it open and perused the contents for a moment. "He…ah…he died. Four years ago. Pancreatic cancer."

'Eli, tell my dad I said sorry. Tell him I will ring him as soon as I can.'

Max's voice, from all those years ago, faded away as she looked at the adult version of him, feeling the need to give him a tight hug. But she didn't move. She had lost that right years ago when she failed to keep her promise to him.

"I'm sorry, Max. I didn't know."

"Why would you? Besides, there's no point talking about it." He bent at his knees to look at the lower shelves. "Do you want something cold? I got water, beer, and ginger ale."

"No, thank you. I'm good."

"I'll go with a beer. If you change your mind, you know where to get one."

"This...this is nice," she said to fill the silence, surveying the copper pots hung over the granite island.

He eyed her from beneath a strand of wet hair that fell over his brow. "You sound surprised." Then he grinned. "I get it. You were expecting a typical bachelor pad. Pizza boxes, takeout containers, beer bottles—the works."

She smiled. "You have to admit you weren't exactly housebroken back when—" She stopped then shrugged.

He took the hint and didn't push her for a trip down the memory lane. Carrying his drink, Max walked to his living room and sat down on the abstract printed rug, his back against the recliner. He stretched his legs and sipped his beer, seeming to savor the drink. "Come, Eli. Sit with me."

She didn't move. There was nothing teasing or seductive about his invitation, yet the sight of him lounging back half naked made her acutely aware of him as a man.

Hello, anybody there? Where the hell was her subconscious? The bitch was supposed to stop her mind from wandering off into unchartered territories.

Max leaned forward, staring into her eyes, and waved an arm like an air traffic controller. "Hey—Earth to Eli."

"Huh? Yeah." She took the three steps that took her to his side and sat on the leather sofa, nervous as hell.

He angled his head and looked at her, his eyes dark. She had the feeling he could see right into her—into all the secrets she tried desperately to bury under her lies.

"Tell me."

She swallowed hard and shook her head. His eyes didn't blink, and that direct gaze was more unnerving than his silence.

Elena licked her lower lip. Her throat was swelling on her. "I need a favor."

He brushed his palm across his stubbled chin. "I'm listening."

Say it. Just say it and get it over with. "I need a place to stay. For two days. Three days, max. I—I'm in a bit of trouble."

An awkward silence fell between them. She was suddenly aware of her hands, clasped tight on her knees. She unclasped them, wiped her palms on her thighs, then stopped, then placed them back on her knees. More silence followed.

At that Max couldn't suppress a scowl. "What kind?"

"I'm on the run." There. She'd said it.

Max rolled the bottle between his palms, little droplets of condensation flying from the bottle to his thighs. "Trust me, I figured that much. But from who?"

She eyed the long neck of the bottle, wishing she hadn't rescinded his offer for that drink. "A—a man."

He paused, mid-sip, and then set his bottle next to his thigh. "This guy, is he an ex-boyfriend? A psycho stalker? Your husband?"

A rumble of thunder sounded in the distance, with the promise of rain. She swallowed, words stuck to her vocal cords, as if they never wanted to leave. "We went out a couple of times. But it wasn't anything serious. I certainly wouldn't call him my boyfriend. But, yes, he is the monster I'm running from."

Max's expression didn't change, but she felt the change in him. He had looked relaxed, sprawled out on his living area rug, drinking his beer. Now, savage fury swirled around him like a dark thundercloud. An icy hollow formed in her gut. By God, what was she doing? Hadn't she done enough? Three lives were lost due to her stupidity. Knowing Max, he would now want to dig up everything. Fix everything for her.

"Why not go to the cops?"

She gave him a wry smile at his question. "It's complicated."

"How?"

She shrugged, then picked a piece of lint from her jumper. "Because he *is* a cop."

A long beat of silence followed. Then Max shook his head, as if trying to clear the cobwebs. He sat up straight. "All right. You better start at the beginning, Eli."

Fuck.

თთთ

The clock on the wall read eight-fifty p.m. They had been sitting quietly in his living room for about twenty minutes now. Eli was busy studying her blunt fingernails as if she was seeing them for the first time. She had small hands, soft and slim. He knew she was having trouble opening up to him. As much as he wanted to prod her into revealing her past, he knew he had to be patient.

"Eli, it's okay," he said. He couldn't quite remember the last time he'd felt so desperate, but then he remembered that night fourteen years ago when he had driven through Mitchell freeway with a dead body, wrapped in a sunblock curtain, in his front seat. But of course, things had worked out okay for him that night.

Eli lifted her head and looked at him with those big gray eyes. There was a hesitation. Then she began, "I met him at Midland police headquarters." She started picking at the imaginary specks of dirt under her fingernails. That's when he noticed the scar on her right arm, hidden above the three-quarter sleeve of her blue jumper. From his vantage point, he didn't know what it really looked like. But something told him it was an old wound, irregular, the tissues dense and thick. It reminded him of the marks he had seen on the wrists of a teenage girl at the Outreach shelter, the one who used to cut herself for fun.

"I had a temp job there as a receptionist. He worked for the criminal records department. We weren't friends. But we used to…you know…just smile politely. So, when he asked me out for dinner, I was quite surprised. Everything went well that first night. He took me out to this riverside restaurant in Mosman Park. After that, we went out on three more dates. Then something started to feel off. Little things. I started to notice how possessive he was, how unreasonable. Slowly he started controlling me, choosing the clothes I should wear, picking out the foods I should eat, even telling me who I should be friends with. If I resisted, he would make up some way to make me feel horrible about all this. He had this way of making me feel stupid. One day I realized I'd had enough. So, I broke it off with him." She stopped for a moment, looking confused. Her eyes had filled with tears, but she blinked them away.

He looked at her cracked lips and anxious face, and the image ripped at the blinding fury he hadn't known he still possessed. Anger at her stalker. Anger at himself. Anger at the bitchy fates who enjoyed fucking up their lives. Goddammit! He hadn't gone through hell and back only to have her suffer like this. She shouldn't have gone through any of this shit. The compulsion to wrap his hands around the neck of the bastard who had scared his Eli was strong enough that Max knew it was a warning. The last time he had let his emotions get in his way, he'd put a fist-sized dent in his wall. The time before, he'd killed a man.

Eli looked up at that moment, and Max saw something terrible in her expression, as if she was reliving the moments in her past. Her hands clenched and unclenched compulsively on her lap. The fear in her eyes was a welcome reinforcement, it helped him corral his fury. For now.

"Eli." He called her softly and saw her jerk. "Is that when he started stalking you, baby?"

"Yes," she said, without looking at him.

"Didn't you complain?"

"I threatened to inform his boss, but then he stopped bothering me. I thought that was the end of it. Once I finished my temp job, they offered me a part-time position. But after what happened with him, I didn't want to be around him. So, I said no and moved on. I got a job at an indoor play center. For months, I didn't hear from him. But then one day, I saw him in my apartment building. He told me he had bought an apartment across the corridor from mine. Then he started popping up everywhere I went. Laundry. Shops. My workplace. That's when I knew he really was trouble."

"Then?"

"I had no solid evidence to go to the police. What would I say? The guy I used to date now bought an apartment, next to mine, and I keep seeing him everywhere I go? They would have laughed at me. It was his word against mine. So, I didn't. But then I started to notice that things were missing from my place like my yearbook, my diary, my photos—even my...underwear. I did what I thought was best and convinced Harry, my super to change the locks on my apartment. But next day when I came home, I saw that my front door was open. The lock looked new too. It wasn't the one Harry installed for me. I went inside and, on my bed, there was this set of keys and a note explaining that they were my new set of keys and he had taken one."

"Why didn't you take it to the cops, or Harry?"

"Why? To make a complete fool of myself? I knew there wouldn't be any fingerprints left on that note. The man is a cop. He knew how the system worked. Besides, he was good friends with Harry. Harry wouldn't have believed me either."

Once again, he saw her picking the imaginary stuff under her fingernails. This time, the act was accompanied by gentle rocking of her body.

To and fro.

To and fro.

He could see that she wasn't right, could sense that the girl from his past, who always had a smile for him, was slowly coming undone in front of his eyes.

"About that time, I started seeing this other guy. Jerry. A sweet guy I met through friends. We went out on a couple of dates. For our fourth date, we were supposed to go to a house party at his friend's place. Jerry was very much into music, his band was planning to play that night. Only, he never turned up. He just…vanished. Two weeks later, his roommate lodged a missing person complaint. Later that day, police found a note in Jerry's work desk, explaining he had many debts and no means to pay them off. Also, that he was taking a long trip and no one should look for him. The case was closed, written off as a runaway. But I knew. I just knew."

He went motionless. "You think the fucker killed him?"

She nodded, shuddering with exhalation.

The vein in his neck began to pulse and tick. His jaw was sore from clenching it so damn tight, but he welcomed the pain.

Rage. The fucking rage he felt! It pulsed through his veins, filled his chest, seeped out of his pores. All he wanted at that moment was to track down the fucker who'd scared his Eli and kill him inch by inch.

The garbage truck, from the sound of it, passed by on the street. Eli's eyes turned to the window and stayed fixed for a long beat. Then she looked back at him, her gaze haunted, and too tired. "Poor Jerry. I should have warned him. He died because of me." It was uttered in a whisper, and he heard everything she never said. Her regret, her fear, her pain. He held her gaze, trying hard to read what she wouldn't say, until the pain in her eyes became too much for him and forced him to look away.

She smiled, not a pleasant one, but a harsh parody of a smile. "I packed up my bag, wrote a letter to Harry, and took off that night. I've been running ever since."

Max stared at the woman before him in dismay, at the bedraggled clothes, the tired eyes, and tried to reconcile her with the girl in pigtails from his past. He simply couldn't. She was there all right, but it was just her shell. And now he knew why.

Jesus Christ!

He took a deep drag from his bottle, anesthetized to the chilled liquid as it trickled down his throat. "How long ago did this happen?" Max asked, softly, as if not to spook her.

"About six months," she said, without looking at him, and he knew that her immediate, premeditated answer was a lie. Everything she had said so far was delivered with hesitation. But the final answer was delivered with an immediacy that told him it was a lie. That and the fact that she wouldn't meet his eyes. He didn't know why she felt the need to lie to him at this point, but he let his doubts fall by the wayside.

"And this guy, has he been bothering you again?"

Silence.

He didn't dare touch her. Even though he so wanted to wrap his arms around her and draw her to his chest. Maybe carry her away somewhere he could scrub all her memories and replace them with fresh, happy ones. But he couldn't. So, he folded his arms and leveled her with a straight-faced look. "We should go to the police. You know that's the right thing to do. You shouldn't let that bastard get away with this."

"No." She jumped up in a panic. "No cops. You hear me." Her voice was shaking. Her eyes unsteady.

That gave him another pause, the vehemence he heard in her voice. "But why?"

"Didn't you hear a word I said? He is a cop."

"Then we'll go to another station. I know a cop who can—"

"No!" She started trembling.

His grasp on his rage was beginning to slip, but he held on with his fingertips. "Then give me his name, baby. I'll take care of the bastard," he ground out through gritted teeth, staring directly into her eyes.

His words made her snap. Each word she uttered came out in rage. "No, you fucking idiot. I'm not going to give you his name. You're not responsible for me, you hear me? I got into this shit, and I'll get out."

He shot to his feet at the desperation in her voice and towered above her. "I don't get it. The sensible thing to do is to put this bastard behind bars. If one cop doesn't believe your story, we'll go to another. One way or another, we can put an end to this shit. Or do you plan to live in the shadows forever?"

She sniffled then wiped her nose on her sleeve. "Fuck off. I'm done explaining myself to you." She looked up, met his gaze. "This was a mistake. I shouldn't have come here. What was I thinking?" She walked to the front door and grabbed the handle. But he beat her to it and grabbed her wrist, stopping her from opening the door and walking away from his life.

"I'm sorry. Okay. I shouldn't have pushed you. Obviously, you got everything under control. And I should mind my own business. I get that now. But please...stay."

She turned her head to him and sighed. He dropped his arm and took a wide step back, giving her breathing space. "Listen, Max, no cops. And don't think for a minute to play hero. I know that's what you want to do. You feel sorry for me. I appreciate your concern, but it really is not your business. Just let me stay here for a few days. I don't have any money. It's too much bother to find a place where they won't ask me many questions. Three days maybe, but no longer than a week. That's all I need to sort out my shit. Then I'll go."

"Where? What have you planned?"

She peered toward the thick rug, as people often did when they were nervous. "My mom. I'm waiting for my mom. Once she gets here, I'll go with her. Somewhere far. Somewhere he can't reach me."

"Your mom?" In all honesty, he had completely forgotten about her mom. "Aunt Rosie is here in Perth?"

She gave him a sideways glance. "No. I don't know where she is at the moment. But I've sent her an email. She should come. I know she will." Her lips tightened into a thin line.

He continued to stare at her, his fury cooling down to a small boil. "Did you ever tell her—"

She laced her hands in front of her and nodded. "After you left, Mom started wondering about Mark. After all, she had only seen his loving, caring side. 'Mark is a miracle,' she used to tell me. Obviously, she was worried about him. At one point, she said she was going to file a missing person report. I knew I had to do something. I couldn't let the police dig into the matter. So I told her everything."

He let that sink in for a moment then dragged a palm over his face, trying to process it all. "Is that why you left Sunset Bay?"

She nodded. "I had no choice, Max. I had to leave. Or she would have gone to the police. But after I told her, something snapped inside her. She got worried and started acting really weird. Part of it could have been lack of drugs. After Mark, she had no means to get her hands on Meth and crack. She was going through withdrawal. I knew she needed help, but I had no clue how to get help for her. Once I spoke to your dad and Father Richard, but she yelled at them when they tried to help. After that, no one bothered. One day she told me to pack our bags. She had to leave Sunset Bay." Eli straightened her shoulders and looked directly into his eyes. "You see, Max, I had no choice. I wanted to wait for you. But she was my mother. and I didn't know what else to do for her. So, we left."

He crossed his arms over his chest, trying to contain the disappointment flowing through him. He had thought he was over it and had come to terms with the fact that she had left him, despite her promise. Apparently not. "Where did you go?"

"Here and there. For a while. we were at Geraldton. That's where I did my high school and TAFE."

She spoke in a soft, lilting accent that he always associated with Sunset Bay. But it was the pain in her words that clenched his guts. "I'm not blaming you, Eli, if that's what you think. For God's sake, you were a child." That at least was true. The rational part of him knew she had only done what she thought was best for her family.

She shook her head. "I know that. But when things

got really tough—I often wondered what would have happened if I had stayed. Maybe you would have come back. Maybe we could have had a different kind of life. No Mark. No psychopathic stalkers. Just us."

Ah, fuck.

An uncomfortable silence followed, and he said the first thing that he could think of, "Where's Aunt Rosie now?"

A wan smile took over her face. "Mom met Ivan in Geraldton. He's her third husband by the way. They travel, a lot. He's got a caravan, and they take these trips around the outback. God knows where they are now. But she usually drops an email now and then. That's how we keep in touch. I'm hoping she's on her way now. I'll give her three more days. Then—I've got other plans." Her tone went from gentle to fierce in seconds.

Blowing out a deep breath, he said, "Aunt Rosie, does she know about…"

Her head shot up. "About Ju—I mean *him*? No. It would kill her. She's completely on the bend now. I don't want anything to upset that."

He struggled to keep his voice void of any judgment. "I still think you're making a mistake, Eli. We need to bring this bastard to justice."

She shook her head, and he got the impression that she wasn't telling him the whole story. Something was off. Maybe she was embarrassed. Maybe she didn't trust him completely.

But what mattered was that she was here, and he would get to her. One way or another, the bastard who touched his Eli would pay for it.

"Do you have anything to eat? I haven't had anything to eat today."

He swallowed his snort before she caught a whiff of it. *Change the subject. Get the focus off of her. Very clev-*

er, Eli. "I was just about to go get some dinner when you caught me. Do you want to go with me? There's a nice burger place around the corner."

She shook her head. "I would rather not."

"Okay. Then…uh…Cornflakes okay with you? That's about the only thing I got in my pantry at the moment."

She nodded.

He walked to his kitchen, opened his pantry cupboard, and pulled out the box of dry cereal. He took a bowl from the overhead cabinet, dropped in a handful of cornflakes, and poured a generous amount of cold milk. Eli devoured her meal in silence, plunging spoonfuls into her mouth. He leaned against the kitchen benchtop and watched her silently. When was the last time she had a proper meal? She had lost weight since he had last seen her. Where had she slept for the last few weeks?

When the meal was through, she set down the spoon and rose from her chair. Then she took the bowl to the sink and rinsed the bowl and spoon, before placing it on the drying rack.

That done, she turned to him. "Thanks."

"Come with me," he said, walking toward his spare bedroom. He used the room for folding his clothes. Occasionally Jake crashed there, only when he was too sloshed to drive. Eli could sleep there.

He pushed his way through to the room, picked up the dozens of socks and underwear off the floor and the bed, dumped them all in the wicker basket at the foot of the bed, before inviting her in. "You can sleep here. This is a three by one. So, there's only one bathroom. That's through there." He pointed to the door behind her.

She stood at the threshold, staring first at the bed, then at him. Her lips wobbled. "Thank you. I really appreciate this, Max."

He shrugged. "I will get you some sheets." He by-passed her at the doorway then rushed to his linen closet for a new set of sheets. He was at the end of his laundry cycle. Chances were, the cupboards were empty. *Please let there be at least one new sheet.*

He returned in a few minutes, armed with new sheets and a towel, the only fresh one he could find. He set them on the mattress and walked back to her. "Take rest and try to get some sleep. We'll talk in the morning. If you need..." His thoughts trailed off as she slipped her arms around him for a hug. The simple gesture coming from her surprised him. The Eli he'd known used to be a chronic hugger. But this Eli, he knew had an invisible hands-off sign stamped on her forehead.

Tentatively, he brought his arms around her and hugged her back. He could totally do this. Even though this certain someone smelled like cinnamon-coated sin.

Block that thought, Logan.

"Thanks, Max." She lifted her face up the same moment he dipped his head down to smell her hair. Their lips met. For one heartbeat. One painfully intense heartbeat.

He dropped his arm as if burnt. She pulled away with the same urgency.

Awkward.

Just play it cool. No reason to make a production out of it.

He saw the surprise, the dismay, but then she was composing her face, pasting on a fake smile. "Goodnight, Max."

He couldn't move, not a single muscle, even after she shut the door.

It was the ring of his phone that finally yanked him from the frozen state.

Friend, he told himself. She was his friend.

He patted his pockets, located his phone, then pressed the answer button, noticing his hands were trembling.

Dammit!

She trusted him, and he shouldn't take advantage of that trust, he reminded himself again. They had a history, and she had turned to him in her moment of need. He shouldn't forget that for a moment.

Not for a moment.

CHAPTER 9

Elena rang the agent. She thought it was going to be an awkward conversation, and it was. So far as she knew, the woman hadn't made any progress in tracking down the last two babies on the list, and she responded to Elena with nothing more than fake politeness.

"I told you before, Ms. Martin, I haven't been able to do much about your case."

"I know. It's just that—"

The woman at the other end sighed. "Listen, I know how desperate you feel. But these things take time."

"You sound just like your boss."

The woman laughed. Elena could picture her sitting at the small wooden desk in her cramped office, files thrown haphazardly around, her long ginger hair pulled up in a messy bun. "Give me two days, Elena. Then call me. Or better, I'll call you the moment I hear anything."

"No," Elena said quickly. "Don't call me on this number. I won't be here for long. Message me."

There was a long pause. "All right."

"Thanks, Erin. I really appreciate it."

❧❧❧

He was just a regular guy, back from his weekly

shopping, he told himself as he pulled into his garage the next morning, his car boot full of groceries and fresh veggies. If anyone happened to ask, that was his story, and he was sticking by it.

He wasn't in a relationship with Eli. This was not some fantasy roleplay. He wasn't doing this because he felt sorry for her. He was just trying to make her feel comfortable. She had to eat, and he had no clue what she preferred. So, he did the intelligent thing and bought a bit of everything. He knew she liked tea, but what kind? There were freaking mile-long aisles packed chock-a-block with different varieties of tea. Green snail spring tea? Strawberry pomegranate tea? Who on earth drank that crap? But hey, he had given in and bought one of each. He'd also gotten some top-grade locks from Bunnings, safety chains, and window sensors. If she felt relaxed and safe, she wouldn't feel the constant need to pack up and leave.

What about the security alarm you've ordered from RAC? Or the two hundred buck GPS tracker?

Okay, so maybe he had gone a bit overboard with the security detail. But if what she said was true, and this guy after her was indeed a psychopathic stalker, it wouldn't hurt to be extra careful. The key, he'd learned the hard way, was to stay one step ahead of your enemy.

Still, there were bits about her story that he thought were a bit glossed over. Maybe she was embarrassed. Or she didn't trust him completely. Or…he didn't know all they why's and how's. But when all said and done, he still considered her his woman. She hadn't given him the green light so far. Probably wouldn't ever. But something about her softened something inside him. It had been that way forever. Almost from the moment he'd met her, she had wormed her way through to his heart, making him feel stuff he didn't have any right to feel.

He simply didn't know how to stop caring for her.

And he wasn't sure he even wanted to. Because she, and she alone, held the power to turn him inside out. Yeah, sounded corny, but it was the simple truth.

God, how he wished things were different. He'd give anything to make her feel safe, a woman capable of smiling, and enjoying her life. But things were as they were, and he could only hope that he was doing the right thing by her.

He still didn't like the idea of her hiding from this crazy bastard. At some point, he would have to talk her into going to the police. Elena thought her stay with him was a temporary option, but the truth was he had no intention of letting her go. She'd trusted him, for now, he didn't want to do anything to rock the boat. What he wanted was her. But it would have to wait. He had the added predicament of convincing her to stay without coming across as a pushy bastard. And that's why he would have to be careful around her. She was fragile and vulnerable, and he was a walking hard-on around her. Not that he could do anything about it. But, yes, it was there, a constant reminder that he needed to get laid ASAP or suffer a self-detonation.

Sighing, he pressed the remote and let the garage door roll down.

Just as he opened the door and stepped inside, armed with grocery bags in both hands, she walked out of the shower, a look of surprise in her big, gray eyes.

Then she smiled.

Hot, incredibly hot. And utterly clueless.

Her face looked pink and kind of dewy, her hair a tumble of wet, golden strands down her back. She was wearing a loose-fitting green sweater that reached up to her mid-thigh, and nothing else. The damn sweater slid off one shoulder as she moved, baring creamy skin.

Christ, where was the bra strap? May there was no bra. He suddenly had a visual of him stepping behind her, sliding his hand under her sweater, up her flat belly, over her ribcage, then cupping her breasts. Speaking of breasts, what size was she? Thirty-four C?

"Fuck," he whispered, his jaws clenching.

Lust, high-octane, shot through his bloodstream. All those little pep talks about exercising self-restraint—they went right out his brainbox, along with his common sense. Dammit, why did she have to look so fucking beautiful?

She started toward him, confusion washing over her expression. "Are you okay, Max?"

Then she stopped and bit her lip.

Bit. Her. Lip.

Holy mother of God. I can't take it anymore.

"Yeah. I'm good," he murmured, breathing hard through the adrenaline rush.

As she looked over at him again, one eyebrow went up. Her concern was sweet, but the heated scrutiny sucked the air right out of his lungs. Taking a step away from her, emotionally and physically, he dumped the groceries on the kitchen benchtop and hurried out of his kitchen.

Cold shower. Now.

"Max!"

He didn't reply. She had nothing to say that he wanted to hear. Well, unless she had had a change of mind and was ready to roll around the sheets with him.

He looked back, and she was standing where he'd left her, her eyebrows drawn together in obvious confusion.

Nope. He wasn't that lucky. Not yet anyway.

⁊⁋⁊

Three nights turned into five.

Then five turned into seven.

She didn't know how it happened, but as she sat there in his living room, breathing through some relaxation moves, she suddenly realized she had to move out. It was probably the woman phoning Max earlier on his landline looking for him that clinched it. Jealousy wasn't exactly what Eli felt when she'd heard the throaty voice of the unknown bitch. But close enough.

She waited for Max to come home from work, ready to tell him that she was moving out. She repeated the words in her head, polished them, all the right things with the right hint of emotion that would make him believe her—enough for him to let her go.

She had already scouted out a homeless shelter twenty miles out of the city limits. A place where neither Justin nor Max would think to look for her.

She had twenty bucks she'd nicked from Max's wallet. That should be enough to catch public transport three-quarters of the way. The rest, she would walk.

A jagged streak of lightning zigzagged across the night sky when Max walked in. Behind him, through the open door, she saw the rain fall—cold, thick, unforgiving. He stood there at the threshold, hair plastered to his head, his clothes a soggy mess, and his lips curved into the most endearing smile.

Then he sneezed.

Once. Then twice.

She ran to him. "Max."

"Hi, Eli." He squeezed her shoulder then took a deep breath. "Hmm…what's that smell?"

"Chicken potpie."

Another sneeze.

"Bloody hell, Max. You're soaking. Where's your umbrella?"

A manly sniffle. "Left it at the Dojo."

He took off his jacket and hung it on the hook by the door to the garage. "You better stay away, baby." Sniffle. "I think I'm coming down with something."

Shaking her head at the misery she heard in his voice, she led him to the kitchen, made him sit on one of the wooden bar stools. For the next half hour, she ran around like a headless chook, making him drink lemon tea, drying his hair, taking care of the manly flu that made him impatient.

When she finally got him to bed and rubbed a generous amount of Vicks on his forehead, he looked at her with those tired moss-green eyes and mumbled: "I'm so glad you're here, Eli. Thank you."

Sighing, she left his bedroom, leaving the door partially open behind her.

Her plans could wait another day. Or two.

સ્જ

They met at Paddy's, their usual place. For a change, they were able to secure a table by the fireplace, one of the advantages of not having Paddy around, and ordered a large Pepperoni pizza to split.

Shortly after their food arrived, Max brought up the subject that was foremost on his mind. "I have asked Elena to stay with me."

Jake froze, pizza caught mid-air. "Elena? The chick who dropped out of the dojo? The one you said you weren't into?"

Max nodded.

For a moment Jake didn't move. Slowly, he took a bite. Max knew the silence meant trouble. Clearly, in the light of recent events, he was going to get a dressing down.

Sometimes, having best friends sucked.

"She is in a bad place at the moment," he told Jake. "Until I figure out an alternative, she'll be staying with me."

Silence.

"Jesus, man, don't give me that look. You're thinking I'm making a mistake. But I can't throw her back out onto the streets. I just can't. She won't survive. You know how it is out there."

Jake finished chewing, took a large sip of his Hahns dry, then set down the bottle. "Why isn't she with her family?"

"She doesn't have any family." There was her crackpot mom, but he thought it best if he didn't bring that up in this conversation. That would be like pouring fat into the fire. Jake hated druggies with a passion.

Jake looked at him for a moment. "Of all the people in the universe, she decided to come to you for help. Who the hell are you? Mother Theresa of Perth?"

Max looked away.

"What the hell, dude? Is there something you aren't telling me?"

"No. It's nothing like that."

"Fuck, Max, you're sleeping with her?"

Max gave Jake a "*Come on*" look. "Do you mind repeating it a bit louder? I don't think the people in Bali heard you." He leaned closer. "For your information, I'm not sleeping with her. It's not like that between us."

Jake shook his head. "But you want to. And I'm telling you that being involved with this woman is a very bad idea. Oh, hang on." He paused. "That's right. I've told that already. Like a million freaking times."

Max let it roll right off him. "Don't worry. I've got it under control, okay?"

Jake took another bite of his pizza. "If you, for once,

stop thinking with your penis, and start using your brain, you'll know what a stupid thing you're doing. Besides—" He took another bite. "What is this big problem she got? Money trouble, visa issues, crazy boyfriend?"

Max nodded. "Something like that."

Jake snorted. "How convenient. Even if that's the case, why doesn't she go to the cops? I know there are things like restraining orders."

Max took a deep breath. "It's complicated."

"Yeah, right. You just want to play the white knight to score with this chick."

Max shook his head and set down his beer. Then he leaned closer and dropped his voice. "The crazy-assed boyfriend *is* a cop. That's the problem."

Jake gave him an amused look. "Man, I'd hate to see your pretty face when he gets a hold of you."

Max scoffed. "He sure can try. But he won't like the results."

Jake rolled his eyes. "Messing with a cop? You know this is not going to end well. I know you're a bleeding heart. But all this trouble for a chick? *Come* on, man. She's a knockout, I'll give you that. But I've never seen you go all ga-ga over one before. Especially one you haven't slept with."

Max snorted. "Hey—I always treat my ladies well."

Jake looked at him over the rim of his bottle. "Is that what she is now? Your lady friend?"

Busted.

Max sipped his beer and chose to exercise his right to remain silent. He hated, *hated,* keeping things from Jake.

Jake smiled, point made. "I'm just saying that I don't get what's going on between you and that woman. It's obvious you want to bang her. But if that's all there is to it, then stop being such a freaking saint and bang her, then let her go on her way. Or you will be counting bars in a jail cell," He moved his fingers in the air, demonstrating. "See that?" He repeated the move.

Before he could stop himself, Max thumped his fist on the table. "Elena is not just a random chick for me, okay? She's Eli. I've known her for a long time. She used to be my…" He stumbled over that one. "…my friend."

There. It was out. Forced out of his mouth.

Jake stared at him. A nervy kind of stare. "Say that again."

Max was slow to respond. But then he shook his head, squared his shoulders. What the hell. The cat was out of the bag anyway. He might as well suck it up and tell the whole truth. He pushed his chair closer to Jake, the loud scraping noise drowning under the pub music. His voice dropped into a whisper as he spoke: "Do you remember that night we met for the first time?"

Jake's eyebrows furrowed, confusion evident on his face. "What's that got to do with her?"

"Do you?"

"Yes. Of course. You came up to the Outreach shelter and told the supervisor you needed a place to stay. She put you up with me for the night. And I asked you—"

"If I'm in trouble."

Jake nodded. "Yes. So?"

Max began picking at the edge of the table runner. His eyes refused to meet with Jake. "I lied to you then. Or rather, I only told you half the truth."

Jake did a slow blink. "What are you getting at, Max?"

An invisible wall went up around Max. He didn't like talking about his past. He never did well with questioning. But he knew he had no choice today. He brought this on himself. So, he lowered his voice again. "I—I killed a man that day."

Jake's eyes rose to his. Blue eyes that carried fatigue and baggage that far outweighed his age. Max shifted in his seat. Desperate. Waiting to be judged. Jake opened his mouth to speak. Then he snapped it shut.

"His name was Mark. He was Eli's stepfather. He was…a fucking pedophile. I never liked him. Never liked the way he used to touch or look at her. I used to love her—Eli, you know. I was only seventeen, and she was fourteen, but I always thought of her as mine. Then one day she came running to me. The bastard had tried to—" He took a deep breath. "In between the struggle, she knocked him on his head with a candlestick. He passed out on her bedroom floor. And there was blood. So much blood. She panicked and came running to me. And I did what I thought was best for her. I finished the job she started, wrapped his body in a curtain from my bedroom. Then I stuffed his body into the front seat of his car and drove thirty miles to Perth Hills and dumped it where I thought no one would see."

Jake shook his head. "So, where was this girl all this time?"

"After what happened, I stayed away from Sunset Bay. It took me three years to work up the nerve to go back. By then, Eli and her mom had left. I had no means to reach her."

Jake cocked his brows. "Let me get this straight. You killed a guy for her, and she did a runner on you?"

Max shook his head. "It wasn't like that. Her mom had issues, and Eli had no choice but to leave."

Jake smirked, an ugly sound. "The way I see it, this girl's a user. She used you to get rid of her stepdaddy. Then she went on her merry way. Now that she got more guy trouble, she wants you to take care of that for her. You see the pattern here, mate?"

Max sighed. "You're wrong. Eli is not that type."

A mocking smile twisted Jake's lips. When he spoke, Max could hear the emotion in his voice, the disappointment that roughened it. "You know what I'm thinking, mate? Fifteen years. Fifteen fucking years, Max. We've been through a lot together, haven't we? And you never bothered to tell me about any of this, until now."

Fingers curling into fists, Max faced him. "I never told you any of this before because I wanted to move on, forget that shit ever happened. But now Eli's back in my life, and she's in trouble. And you're my best friend. So…" His shoulders lifted and fell in a shrug. "Come on, man. Give me a break."

Jake didn't speak for a while. Max waited. For how long, he didn't care. Behind his temples, the mother of all headaches arrived, without warning. Still he sat there, staring at his drink, until he began to loathe the silence.

"Max?"

A waitress in black skirt stopped at the table to check if they needed a refill and Max jumped. "Ah…no. We're good. Aren't we?"

Max felt his heart drum loudly in his chest, overwhelmed by the sense of guilt. The situation was out of his control. He was powerless. His friendship with Jake had lasted for over fifteen years, and now it was at a pivotal point. For one split second, he wished things hadn't come to this stage. Then he thought about Eli, her anxious face. No. She meant a lot to him. He was glad she had turned to him in her moment of need.

The waitress coughed, bringing his attention back to her and Jake. Max cocked a brow at Jake, waiting. *Come on, dude. Say something.*

Jake lifted the bottle to his mouth and drained it, then he plonked it back on the table, lips curved into a smile. "Yes, Tanya. We're good. All good."

Phew.

With a wry grin, Max took a sip of his beer. Time to steer the topic away from Eli. "So, what's going on with you these days?"

CHAPTER 10

S he woke in the dark, unable to move or see. Her arms throbbed like a bitch, while the little dinner she had earlier churned in her stomach like contents in a seven-hundred-watt blender on full throttle. Disoriented, confused, she struggled, then stilled with the realization that her arms were pinned overhead.

She tested one leg, then the other. Bound.

An angry scream welled up deep inside her throat, but it didn't make past the duct tape over her mouth. Fucking hell.

She heard a plaintive cry.

Her baby! Alex!

Fresh panic erupted. She had no idea how long she had been sleeping.

A door opened with a whiny creak then closed with a soft click. Steady footsteps sounded on the floorboards. She heard another door open somewhere. Her baby stopped crying, as if someone stuffed something inside his little mouth. She hoped to hell that something was a bottle of milk. Or the very least his favorite dummy. Alex could be difficult when he decided to chuck a tantrum, which was pretty much whenever his mood struck. And if he decided to throw a hissy fit today of all days, things could get ugly, real fast.

Jeez, listen to her bitching about her own kid. No wonder Justin thought she wasn't cut out to be a mom.

God, this wait was killing her. What was taking him so long?

Seconds segregated to long minutes. Or was it hours? Where the hell was he?

Footfalls returned. He was getting closer, then closer still.

She knew what was coming, but knowing didn't lessen the complexity of emotions one bit.

She felt his cold touch as he removed the band around her eyes. Then he came into view. The familiar smile, his soft blue eyes—something in those eyes warned her—an instant before the pain hit.

She was glad that he hadn't given her any verbal warning. Sometimes it helped. Not always, but sometimes.

The whip struck again. Like lightning.

Closing her eyes, she concentrated.

"Is that enough?" he whispered in her ear, his breath heavy, hot like acid.

She shook her head. She had to come. That was the deal.

She struggled to find purchase, only to cut the ropes into her skin until she smelled her own blood.

Pain spun in her head, her limbs began shaking. Thoughts continued to pelt their way through her brain. And somewhere in the midst of all, an orgasm exploded through her.

Blessed peace.

Something fell on her face. She snapped her eyes open. Even as her vision went in and out of focus, she saw Justin's face, his tear-stained gaze. He was shaking his head at her, his expression one of abject defeat.

"Why do you insist I hurt you, Elizabeth? Why, baby?" He reached out and touched her thigh, and she hissed.

"Oh God, your skin—" He began to sob, lifting his bloody hand to wipe his nose. She hated his tears on her, made her feel dirty. Unclean.

"There has to be another way, baby. Don't make me do this to you anymore. Please. I can't—" His words shuddered out in a gasp. "—I can't take it anymore."

She drew a breath in, prepared for the inevitable. In some perverse part of her brain, she even welcomed it.

Slowly, her world turned black.

She woke up screaming.

Dream.

Just another dream where she felt angry, helpless, trapped.

All those things and more.

The memories became a flood, driving her out of the bed and into a tense pacing that took her from one end of Max's guest room to another.

Six steps forward...six steps back.

Six steps forward...six steps...

Yes, she was pissed. Ever since her escape, she hadn't gotten more than three hours of sleep each night. Either the nightmares would wake her, or she would lie awake, listening for footsteps and wondering if someone was in her house. She had honestly thought tonight would be different.

It wasn't just that. Now she'd been forced to persuade Max to let her stay, essentially, and that didn't sit well with her. She was putting him in danger by simply being near him. She knew she needed to be practical, she was a woman on the run, penniless, and she needed time and resources to make her plan work. Staying made a lot of sense.

Do you really think this is a good idea? You know

Max is bound to have some doubts about your cover story. Do you have a backup plan in case he starts digging too much?

Great. Even her sassy subconscious wasn't on her team.

No, there was no way she could sleep now.

Air.

Maybe she all she needed was some fresh air to clear her head.

A moment later, she was stealthily feeling her way through Max's living room to the small alfresco area beyond his dining hall.

"I don't think you've got much future as a thief. You suck."

She whirled around as Max's voice came from behind her in the darkness. "Dammit, Max, you scared me."

As she stared, he stepped from the shadows near his bedroom door where he had been standing. It was obvious he had not yet gone to bed. In the pale moonlight, she saw he was still wearing the custom-made black dojo T-shirt and the white gi pants.

He flipped the light switch on, flooding the room with soft yellow light. "Couldn't sleep?"

She looked away. "I just needed some air."

"Bad dreams? I heard you cry."

She stiffened. "Something like that."

"About him?"

She looked up, met his gaze. She tried to read the expression in his eyes. She could feel there was sympathy in his eyes, she could feel it reaching out to envelop her. "Yes. About him."

His lips pursed as he blew out a frustrated breath. "I need his name, Elizabeth."

"Nope. You're not getting it."

She tried walking away, because he was too close for

her comfort, and she needed to get away from his shrewd probing eyes. But he blocked her path, stopping her. "Wanna talk about it?"

She tried to play it off, injecting a good dose of snark into her words. "Who are you, Dr. Phil? Jeez, Max. Give me a break."

His eyes searched hers. "You're getting mouthy again, Eli. Which means you're scared." He ran a hand over his jaw and then nodded. "Very well, I won't push. How about I get you a cup of warm milk instead?"

She blinked, caught off guard by his sudden switch in topics. She felt a little sick about her behavior. Flustered, especially at how smoothly he'd handled her bitchy self, she continued. "How—how do you put up with me? Even when I behave like a total bitch, how can you be so nice to me?"

He stepped closer, his expression a mixture of sympathy and something else she couldn't decipher. "Because you mean a lot to me. And if our roles were reversed, you would've done the same for me." He paused then added cheekily. "You would've—right?"

"Yes, of course," she said, feeling horrible he even had to ask.

"Then tell me what's going on?" His gaze softened. "I just want to help."

She looked away from his face, needing that fleeting moment to compose, and then met his gaze. "I have these nightmares. They're memories mostly. And they keep me up at nights. Today I saw that I was at his house, and he was—" She drew a deep breath. "He was always—" Her teeth sank into her lower lip, shame creeping up to her face like an ugly rash.

Max swore. "Don't."

She kept her gaze fixed on his, speaking determinedly. Now that she opened the floodgates, it just kept on coming. "He had this—had this way of pretending that he did what he did because I asked for it. Like it was every woman's secret fantasy to be stalked by a guy. I guess it was his way of convincing his twisted, convoluted mind that he was doing the right thing. And now—after going through all that shit, I feel so messed up in here." She tapped her temple with her forefinger. "And I don't know what to do, Max. I've no freaking clue how to get over this and be normal."

She fell quiet then, standing still as she waited for his reaction. Any moment now he would turn away from her. She would see pity morph into revulsion in his pretty green eyes.

Oh, fuck, don't fall apart, Eli.

She inhaled sharply as Max cupped her shoulders and drew her to his chest. "Sshh…it's over, baby. It's over. I've got you now."

Her eyes filled with tears, her heart suddenly vulnerable. His capable hands stroked her hair, her shoulders, her back. Not demanding, just soothing.

Up and down.

Up and down.

For one moment, she was overpowered with longing to simply surrender to his heat and strength. How she hated this self-imposed solitude and restraint. For once, she just wanted to feel. She knew it wouldn't be like those times with Justin, because Max would be her choice. Maybe she could rise on her tiptoes, press a soft kiss to his throat, nibble on his earlobes, and see where it would lead? The temptation wasn't wholly unexpected, or beyond her imagination. Unfortunately, right on cue, memories of a decade spent in a dark, dank basement surged to the surface.

She pressed her lips hard to stop them from trembling. "Post-traumatic stress, panic attacks, OCD—I'm so fucked up," she mumbled into his chest. She wrenched herself free before he could respond and began pacing. And he let her. He simply folded his arms across his chest and leaned against the door jamb, those intense eyes never leaving her face a second.

"I—I've got to do something. I—I feel so helpless. It's like I'm letting him win. I can't do that. I've got to—I've got to—do something."

He watched her for a long moment and then straightened. He took one step forward and extended his hand. "Come with me."

She stilled. "Where?"

He caught her wrist and pulled her along. "Outside."

She frowned. "Why?"

"Because you need sleep, and something tells me a good fight will help you do that."

She dug her heels into the carpet, bringing him to a halt with her. "You're going to fight me? Now? I don't want you to do that. Go back to bed."

He looked over his shoulder as he unlocked the sliding door and stepped outside. It was sweet, the way he pretended not to notice the row of tin cans she had arranged before the glass door, her personal security alert.

"Are you scared I'll kick your ass, Eli?"

She snorted as she stepped over the cans. "I know what you're doing. And it's really sweet. But this kind of therapy—"

He moved like a bolt of lightning, kicking his left leg out in a practiced move. His toes connected with her knee. The shock far outweighed the pain. Then there was no time to reflect, as she crumpled to the ground.

Far out!

He ran toward her, right arm raised to deliver a knife-hand strike to her collarbone. Reflex kicked in, and she rolled over, grabbed both his legs and toppled him over. She surged to her feet and delivered a well-timed inverted punch to his rib cage before he could find his feet.

He cleared his throat, which may have been his version of a painful grunt, then he was grabbing her around her thighs and bringing her down. She tried to block, but he still managed to sneak in a couple of punches. A few minutes into the scuffle, fun vanished, and Elena felt the first stirrings of unease and anger. So, when he brought his hand down again, she curled forward, grabbed his ankle and gave it a lift and twist. When that wasn't enough, she brought her hand down and pummeled his shin. He caught her fist in one palm and yanked her up. Before she could blink, he was straddling her, not resting his weight completely on her hips to crush her, but it was enough to pin her. He grabbed both her wrists and brought them to his chest.

He grinned down at her. "Is that all you got? I hate to say it, but you hit like a girl."

"I am a girl, you asshole," she growled as she planted her feet on the tiles and tried to buck him off.

Above her, he stilled. Catching his sudden stillness, she stared at him, her breasts rising and falling with every breath. His gaze dropped, and she could feel him openly checking out her breasts.

"Trust me. I know," he said after a long beat.

She felt as if someone had yanked the thick blanket of adrenaline off of her. Thoughts started to stream in. Time for a reality check. She was on the ground, and he was on top of her. If he moved a couple of inches back, he would be—

This was crazy. Then why did it feel so right?

"Uhmm…Max? Could you…let me up?"

He blinked. "Yeah." He moved fluidly then stood over her, one arm extended to pull her up. "Better?" he asked as she wiped her sweaty face on the sleeve of her PJ top.

"Yes." She looked up. "Thank you. As far as therapies went, that was crazy, but I guess it worked."

It took him a moment, then he grinned. "Am I good or what?"

She rolled her eyes. "Yup. But please don't make a practice of this. Or I won't be able to walk straight for a week."

"It was this, or kissing you until you saw stars and heard angels. Somehow, I didn't think you're ready for that. But don't worry, we'll get there."

She blinked.

Did he just...what did he say? "Max? You...I mean...we can't..."

He stepped inside and waited for her to follow. "Do you think you can sleep now?"

So, they were going to ignore the bomb he just dropped? Well, fine by her. She, herself, was a great believer in ignoring the big, fat elephants in the room anyway. "Yeah, I think so."

She stole another look at Max, who had moved into the kitchen for a drink of water. A small smile played on his lips as he opened the fridge and scanned its contents. He knew all right. He knew damn well what he was doing to her.

"I'll—I'll get back to my bed now."

From the kitchen, Max looked over and gave her an all-too-innocent smile. "Night, Eli. Sweet dreams."

Yep, he knew. The sneaky bastard.

❧❧❧

After leaving the Dojo, Jake drove to the busy St. George Terrace in the business district and parked his car in an empty bay closer to the Red Cross Blood Bank. A quick word with his mortgage broker, and then he would head back home to fix up that leaky pipe in his bathroom. Well. Unlike his life, at least that was one problem he could actually fix.

A red BMW came roaring down the street and ran the red light as he waited at the Zebra crossing for the signal to change. Holy crap. The guy must have been zooming at a hundred in the fifty-mile zone. He saw a group of seniors waiting at the side of the road shaking their heads in disgust. He shrugged at them. *Well, what can you do? Some morons will only learn things the hard way.*

Smiling, he let his gaze drift along the buildings with brightly colored awnings stretched along the opposite side of the street. Then he noticed.

Elena Martin.

Dressed in a sexy blue suit, and sky-high pumps, she walked briskly to a sleek, sophisticated building that stood independently, and slowed to a stop in front of its frosted glass and chrome door. The automatic door opened, and a couple in their late thirties exited, their faces bright with excitement. Elena stood where she was on the sidewalk, seemingly hesitant. Jake looked up and saw the board.

Jigsaw Adoptions and Counselling Services.

What was she doing at an adoption agency?

He saw her look to her left and right, then all around. She swiveled her head, and, for a split second, he was sure she saw him.

The walk signal changed at that moment. Someone bumped into him from behind. He resumed walking. When he reached the opposite end of the road, he looked for her.

But she was gone already.

Jake whistled and walked to his broker's office.
No clue what all that was about.

ఌఌఌ

She woke up feeling nauseous, strands of hair stuck
to her face, dizziness a tight blanket enveloping her senses. Her mouth was sandpaper dry. She shifted to left,
hoping to sit upright, then quickly dropped that idea as
pain flared in her lower abdomen. Through half opened
eyes, she scanned the immediate surroundings. The room
was slightly spinning, everything a blur, as if she was
caught in a merry-go-round.

She closed her eyes again, anxiety growing. Where
was she?

The next time she surfaced, she opened her eyes
wider and strained to keep it that way. A slight shift of
her head to the right showed her an aseptic hospital room
painted a stark white, a small desk and a plastic chair left
for visitors. The meal trolley placed next to her chrome-
railed bed held a plastic cup half filled with clear liquid.
Water. Sweet Jesus, she hadn't realized just how dry her
throat was.

Getting vertical took some intense gymnastic moves
on her part, considering the IV tubes attached to her arms.
Still, when she did it, she felt a small sense of achieve-
ment. One deep drag, and the water was gone. Half a cup
of water wouldn't cut it. She needed more.

She tried to shift her legs, felt the weight between her
thighs. She pushed down the wrinkled white top sheet,
saw the catheter bag and the long tube attached to it. A
violent shudder ripped through her as memories surfaced
like a surfer breaking out of a rampaging wave. *No. It
couldn't be.* Icy sweat frosted over her forehead as her
hands moved to drag the hem of her hospital gown up,

past her thighs, past her hips, until she could see her abdomen.

There it was, a huge white bandage covering her lower abdomen, just above her pubic line. Her hands trembled as she touched the dressing. She had to see. Had to know what they had done to her. Pulling at the edges of the bandage, she pulled the dressing halfway open and retched when her gaze met the grotesque line of stitches that lay like a hairy caterpillar amidst a wide patch of stinky betadine.

She knew it then, she had lost the battle. Still, she wondered how much he had instructed them to take. Because, depending on the answer to that question, she could make up her mind whether she should die, or spend the rest of her days in a jail cell.

A shiver of awareness prickled across the back of her neck. The door to her room opened. In the late afternoon sun that filtered through the window, she saw him.

He was smiling at her, no, make that a smirk.

He drew closer, blue eyes glinting, filled with the intent to hurt. Frantic, she struggled to get away, but realized the IV tubes held her arms in place.

"Please. No."

She jack-knifed to a sitting position, the sheets twisted around her, confining her arms against her sides. The tank top and cotton shorts she had worn to bed were both soaked with her sweat. Her eyes darted around. Nothing moved in the darkness of her bedroom. No one stood over her bed. Dream. It was just a stupid dream. She was safe. She had to be.

She breathed hard, trying to bring her heart rate to semi-normal. Thoughts swirled in her mind, mingling with the fuzzy memory of that sterile hospital room. For the first time since she broke free of her prison, she wished she wasn't alone.

The single light in the room came to life, startling her. Her pulse spiked.

Max.

Embarrassment heated her face. He must've heard her scream. Great! He must think she was nothing but a sissy.

He stood at the door, wearing satin shorts with a suggestive caption that read *Down under*. The sight would have made her smile. But then she looked up, met his perceptive green gaze. He looked so tense, muscles coiled tight, the skin on his face so taut as if it was being sucked against the bone. He didn't say a word, just strode forward and gathered her into his arms.

"Was it another nightmare, sweetheart?" His voice was dangerously quiet as he stroked back her hair and peered into her eyes.

Elena pressed her lips together as her words died down in her mouth. A hundred retorts flooded her brain, but she wanted none to make it past her lips. As much as she wanted to prove to him she wasn't a scared sissy, she knew *he* was in an even worse mood than her. She didn't dare push him. Besides, the perverted part of her was enjoying the skin-on-skin closeness to him. His warmth, the spicy Davidoff scent. She raised her arm to twine around his shoulder then stopped just in time before she made contact.

What the hell was she doing? This was wrong, on so many levels.

Irritated by her reaction, she pushed against his chest. He dropped his arms, but didn't move away. His gaze never left her face. She saw the brooding shadows in his eyes, saw them morph into something deeper, and felt her pulse kick up again. A sensual awareness tingled through her. Dammit, she could not allow this to happen, not now, not until she took care of Justin.

"I'm fine, Max," she said, scooting back. She wrapped her arms around her knees and allowed herself to relax against the headboard.

"You don't sound fine," he said, straightening to his full length. "You wanna talk about it?"

Embarrassment mingled with an upwelling of shame. Tears prickled behind her eyelids. She looked away from him. "I said I'm fine, Max."

He climbed onto the bed, his movements lithe as a sleek tiger, and closed the gap between them. Sitting on his knees, he put his hands on her shoulders. "You don't have to hide anymore, remember? That means that you can tell me whatever it is that's bothering you. If you don't feel safe here, or feel uncomfortable about something."

She raised her chin. "I'm fine, Max," she said roughly. "And I feel quite safe in your home. But I think it might be a good idea if I move out of here. I've been thinking about it. I'm cramping your life. I think I should—"

He gripped her forearm tight. Then dropped it the next second as if she burned his palm. "Look," he said, stroking her elbow. "Let's stop this crazy talk right here, right now. You're not going anywhere. At least until we figure out a way to get hold of your mom. And, you're not cramping my life. I like having you here."

"But this is the third night in a row I've been disturbing your sleep. You don't have to put up with my shit. That's not fair to you."

He smiled. "Hey, you put up with my snoring. I put up with your bad dreams. I would say it's pretty even."

"Max—"

"Come on." He caught her wrist and pulled her out of the bedroom. "Let's get you some warm milk."

She pulled back. "You think warm milk will stop my bad dreams?"

"No idea. But I've been told my snores are like a one-man heavy metal concert. Hopefully, the milk will help you sleep right through it." He moved his right hand forward in a sliding motion.

She smiled. They were back in neutral territory. Playful, silly Max, she could handle. It was the dark and enigmatic version she had no clue how to deal with.

Max got the milk from the fridge, nuked it for a minute, and handed it to her. They sat together at the dining table while she drank it. Neither spoke. But the silence between them was comfortable, not awkward at all. When she finished the drink, he took her back to her room and tucked her into her bed.

He yawned as he switched the light off. "If you can't go to sleep, go and watch TV, or read something. Don't worry about bothering me."

She smiled. "All right."

She expected him to leave, but he stood there watching her, looking oddly hesitant. "Did I tell you about the one time I socked Jake in my sleep and gave him a black eye?"

She shook her head, wondering where he was going with this.

"Well, after I left Sunset Bay, I used to have nightmares. Pretty bad ones. One night, Jake tried to wake me while I was in the middle of one. I thought it was Mark. I socked the shit out of him, and he went flying across the room."

Elena gasped.

"My point," he said, grinning, "Your nightmares, it's not a bother to me. Because I get it. Been there, done that. If you ever feel the need to punch someone, baby, I'm your guy."

Her throat ached, and her eyes welled, but she didn't cry. She felt solid in a way she hadn't felt in a long time. "I'll keep that in mind."

"Goodnight, Eli." He turned to leave.

"Max?"

"Hmm?"

"Thanks. For everything. I never got a chance to say that before." She was referring to a night that happened so long ago.

There was a lengthy pause. For a few seconds, she thought he wasn't going to speak. Then he did. "If I had to do it all over again, I'd still do it. For you. You know that, right?"

She knew what he meant. God, she knew exactly what he meant. He would take out Justin. For her. And he wouldn't think twice about it.

For now, those words were enough. The certainty in his voice was enough. They worked like magic.

"Yes." Her voice was a bare whisper.

He closed the door after him.

As she closed her eyes and tried to sleep, she felt steadier, calmer.

Nightmares would come. But now she had a talisman.

CHAPTER 11

Max hadn't planned on meeting up with Jake. Truth be told, he had been avoiding Jake, and everyone in their friends' circle, like the plague for the last two weeks. The situation with Eli was very much volatile. Her mom had gone AWOL. The bastard who terrorized her was still out there, hunting for her. Whenever Jake rung, Max either hung up mumbling some piss-poor excuses or switched off his cell. He'd taken a month off from the dojo, not wanting to give the peanut gallery another show. Jake, he knew, wasn't the best when it came to admin work, but until he figured out how to handle the shit storm that was Eli's life, Max thought it was best to lay low.

When Jake texted him and told him in his no-nonsense terms that unless Max showed up for Sunday morning class gradings, Jake would pay a visit to Elena later, Max knew he had to do something. Hence the impromptu lunch date.

They met up at Paddy's little tavern in North Bridge just after two. Everything felt awkward. From the handshakes to chest bumps to back slaps. In the end, they settled for a chin tip and a *What's up?* before parking their asses on two low-backed bar stools. Paddy wasn't around, which was a relief. The usually crowded place was empty, save the few seniors out to splash their pension money.

Max settled for a lemon-lime bitter and a bowl of Nachos while Jake ordered a Vodka on the rocks.

As soon as Cherry, their waitress, turned her back, Jake hissed. "Are you fucking kidding me? Lime lemon bitter? What's next? A mani-pedi package?"

Max shrugged. He wasn't about to tell Jake that Elena didn't like hard drinkers. And Max wasn't about to push his luck by turning up plastered with her in his residence.

That would pretty much put a full stop to her trust and his peace of mind. So yeah—he would settle for a sissy drink.

Cue the awkward silence.

"So?" Jake cocked one brow at Max as Cherry returned with their order.

It pained him to admit, but there was no other choice. "Eli doesn't like the hard stuff."

Jake grinned, flashing a glimpse of the carefree guy he used to be. "Man, I've heard about guys who ended up pussy-whipped. But this…"

Feeling uneasy about discussing his relationship with Eli, Max attempted to steer the conversation away. A pansy move on his part. "Jake, about the classes. I'll need more—"

Jake waved his hand in a slicing motion. "It's all under control. And I didn't come here to talk about that."

No shit. "Okay…"

Jake took a large sip of his drink and closed his eyes for a second. Then he opened them and looked directly at Max. "Buddy, I've known you for nearly fifteen years. I know I reacted badly when I heard about you and that woman. But—"

Max strummed his fingers on the granite benchtop.

He kept his gaze deliberately fixed on the bowl of Nachos in front of him. "She's got a name, Jake."

Max looked at his buddy and found him staring moodily into his drink. "Do you have any fucking idea what you're doing, mate?"

"Yes." A pause. "Yes, Jake, I do."

The silence between them grew louder than a scream. Max took a large gulp of his drink. God, why in the heaven's name had he ordered this crap? He wanted something stronger, something that would go straight to his head and make everything seem fuzzy and soft.

Jake shook his head after so much deliberation. "I don't think you do. Forget about what you did for her when she was your teenage love. That was then. Done. Dusted. History. But this—now—you're playing with fire."

"I don't see how. Even if it is, it doesn't matter."

Jake looked at him, his gaze steady. "What the hell does that mean? From where I sit, this woman has been messing with you forever. She turned your life upside down, destroyed your peace, and now she has turned you into a complete pansy. How can any of this be okay?"

"I love her. Always have." There. It was that simple when it came to her.

More head shakes. A string of uncensored curses. "Lust. Chemistry. Pure and simple. It's known to make grown men act like boneheads. I should know. I've been in your shoes once."

"Fuck off, Jake."

Jake looked at him, his cobalt blue eyes flashing with anger.

Max wasn't about to back down. He didn't come here to argue with Jake. But it seemed to him, that unless he made Jake see what he really felt about Eli, they would forever be stuck at an impasse. "Listen." He quick-

ly scanned the place to make sure there were no Nosy
Nelly's around. Then he looked back at Jake. "I've been
in lust before. I've fucked enough women to know when
I see the real deal. Eli is the real deal for me, Jake. It has
always been her. The sooner you accept that, the sooner
we can get past this shit and move on with our lives."

Jake gave him a funny, twisted grin over the rim of
his glass. "Mark my words, buddy. You'll regret this. Big
time."

Max shook his head. It was like preaching to a lamp
post. Nothing would get through to Jake until he was
ready.

Jake took a deep swig, drained the glass and
slammed it on the bench. "This woman, Elena, she is a
beautiful piece of ass. But at the end of the day, that's all
she is. All she should be. Fuck her seven ways until Sunday if you want to, but then, let her go."

And we're back to square one.

Another silence stretched out. Eventually Jake cursed
under his breath.

"Bye, Jake." Max pushed back his stool and stood. "I
think we're done here." He moved past Jake then
frowned when he felt the heavy grip around his wrist.
"What?"

As Jake released his hold, his eyes never wavered.
"Justin Adams was at the dojo, yesterday."

"Who?"

"Justin Adams. Elena's husband."

Max felt his jaw drop in sincere shock. "What the
fuck are you talking about?"

"Max." Jake's voice took on the tone of pity. "She's
been lying to you, buddy. She's married. Her husband is
Justin Adams. A nice guy. He's been looking for her
since she did a runner on him."

Fucking hell.

He grabbed Jake by shoulders and leaned in. "Listen to me. Stay the fuck away from him. He's bad news."

Jake's gaze fired into his, blue sheathed in ice. "All he wants is his wife back."

Shit.

"She is not his wife, Jake. He's a crazy bastard," Max ground out through gritted teeth.

Jake's expression shifted into frustration, and he swatted Max's hands away. "I don't know what stories she had been spinning to you. But there are always two sides to every coin."

"That's a load of crap."

Jake looked away then turned back to Max. "He wants to talk to you."

Max snorted.

"You stole his wife, bro." Max opened his mouth to refute, but Jake silenced him with a hand. "You did. There's no two ways about it. The poor sod ought to have something to say about it. And in my books, you damn well should give him a chance to talk. You owe him that much."

Anger mingled with frustration, and guilt wrapped them both in a tight bow. Fuck!

"Listen, things aren't that simple."

Jake waved a hand, dismissing him. "You should go talk to him."

He nodded. "I'll think about it." He straightened. Now that he thought about it, maybe meeting the fucker wasn't such a bad idea.

He whispered the name in his mind. *Justin Adams.* If that was indeed his real name. Max highly doubted it.

Eli still refused to go to the cops. And she wouldn't give up the fucker's real name even if her life depended on it. He'd tried, so he should know. The woman was as stubborn as they came. He knew her reservations, the reasons behind them, and couldn't blame her. Unless one was determined to cash in on the sob story, no woman would want to publicize the fact that she had been terrorized by a man she had gone out with. Add to the fact that the fucker was a cop, the media would have a field day with the story if it ever got out. She wouldn't ever have peace of mind. She would forever be a victim.

So where did that leave them?

The woman was his. And there was nothing Max wouldn't do if it meant ensuring her safety and their future together.

Even if it meant killing a cop.

⌁⌁⌁

As Max walked out of the gym after his work out, his cell phone rang. A stiff wind caught his jacket as he reached into the inner pocket and withdrew his phone. An unknown number flashed on the screen.

"Hello?"

"Max Logan? This is Justin Adams."

A long pause.

"I'm—I'm Elizabeth's husband."

Crazy and delusional.

The rage he had been unable to contain since Eli turned up at his doorstep came back with a bite. "I heard you've been checking up on me, mate."

"I—Yes—I mean no—It's nothing like that. I like to talk to you. Alone. If it's not too much bother."

Max didn't know whether the guy was layering it thick with his fake politeness, or that's the way he always spoke. It would have helped a big deal if the guy had dropped a few F-bombs as his opening shot. This was unexpected. "Name the place, Adams, I'll be there."

At the other end, Justin Adams let out a deep yet unsteady breath, as if he had been unsure of his reception. "How about my place? I live at twenty-five Sandalford Avenue, Kalamunda."

Huh? He gave up the location of his hidy hole that easily?

Max did some quick math in his head. Kalamunda was all the way up in the hills. It would take him a good hour. The sensible thing was to ask Justin to meet him at a place of his choosing. That way he could avoid any unexpected surprises. You never knew what kind of booby traps the crazy bastard had in store for him. But some morbidly curious part of him was jumping at the opportunity to meet the bastard on his home turf. "Around five?"

"Thanks, Mr. Logan. Appreciate it." Justin hung up.

Max decided he would go. So, it would be just him and Justin.

Perfect.

CHAPTER 12

Justin Adams was a disappointment.

In the movies, there was always something that gave away the silent perpetrator. A jaw tic, nails bitten down to the quick, drug-glazed eyes. Something. Justin looked rather normal, not wired at all, and when he shook hands with Max, rather nervous. There were no sociopathic vibes that Max could pick up, and his internal alarms weren't buzzing like crazy.

He had always thought blue cop uniforms added depth to a man's image. At least until this evening. On Justin, the uniform was wasted. Everything about him screamed geek. He was short, maybe five-foot-eight, with a mop of curly blond hair that was a bit greasy. Thin nose, thin lips, even a thin frame. The only arresting feature was his blue eyes. They were huge and wide apart in his longish, smooth-shaven face. *This* was the guy who had terrorized his Eli?

Evil came in all shapes and sizes, Max reminded himself, and it would be horribly short-sighted of him if took this guy for granted based on his appearance alone.

Taking a deep breath, Max looked around at his surroundings. If Justin Adams was a disappointment, it was nothing compared to what Max felt when he saw his house. He'd expected the guy to be living in a haunted cabin in the middle of the hundred acres wood, some-place so remote even Google maps wouldn't have any luck locating it. But the charming colonial home was starkly beautiful in its lines, rich with character that came with age, it might have been a photograph shot for a calendar.

Nestled on the edge of Gooseberry Hill National Park, the house, with its wide French doors opening to a wraparound porch and glorious rose gardens stood a few yards away from the main road. As if those trappings weren't enough, there was a freaking bird bath and a cherub shaped water fountain he kept in good condition.

"Please come in," Justin led him down into his house, and when he stepped into the neatly kept living area, Max felt the second stirrings of unease.

On the wall facing the front door were three huge sepia photographs of Eli, each more potent than the other. It was said that one single photograph cannot capture the essence of the subject, a layer maybe. But these photographs of Eli, Max had to admit, they were spot on. As soon as Max saw that, he started to notice other things. Little things. Like the basket of wool and some half-knitted baby garments left at the foot of a reclining chair. A river landscape with the name—Elizabeth Adams—signed in her bold, slashing hand on the narrow wall between the windows. Several pictures of Justin and Eli together tacked onto the pin-up board above the computer nook. She had her arms around him in one of them, and she was smiling, like a woman in love.

Something was wrong. Deep in his gut, Max knew it. Everything about this place said it was a home. If Justin had intended to spook him with this shrine-for-Elizabeth setup, he had definitely achieved that. But Max wasn't about to admit it to the other guy.

"Can I get you tea or coffee? I, myself, prefer coffee,

but Elizabeth loved her tea. She always stocked a variety of them."

Max shook his head. "Look, mate," he said with some effort, because the whole situation was starting to piss him off. "We both know this is awkward. So, let's cut to the chase. What do you want from me?"

For a long moment, Justin said nothing. Then he gestured Max to sit down on the black leather couch. With a sigh, Max sat. Justin took the seat opposite to him. Max watched the other guy as he dragged a hand over his face. In the tight, awkward silence of the beautiful house, Max thought how alone they both were.

Eli's voice barged into his head: '*He is the monster I'm running from.*'

What the hell had he agreed to?

"I haven't slept since the day she left. I am so worried about her."

Max snorted and lounged back. "Worried she might blab what a crazy son of a bitch you are? Worried you might lose your job? Enough with this bullshit, Adams. The game's up. I get that you're mad things didn't go according to your plan. But—"

"Mad? Do I look mad to you?" Justin angled his head, his baby blue eyes all earnest.

No, he didn't look mad. He looked sad, pathetic even.

Suddenly he put his face in his hands. "I miss her so damn much," he whimpered, and with horror, Max realized that the other guy was crying.

What the fuck?

"Justin," Max said carefully. He had no clue what this guy was up to. For all he knew, the clever son of a bitch was putting up a show for his benefit. If Justin was a hair-trigger psycho as Eli described, then Max had to tread very carefully around him. His intention was to get

Justin to stop stalking Eli, not piss him off. "Elizabeth wasn't happy in your relationship. She wants you to stop doing whatever you're planning to do. Sometimes people fall out of love as fast as they fall in love. If you care about her as you say, then it will be in her best interest if you let her go."

Justin lifted his gaze to Max. It glittered with a sheen of tears. Then he looked away, as if embarrassed, and wiped his tears on his blue shirt sleeve. Max was left to stare at him. What the hell was going on with this guy?

A tense quiet followed.

"That's where you are wrong, Mr. Logan. Elizabeth had been happy. We had a wonderful marriage, until—" He gulped and looked around his house. "We were happy here. This was our home. Alex, me, and Elizabeth. We were a unit. And now…" He trailed off.

Max ignored the remark about marriage and focused on the new name that cropped up. "Who is Alex?"

For a moment, Justin stared at Max, and a look of surprise crept onto his face. "She didn't tell you about Alex?" A noise came out of his mouth that was half sob, half growl. "Alex is—he was—excuse me for a second." He jumped to his feet and hurried through a door to the left.

For a few moments, Max was left to ponder the mystery that was Justin Adams. What the hell was going on here? Justin seemed seriously delusional. There would be no getting through to him. Max had come here prepared to kill the bastard, but now he was having serious second thoughts. It would be like kicking a puppy, or smacking a baby. Too easy. Maybe what the guy really needed was medical attention.

"Look," Justin came back carrying a red velvet covered photo album. He held it open before Max. Inside, there were rows after rows of pictures of a beautiful little boy. About a year old. Max didn't have to be a rocket scientist to figure out that the boy with sharp blue eyes and mop of blond hair was a by-product of Justin. He couldn't make himself look away. A question lingered: why the hell hadn't Eli told him about this little boy? If she had omitted to tell him about the kid, then what else had she kept from him?

"Alex. My son. We lost him a year ago."

"How?" Max asked, rooted to the spot. No, it wasn't anger that was burning in his gut, it was disappointment.

Justin closed the album and placed it on the coffee table with care. His fingers trembled as he groped for the armrest. "He…ah…drowned. In the bathtub. A freak accident, that's what the investigating officer said. But—I knew it wasn't. If I had told them the truth, I would've lost both my son and my wife, so I kept quiet."

"What the hell are you saying, mate?" Max tried to keep his voice steady, but it came out as a ragged gasp.

There was a long pause as Justin lowered himself to the leather seat. "Alex's death wasn't an accident. Elizabeth, my poor Elizabeth did it."

Max let out a humorless laugh. "Are you fucking kidding me, mate? You stalked her until she was forced to give up her home and run away, and now you're blaming *her* for the death of your son? You're sick." Max got to his feet and went up close to Justin. To hell with the consequences. The bastard might pull his gun on him. But Max couldn't sit and listen to the crap another second. "Do yourself a favor, mate. See a good doctor. You need help."

"You don't know Elizabeth like I do," Justin said as if Max hadn't spoken. "She is a beautiful person inside and out. But post-natal depression is a bitch. It did a number on my poor Elizabeth. After we had Alex, she was always moody and sad. I put it down to stress. New baby, new house. She didn't have many friends. And I was busy with my job," he gulped. "No. It was my fault. I should have paid more attention to her. The signs were all there."

Max straightened to his full height. "Nice story. But I'm not buying it. I know Eli. She is not the nutcase. You are."

Max walked to the door.

"She has been stalking you, you know."

He froze, feeling a ripple of alarm skate down his spine. He turned and stared pointedly at Justin. "What the hell are you talking about?"

"Eli. She has done this before. So, I know."

Max cleared his throat once. Twice. "Done what before?"

"Running away from me. Stalking guys she felt attracted to. Playing house with someone. It didn't end well for the other guy. I hope the same thing doesn't happen to you."

Max took a step forward. "Are you threatening me, officer?"

For the first time, Justin snorted. He got to his feet and crossed over to where Max stood with his hands jammed into the front pockets of his jeans. "No. I'm warning you. Elizabeth's got a problem. Ignoring it isn't going to make it go away."

"No, mate, you've got a problem."

As the blue eyes stared into his, the air between them shifted, and Max had the feeling that the other guy had reached his limit.

"Listen, Elizabeth's problem must have started out when she was young, but it never got treated. Having Alex, the hormonal changes, it just made it worse. Often, she gets fixated on something, or someone. It started off as harmless hobbies. For a while it was knitting. Then she took up painting. I can show you her paintings if you like. Crazy, nonsense that she called art. There are two rooms full of them. But then she lost interest in them, as she always does."

Max winced and rubbed his temples. He could feel a headache brewing there. "Why the hell are you doing this? Can't you just accept that she is not into you anymore and move on?"

Justin rushed through the rest, "After Alex was gone, we weren't on good terms. I loved her, but a part of me couldn't get past the thought that she'd killed our son. It was at that time she saw my colleague, Derrick. For months, she would leave the house after me, and stalk him. She even broke into his house twice to learn more about him. His taste in music, his friends, his favorite restaurants. I am not making this up. I know this because she told me. She said she often made up situations just to be around him. At first, I didn't notice any of this. By the time I caught on, she had already left. One day, she turned up at his place claiming I was abusing her. Derrick, the idiot, he was crazy about her. He didn't believe a word I said. He let her stay. Two weeks later, Elizabeth came back to me and said she had made a mistake. Three days after that, Derrick wound up dead. Accident. Brake failure. How convenient."

Max swallowed. There were sharp needles in his throat. He looked at Justin, who seemed to have aged right in front of his eyes. Was any of this true? He could either trust Eli and go mad wondering about Justin's words, or trust Justin and lose Eli. Either way, he felt he had walked into an alternate universe.

"Why the hell should I trust you?"

"You don't have to. But you should, for your own sake."

Max chuckled in a short burst. "If she's a crazy bitch

as you say, then why the hell do you want her back?"

"Because I know she's sick, and she can't help what she thinks or does."

Determined to keep it together, Max took a deep breath. "Let me get this straight. Are you saying you never stalked Elizabeth in your life? You never broke into her apartment, stole her things, kept them as little mementos maybe?" Max took another step forward until he was nose to chest with the other guy. It gave him a small amount of satisfaction when Justin shrank back an inch as if intimidated by Max's tactics. "And you didn't have anything to do with the death of her friend Jerry?"

When Justin just blinked at him, Max smiled. The bastard was worried.

Justin coughed twice, as if his throat was so dry he couldn't get the words out. "Me? Stalking? I can see how much thought she has put into all of this." He looked at Max. "I never stalked Elizabeth, Mr. Logan. Never had to. We both met, fell in love, got engaged and married, as normal couples do. And Jerry—She once told me she had a friend named Jerry. But as far as I know, the guy committed suicide due to depression."

Max shook his head. "You're full of shit, Adams."

Justin took a deep breath. He looked baffled, in pain. "I can see you like playing the knight in shining armor. Elizabeth often has that effect on guys. But you're wrong. This whole thing is a mistake."

Christ, why was he getting so worked up over this guy's words?

"Goodbye, Justin. Get some help."

Max walked past him and opened the front door. A soft rain was pattering outside. In the silence that followed, Max stared at Justin's beautiful gardens. There was a conflict raging inside him, a bizarre internal war between half-lies and half-truths. Who to believe, who not to? He didn't want to think of Eli in the wrong, but the rational part of him was urging him to think twice about Justin's words.

Justin fell into step. "Do you want a word of advice? Leave her while you can. I know her. She will fuck you up."

Max snorted. "Yeah, right. Nice try."

A trembling hand covered his forearm. "She might be a novelty to you. A good fuck. Beautiful company. But she's my life. She's all I've got. Please, give her back to me."

"You'd like that, wouldn't you?" Max asked over his shoulder. "You give one hell of a performance, Adams. I'll give you that. But I'm not about to play right into your hands. For now, I'll stick with Eli."

Justin dropped his arm. "You're making a mistake."

Max bound down the two steps to Justin's garden. Then he turned. "Forget her, Adams. She's mine now."

Justin gave another baffled, sympathetic smile. "You won't get to keep her, Mr. Logan. No one ever does."

CHAPTER 13

Eli was going through her routine drill when he walked into her bedroom. Smart girl. She was keeping up her practice and, from what he'd seen so far, she was darn good at it. After meeting Justin, he wouldn't blame her. Now that he had some time to calm the hell down and think about it, Max was certain that the bastard was more dangerous than he looked. The sick fuck was unpredictable, wily, and smooth as an eel. His wouldn't-hurt-a-fly expression and unbanked concern for his, seemingly crazy, wife was all an act. He was delusional and crazy. And that made him doubly dangerous in Max's book.

So now what? He had met the bastard, let him know that Eli was off-limits to him. But the million-dollar question now: would he listen?

If he didn't, then what? So far Eli was safe in his house. But for how long?

The good thing, he thought, he wasn't completely without resources, or holds. There was always an option of reaching out to Chief Chalker. So far, he had left it as a last resort. And Eli had mixed feelings about approaching the police. And who could blame her? Getting her to file a report against Justin would take some convincing. He would have to figure out a way to do it. And maybe, just maybe, it wouldn't hurt to keep the chief posted about the situation. Justin Adams was a menace who should be locked up in a looney bin.

Max's gaze narrowed on Eli as she balanced on one foot and performed a complicated move. Should he tell her about meeting Justin? She was a prime target, and Justin had plenty to lose. But if Max opened his big mouth now and blabbed about Justin, she would freak. Her first thought would be to simply pack up and leave.

No, it was better if she didn't know.

Standing there, watching her move fluidly, her features tight with undisguised tension, it hit home again. *I don't want to lose her. Ever.*

She saw him and paused. "Hi."

"Are you almost done?" he asked, parking himself on the edge of her bed.

She nodded. "Why?"

"I'm starving. Shall we go out and get something to eat?"

"I—" She hesitated.

"You could use some fresh air, Eli. You've been cooped up inside this house for days now." He extended an arm. She took it.

"I don't—" She stopped, as if trying to puzzle it out. She didn't look at him. "I don't think it's a good idea."

"I think it's a damn great idea." He pointed to his watch. "You've got ten minutes to shower and show up. Or I'm dragging you out in your workout gear."

That got her hackles up. She placed both hands on her hips. "Maybe I'm not hungry."

"Oh, I think you're," he added with a smile and let his gaze run over her. If anyone had told him a month ago that loose gray sweats and a cami was a sexy outfit on a woman, he would have laughed his head off. But now— *Christ.* Full mast.

"I think we both are," His voice dropped, gaze roaming over her in another deliberate once over.

She sucked in a breath, the movement lifting her breasts up.

Look away. Look away, you jackass.

He finally let his gaze shift away from her. Jesus. He shouldn't stare at her right now. Hell, speaking to her was a mistake, because it made him want to draw her closer and nibble at her pouty lips.

"I don't wanna go. I don't think you should go either. I could make something for both of us."

That got his attention. "We're eating out, and that's final. Your time starts now," he said, studying her expression of exasperation mixed with arousal.

"Max, please."

Did that sound like a moan? It totally did.

Dammit, he was beginning to feel that tingling heat again. Just when he thought he had everything under control, she said or did something that made him hard again.

He didn't speak again until she showed up ten minutes later, dressed in black jeans and a white top, a yellow cardigan over it.

"Ready?"

She shrugged. Then she surprised him by falling into step with him. With her body huddled closer to his, and her hands so soft, her fingers slipped into his, intertwining them.

Since when did an innocent gesture like that switch on his protective instincts?

Since the hands belonged to Elizabeth Campbell.

Jesus. He needed to get his head on straight and fast.

Eli tilted her head, and the curvy tips of her silky hair drifted over his forearm. "Max?"

Her gaze met his then, the innocent look tempting far more than her supple perfection.

"Yeah?" he choked out, his gaze suddenly stuck on her mouth, making it hard for him to breathe. Christ. He was hard—all around.

Space.

He needed to put some space between them.

Pretending to play it cool, he slipped his fingers out of her hold, then jammed it straight into his hair. She had to know that was a dicey move.

Smiling, instead of looking surprised, she said, "I thought I was the only one who got a problem getting touchy feely. Looks like you have it too."

Shit. Play it cool. He cleared his throat. "What do you mean?"

She smiled again. "Come on, Max. You were never good with hugs and stuff. I remember how you used to freeze whenever anyone touched you. God forbid, if I ever gave you a hug. You would go all stiff as if someone rammed a stick up your...you-know-what." Oh, hell. She looked him over. "Me and Mum, we used to talk about it, you know." She lifted one shoulder that had her breast brush against his elbow.

Max gritted his teeth. "Talk about what?"

"Well, it was Mum mostly. But she used to think that—maybe if you were—"

Her soft, husky words did crazy things to him before her words registered. What was she getting at? "What?"

Cue the silence.

"What, Eli?"

Very softly, she said, "Gay."

No fucking way!

Annoyed, pissed, he pulled the brake on his legs and rounded on her. "I'm shocked that you even knew what being gay meant back then, Eli. Besides, what was your mum thinking, talking about such stuff to a fourteen-year-old?"

She tried to look scared, but the twitching smile ruined the effect. To him, she looked cute—not a word he would ever say in public. But there you go.

Breathless eyes wide, she murmured, "So, are you? Gay, I mean."

He looked at her lips then at her eyes. Just to tease her, and to indulge a bit in the masochistic tendencies he hadn't known he possessed, he rubbed his thumb over her soft bottom lip. His dick twitched in response.

Her breath hitched again. Yet, she didn't step away from him. They both knew where this was leading.

"No, Eli, I'm not gay. And if you had any idea about what's going on in my head right now, you wouldn't have brought up this subject."

Pale moonlight washed over her features and gleamed off her hair, making her appear an ethereal fairy. But it was the long, harsh breath she exhaled that captured his attention the most and made him realize how pivotal this moment was in their lives.

"What are your thoughts?" Her words were soft, kitten soft.

He let out an unsteady laugh, and then his gaze zoomed back in on her lips. Her tongue chose that moment to dip out of her mouth to lick her lips.

Far out!

He didn't trust his hands to remain still any longer, so he stuffed them both into the front pockets of his jeans and rocked back on his heels. "I'm fucking crazy about you, Eli. Always have been. Always will be. And before you ask, no, this is not about sex. Although that would be fucking great. But this is about you. Only you."

Amusement fled, now her eyes looked the size of dinner plates. "No." She shook her head in denial when he said nothing. A thick cloud ambled across the moon, sponging up the weak light. A moment later, lightning flashed across the horizon, and the first fat drop of rain fell on the tip of her nose.

Curving an arm around her middle, she took a step back. "No, Max. Don't."

He leveled her a hard stare, worry a tight coil in his gut. "Yes, Elizabeth."

On a sharply inhaled breath, she tried to dart around him in a rush. Acting on reflex, he yanked her back to his side, and damn, it felt right having her close. His resolve not to push her into something she was not ready for weakened as she squirmed. And then she went ahead and bit her lip. He lost the fight.

Maybe his brain, centered on getting her naked, must have short-circuited somehow. Because the next thing he knew, he was grabbing her hair, tipping her head back and covering her mouth with his.

But, damn, she tasted good. Under his fingertips, the frantic pulse at the base of her neck raced. She wriggled like a worm caught on the hook, and he countered by caging her against his chest. She clutched at his biceps, and made a soft sound he interpreted as anticipation. His open mouth had free access to her throat, her shoulder, her earlobe and he made use of his tongue and teeth to drive her out of her ever-lovin' mind. He nipped, he suckled, he licked. All the while she clung to him, letting him kiss her, deeper and hotter.

Stop, you Jackass. Don't scare her off. The rational words came out of nowhere like a well-appointed arrow.

Fuck.

So much temptation. But fuck.

As much as he wanted to be sliding deep inside her right now, he knew he had to put a full stop. This was not a fling, not for him. He wanted so much more from her. And until she was ready…

He caught her head in both hands and slowly broke

the kiss. Eli whipped her head back, her gaze still glazed. Lust had darkened her face, left her gray eyes smoky.

Keeping his expression stony wasn't easy, not when he wanted to pick up where he'd left off and get her under him. But he knew in his bones that the best way with Eli was to ease her into the idea of being with him. Once she trusted him, he could slowly coax her into deepening their relationship. After a bastard like her ex, she deserved so much better.

Until then, he would have to suck it up and take a helluva lot of cold showers.

Sweet Baby Jesus, you better have a sainthood and a pedestal ready for me.

"I—I don't know—I'm so sorry. I shouldn't have—" A hollowness filled her voice as she took a quick step back. Worse than her apology, in her voice, he heard the edge of fear, and maybe a shitload of hurt. What the hell?

Then his brain did some quick reorientation. Everything he had learned about her relationship with fucking Justin came back to him. Bloody hell! No way would he let her take the blame for what had almost happened between them.

Max took two steps that put her chest to chest with him. She held up a hand, as if that would stop him. He stepped right into it, grabbed that hand and looped her arm around his neck.

A deep breath lifted and mashed her breath against his ribcage. She shifted, tilted her head back, her gaze stunned. More than anything else, seeing that particular look on her face convinced him he'd made the right decision.

"Max," she whispered.

Eyes narrowed, teeth locked in tight, he growled. "Why the hell did you just apologize to me?"

He knew why, but he wanted to hear her say it. Frus-

tration and fury punched in his gut as her throat worked
on a hard swallow.

Eli squeezed her eyes shut, as if trying to block out
his anger. "I provoked you. I said things that forced you
to kiss me."

Bloody-fucking-Justin. The bastard messed up this
sweet, lovely woman big time.

The situation warranted some immediate damage
control. Max responded the only way he knew. He
grabbed her chin in one hand and kissed her hard. "Like
hell, you forced me." One kiss. One nip. "I kissed you
because—" Bite. "—I wanted to. I've been waiting nearly
fifteen years for that kiss. Like hell will I let you take all
the credit. It was all me, baby. All me."

Her small hands wrapped around his thick biceps.
"What are you saying, Max?"

Using one hand, he tucked a stray lock of her hair
behind her ear. "I'm fucking crazy about you, Eli." He
pressed his forehead against hers. Looking into her gaze
was not an option any longer. He would just lose it if he
saw fear and embarrassment there. "Remember that day
when you left a feather under my pillow to catch my bad
dreams? That's the day I fell in love with you."

The first tear spilled onto his wrist. "Max, no, that
was a long time ago. We were just kids. You can't be in
love with me."

He choked out a laugh and dropped his arms. She
was not ready. Probably was scared spitless since he was
coming onto her like a freight train with no brakes. "Fine.
I just made that up to make you feel better. Happy?"

He turned to walk away, but she grabbed his arm.
"This thing between us, it can't go anywhere, Max. Not
now, not ever. He is still out there and—"

"That's your hangup. Not mine."

"But there are things—"

He knew what she was about to say. So, he ruthlessly squashed her words before they spilled with another kiss.

Wind lashed the rain against his back. Thunder shook the air around them. Locking her hands around his neck, she moaned.

Heat rolled through him like flash fire. But he was determined not to come on too strongly. He had said far too much as it was. She needed time. Hell, they were both new to this game. It would do them good if they took their time.

So, he tapered off the kisses with throbbing impatience, not devouring, not asking for more. He nibbled on her earlobe closer to his mouth, slipped his tongue into her ear, and grinned when she rewarded him with a shiver. *Can't love you, my ass.*

Slowly, deliberately, he released her and settled back on his heels.

Her fingers played with her gold chain. Tug. Loop. Tug. "Max. I cannot love you. I mean it. I—"

He cut her off. "You better hold it right there, Elizabeth."

Her head whipped up abruptly. Anger flashed in the depths of her gray eyes. He knew it took a lot of effort on her part to let her gaze stay leveled on his. "Dammit, Max. Will you let me finish?"

Confrontation really wasn't her thing. Many women reveled in bringing their man to their knees, but not Eli. *Good for you, Eli.*

"Sorry, baby. You're about to say something which we both know is a lie. So, leave it for now. We'll come back to it and discuss when we both feel ready."

Long pause where there was nothing but the sound of lashing rain and moaning wind.

Damn. He hated the conversational void. But had no idea how to fill it.

Finally, she lifted her hands, as if frustrated, then let them fall. "Fine. Have it your way."

Amusement and desire tangled him in knots. She was so damn beautiful. Brave. And *wet*. Fuck, look at her nipples. *Not the best time, you moron.*

Yeah, right.

To take his mind off the current topic, he looked at his car parked on the verge beyond his front gate. The rain was still going at full throttle. And they were getting drenched. Not that he minded having her wet and wriggly in her arms. But the last thing he wanted was her to catch a cold.

He turned back to her. She was still staring at him, her expression telling him she wasn't happy that he had the last word. Tough.

He gave her an easy grin. "Now that we've settled that, can we go and get that burger? I'm starving."

Frustration was etched deep into her features, but she let him win the round by nodding slightly. "Fine." She started walking, and he followed her, his mouth twitching with a smile. His legs ate up the ground, and he caught up with her in three brisk steps.

The increasing wind slapped against their backs, plastering her hair to her skull. When another lightning flashed, she gasped and ducked against him. Now this, he thought as he guided her into the safety of his car, he could get used to.

ᘓᘓᘓ

His car got totaled that night.

He still had trouble believing it. But the four slashed tires and the sunburst pattern where someone had whacked his windshield with something really heavy told a different story.

Beside him, Eli stood, shaking, looking vulnerable and angry. His lips tightened when he saw the way her hands trembled, the way she wrapped them around her slim waist to stop him from seeing.

"Hey, babe. It's okay. Must be some local kids," he murmured, drawing her closer.

"Like hell, it is," she whirled, eyes glittering. "It's him. I know it. I just know it." At that, she burst into tears.

Max looked around. They had pulled in some crowd. A few passers-by had stopped to stare.

"Easy." He pushed Eli into the house, shut the door, and turned to her. "It's okay." He watched her visibly pale before him. Damn, Justin. Hidden in shadows, the bastard was ripping at his woman, battering her mind and soul, chipping away every last bit of self-confidence she'd had garnered in the last few months.

"I—" she licked her lips. "I've got to leave. I'm putting you in danger." She shook her head, squared her shoulders, as if that would help harden her resolve. "I'll leave tonight."

He caught her forearms and jerked her to his chest. "Like hell, you will."

Big gray eyes stared at him, full of helpless anger and dismay. "Let me go, Max. This is for the best."

"No. You're going to stay right here. With me. And we're going to put an end to this shit once and for all."

"You can't protect me. It's too late for that." She squirmed, and he dropped his arms. She took a step back. "I better go pack."

She was already turning, heading for her bedroom.

"I'll simply follow you. You're not doing this alone. Remember what I said before? I fucking love you. That means I stick up for you."

She stopped, then her eyes lifted to his face. One tear

fell, then another. "Don't do this to me." Her voice was a whisper, a plea.

He stepped forward, took her in his arms, pressed a kiss on her forehead. "Then stay. We'll figure out a way together."

To hell with her fear of cops. First thing tomorrow, he was bundling her up and taking her to Chief Chalker's office.

One way or another, he was going to put an end to this nightmare.

ℰↄℰↄ

Dreams woke her again that night.

Max glanced up from the iPad on his lap as she walked out of her bedroom fifteen minutes later. She paused, lifted a trembling hand to her hair, and found the long strands thoroughly tangled. So, she gathered them in one fist and tucked it over one shoulder. Now what?

A soft smile. "Couldn't sleep?" he asked

She shook her head.

He set the iPad on the coffee table then patted the seat next to him. "Come over here. We'll watch a movie. I got some really boring classics that will put you right to sleep."

She slowly walked over to him, unsure what to say, yet wanting to make all the wrongs right. "I'm so sorry."

He frowned then reached up and tugged her wrist, motioning for her to take the seat beside him. She hesitated and then gave in.

When he wrapped an arm around her shoulders, she didn't stiffen. It simply felt right.

"Why do you keep apologizing?"

"I just—" She could feel the tears stinging her eyes. She tipped her chin and met his gaze. "You've been so good to me and look what happened today. I—I brought this on you."

"For the love of God, not this again, Eli," he said roughly, and she shot him a surprised look. With one hand on the back of her head, he pressed her face into his bare chest.

To level her system from the shock of sudden skin-to-skin contact, she pulled a deep breath into her lungs. Oh, God, his scent. The spicy aftershave. Davidoff Coolwater. That's so—he's so—Better not think about that right now.

"Cry if you want to. Maybe that will help you spring out of this blue funk. But enough with this I'm-responsible-for-the-problems-in-your-world crap."

He began stroking her shoulder.

"That's not what I'm doing," she whispered into his chest, feeling a tad bit pissed.

He pushed her back to look down into her face. "Of course, you are. You like playing the martyr." He began batting his eyelashes like a cheap floozy. "Look at me. Poor Eli," he mocked in a high-pitched nasal voice. "That monster is after me, and it's all my fault. Boo-freaking-hoo."

Oh, that did it.

She smacked his chest. "That doesn't sound anything like me."

"Of course, it does." To drive her further insane, he did his mimicry thing again.

The nerve of the man. "You know what? You've to be the most insensitive man on the face of this planet. And I can't deal with you right—"

He silenced her by crushing his mouth to hers.

Holy hell, she had no idea.

This. So, this was what a kiss was supposed to feel like. Earlier, when he had kissed her, she had been too nervous and shocked to enjoy the full impact of it. But now…

Intoxicating.

Breathtaking.

Terrifying.

Max simply didn't do anything by halves, did he?

He deepened the kiss, angling his head, one hand thrust into her hair. Her breasts crushed against his chest. Then she was sinking. It felt good, beyond good. She slid her hands up the slope of his shoulder for traction, and wow, the man had some serious muscles.

A lick, hot and wet. She squirmed in his arms, feelings she long thought dead coming awake at a rapid rate.

"Don't fight it. We both want this, baby."

She liquefied.

He thrust deep with his tongue, finding the moist recesses, suckling, damn near cutting off her breath. She moaned, kissed him back, fingers gripping his hair, liquid heat pulsing between her thighs. He seemed to want to take more than what she was prepared to give, more than she knew she had to give. A low rumble erupted from her chest when a hand clamped around her thigh.

Quickly, Eli realized that, despite everything that had happened tonight, she really needed this kiss. The way he teased her lips open, the way he seductively dipped his tongue into her mouth as if testing her reaction—it was amazing, and the teeny, tiny part of her brain that always wondered about their chemistry urged her to give in to this…whatever it was…happening between them. And however long it lasted.

Yeah, shouldn't forget that bit.

He kissed her for a long time, as the world bustled by on the street a few feet away. Justin could have made a move on them. She wouldn't have known. For that moment, wedged between his chest and the couch, she was deliriously happy. It was just the two of them that mattered.

Then he bit her where her shoulder met her neck.

She jerked as if he'd electrocuted her. Her toes curled into the soft leather of the couch, her nails sank into his forearm.

He stopped, lifted his head, suddenly looking uncertain, then reached forward and cupped her cheek. "Did I scare you baby?"

The concern, the soft touch. That was enough. She melted, like ice cream on hot asphalt. "More."

Devious sparkle of green eyes. Then he smiled. A sinful smile, full of male arrogance and satisfaction. Then he bit her again. This time he softened the bite with a wet suck over the spot.

The sensible part of her brain warned her not to let things slip out of hand. But her burning shame or helpless anger, none of it did anything to mute the intensity of her reaction to him. As she had proved herself time and again, her self-restraint when it came to him was close to zero.

He pulled back, lifted her right arm up, and suckled the soft skin on her inner elbow. *Oh, make that subzero.*

A hand closed around her left breast. Tentatively, then more firmly. She whimpered, arched into his hand eagerly, and was rewarded by a small roll of her nipple between his thumb and forefinger.

Oh...oh...right there.

Agile fingers jerked the spaghetti strap of her cami down, baring her left breast. It all but spilled into his waiting palm. Light pink nipples puckered under his watch, and he groaned, a sensuous, masculine sound.

"Fuck. You're so beautiful." His head dipped, then he was flicking her nipple with his tongue. Senses sharpened. Squirming, she lifted her lower body against his thigh, needy, ready. She moaned as his mouth closed over the nipple and he tasted her. He sucked her hard and sweet.

Gut tightened, muscles clenched at the onslaught of pleasure. She gasped then groaned, her fingers sliding up his neck to tug his hair. She might come just from this. "Max!"

He jerked back and looked down at her, brows furrowed, eyes no longer green but an intense shade of jade. "Am I going too fast?"

She shook her head. Then unable to resist, she watched as he slid down the length of her body. He kissed the thin strip of her belly visible through the gap between her cami and shorts. Soon the nuzzling turned to soft love bites. But it wasn't enough.

"More," she said raggedly, eyes closed.

"There is no hurry." Chuckling, he slid off the couch to stand at the side, then grabbed her waistband and dragged down her shorts. She always went commando at night, but from the look on his face, he hadn't been expecting that. Breathing hard, he reached out and lightly touched the outer lips of her sex. Thank god, she'd thought to run the razor on her last night.

"Is this okay? Me touching you like this?"

The question threw her off a bit, pulled her back from the haze of arousal. Was any of this okay? This intimacy, this easy camaraderie? What the hell was she doing leading him on anyway? Sex without obligations, or friends with benefits sounded fine in books. But in real life, feelings and desire would creep into the mix, then heartache and sensibility would vie for prime position in your life. Max, by his own admission, had gone off the deep end. Or he believed that he was in love with her.

Dammit! She didn't want to cause him any more pain than she already had. She was acting on borrowed time here. Women like her weren't built for happily ever afters, white picket fences, and school drop-offs.

"Fuck, Eli, you're like silk." Taking her silence as agreement, his thumb and middle finger parted her, and his forefinger touched her glistening clit. The arousal she'd thought she had under control came slamming back.

Still, memories roared in her mind, fighting the waves of lust—maniacal laughter, the pain, soft hands with smooth, finger pads roaming over her belly. A cold burn of anger invaded her veins at the memory of Justin. *Fuck him,* she thought, as the arousal blazed brighter. She wouldn't give the bastard satisfaction to know that he had broken her irreparably. Sex with Justin used to be something she did without thoughts. An everyday thing—like brushing her teeth—and it required no particular effort on her part. Sliding deeper inside her head, she used to pretend herself to be just a vessel, a body for him to do whatever he wished to do. That place had kept her alive. But now, here, *she* wanted this with Max. Just once. To have a taste of normal.

His fingertips brushed over her clit once, twice, three times, sending shudders through her. Then with a low groan, he cupped her and massaged her in slow, easy circles. She liked him touching her like this. She liked being vulnerable before him, she realized. Completely open, at his mercy. Instead of alarming her, that thought settled in peacefully, like a pebble sinking onto the riverbed.

His need to protect her, at the cost of his life, intrigued her. His disregard for her messy past surprised her. His impossible strength, how quickly he accepted her without digging too deep, that meant a lot to—

Holy crap, he sank a thick finger into her wet heat.

"Oh, God."

He chuckled against her throat, his voice rough,

breathing ragged. "I know, and it's only starting."

With his fingertip, he gathered her cream then lathered it all over the inner seams and then the ultrasensitive bud. Her body bowed up into a bridge position then sank down, the hard feel of his finger making everything inside her tense.

Up and down. Round and round. Up and around. Now and then, his finger drove deep, but he quickly withdrew from her heat, as if he feared it would freak her out.

Not bloody likely.

He kept up with his delicious torture, keeping her on a razor-sharp edge, not letting her get used to the slow rhythm.

Her thighs parted, then fell open, giving him better access. "Max!"

Far out! She sounded like a porn star.

"You like that, baby?" He sank to his knees between her thighs, his hand busy stroking her. The fire inside her flared. Her head turned from side to side, her eyes squeezed shut.

More urgently, she cried. "Harder."

He obliged her by reaching out and rolling her nipple again.

Good, but not enough.

Her arms flailed, and nails dug into the skin of his bare chest. An orgasm was building, she could feel it. If only he would put a little more bite into his actions. Maybe she could ask him to pinch her nipples, or slap her clit. She needed the pain. "More, Max. Even harder."

He didn't oblige her. He was in charge of the rhythm, and his fingertips stroked over her in even slower, feather-light circles.

She wriggled, she squirmed. She even tried pinching her own nipples. But it wasn't enough. Planting her feet

firmly on the couch, she lifted her upper body off the
leather. "Dammit, Max. I can't come unless you hurt
me."

He stopped.

A long, still silence.

Her eyes flew open. "Wha—why did you stop?"

He was leaning over her, a funny, puzzled expression
on his face.

"Max…" she said, reaching out, her voice thick with
need.

His eyes, dazed and dark, stared into hers. She saw
pain in them, but it was gone so quickly she thought
she'd imagined it. Then she remembered what she had
asked him to do.

*An image of Justin's stunning blue eyes, the slight
whoosh as the whip descended on her skin, the sharp
pain as skin broke and blood erupted. Then blissful silence.*

A caustic mix of shame and anger warred within the
rigid tension that now encompassed her body. Nothing
excused the way she'd spoken to Max, the way she'd
tried to use him for her pleasure. Max was not Justin, he
was not a man who liked to hurt women on any level. Her
bitchy self-conscious was right all along. He deserved
someone better than her, someone less screwed up. She
had been that woman, before Justin, but this is who she
was now—a woman who got off on pain.

Max shook his head, green eyes filled with remorse,
of determination that had her worried. "That's not how
we are going to do this, Eli."

Shame in her chest, so huge, so damn heavy.

Escape. She needed to escape.

"Well, we're not going to do this at all."

She sat up and swung her legs out of the couch, but
his big body blocked her.

His gaze narrowed on her. "We were doing just fine a moment ago."

She shrugged, crossed her arms over her breasts. "No offense, Max, it just clicked with me that our ideas about sex are totally different. You're all mellow and soft, not that there is anything wrong with it, but I need—" She shook her head, well aware the wrong buttons she was pressing. "I've got needs, darling, needs that may shock someone like you."

It was the reflexive lashing out of an injured animal, harsh, thoughtless. It came from a part of her that was deeply embedded in shame. The part that yearned and failed to maintain some dignity.

But what surprised her was that he saw right through her.

Max chuckled, took a step back, then rubbed a hand over his mouth. Unsure of his reaction, she stood to leave. He easily manacled her shoulders and pushed her back. She fell, felt the slight bounce when her ass hit the couch, then stared up at him. Quickly, frustration morphed into something more visceral. Primal.

"You're so full of shit, Eli."

The comment snapped her out of the solemn mood. Her mouth dropped open. "Beg your pardon?"

He ignored her.

Instead, he dropped to his knees, between her slightly parted knees, placed a hand on each and pried them wide apart. There was nothing easy or mellow about him now. He looked focused, intense, predator mode switched on.

"I could eat you up all day." That came out as a low groan, and she knew he hadn't meant to say that out loud.

"Max!" His name came out high and breathless, and she knew it was anxiety rolled up in anticipation that was making her so squeaky like a high school cheerleader.

For a long moment, he simply stared at her swollen clit. And the jerk took his sweet time. "So…" he murmured in a voice that was erotic as hell, lifting her legs over her shoulders, adjusting her to his liking. "You're saying that you can only come if there is a bit of pain thrown into the mix. Am I right?"

She swallowed hard, then nodded. "What can I say, we all have our quirks." Jeez, where was this coming from? Where the hell was her brain-to-mouth filter?

"There is more to sex than the BDSM shit you're used to, Eli." Anger simmered just below Max's handsome surface, but when he spoke, he was in total control.

She shrugged, or tried to. "Let it go, Max. Some of us fucked up ones need more than plain vanilla to get off."

Crude words. Nonsense words. Lies. All lies.

He flinched. And the pain in his eyes wrapped around her.

I've hurt him again, she thought. He was hurting for her, saddened by her twisted outlook of something considered intimate and precious by most people. She waited for him to counter, say something that would give her a chance to rebuff, to end this, but he didn't. He simply watched her as he ran his knuckle up and down the length of her sex, spreading her wetness.

Minutes dragged, painfully slow, and finally, his efforts began to touch the hidden core of her heart. He never looked away, never smiled. He simply worked over her, patiently, diligently. Something about the eye-to-eye connection—and the fact that it was Max—made it an impossibly intimate moment for her. Shadows continued to linger, but his determination kept them at bay.

"What are you doing?" she asked in a whisper.

"You don't need pain to enjoy this. And I'm going to prove it to you." Quiet words. Simple words.

She squirmed, anticipation wiped out by self-doubts, as she tried to break free. "Is this another one of your pop therapies? Because I'm telling you, it's not going to—"

Without warning, he opened his mouth over her.

An electric jolt. The very strength of her reaction was a shock to her system.

Unable to help herself, she looked down and met his green gaze.

This time they both groaned.

Time began crawling, but all she knew was the heat of him. She squirmed, tried to claw at skin and grab hair that gleamed gold under the overhead light. But then she gave up as waves after waves of pleasure crashed on her. He held her closer, refusing to let go, concentrating on suckling that one right spot, at the same time laving the tender opening leisurely. She cried out, fingers digging into the hand that held her open for his mouth. "Max!"

He thrust a capable finger into her wet heat, then two.

In and out.

In and out.

Memories, painful, never to be forgotten, roared to surface. But pleasure was a tsunami wave that swept them all under. There was no more room for Justin, a dank room saturated with blinding fear—only Max. The softness of his hair on her inner thighs, the occasional scrape of his teeth on her tender flesh, a wash of warm breath.

"You're so close, baby. Next time I'm going to lift your pretty ass and fuck you the way I want, and you're going to come all over my cock."

Dirty talk had never really done anything for her before. With Justin and later with others, it had always come across as a pathetic attempt to get themselves more aroused. But when Max spoke, his words painted an image in her head. Enough to shatter something inside her.

Her breath broke, and she came, arching up her lower body, her inner muscles clenching tightly around his fingers. He rode her through it, wringing pleasure as much as he could. She was aware of him kissing her closed eyelids, her forehead, the tip of her nose. She remained limp, shocked at the easiness with which he had proven her wrong, shocked at the reaction he wrangled from her body. Hope. Vaguely she realized the feeling that was wrapped around her mind was hope.

"Okay, baby?" he crooned into her hair, lifting her up and rearranging her on his lap. His erection dug into her hips.

That got her eyes open. "Max, you didn't—"

"That was for you." He took her mouth, deep and hard, in a tongue-dueling kiss. When he lifted his head, she saw his lips glisten. His chest billowed with his effort to maintain self-control. She shuddered, letting her arm curl around his neck. Her own lips felt swollen, ripe. Her body, deliciously loose. Yet, she wanted more.

She curled up, brought his head down and placed a quick kiss to the side of his neck, up near his jaw.

"That's it. Time for bed, princess." He stood up, with her in his arms.

"But—"

He shook his head. "For the love of God, woman, please don't talk. Don't move. Don't even breathe. I am on edge here."

Clutching at him, she arched into his chest, letting her breasts mash against him, giving him the green signal to proceed. "But I want more."

He paused, looked at her earnestly, his face taut with tension. Then he threw his head back and groaned. "Dammit, Eli. Let me do the right thing."

He resumed walking. As if she weighed nothing, he

carried her to her bedroom and settled her under the covers. He stood looking at her for a long moment. And it
hit her suddenly just how disillusioned she had been all
along. She'd thought uncomplicated sex with him was
enough. But instead, he'd reeled her in with his soft
words, gentle touches, and abundant passion. After expe-
riencing a glimpse of happily-ever-after with him, how
on earth was she going to settle for a life without Max?

CHAPTER 14

Max was stripping to hit the shower when he heard his phone ring from the living room, where he had left it on the coffee table earlier. He was expecting a call from the tow truck company, one he couldn't miss. So, he half opened the bathroom door and yelled, "Eli, could you please get the phone?"

"Hi, Jake," he heard Eli chant into the receiver a moment later.

Shit. Jake must be ringing to know about the term planner and staff schedules. Between getting his car wrecked, and making out with Eli, the thought had completely slipped his mind. He quickly wrapped a bath towel around his waist and hurried to the living room, all the while listening to a protracted conversation between Eli and Jake, about her lessons, how Jonathan was asking after her, and the cooler weather.

He all but grabbed the phone from her hand and barked a hello into the receiver.

"Elena is answering your phone these days." Jake made it like a statement, not a question.

"Yeah, well. I was in the shower." He looked up, saw her watching him with a curious expression. Max smiled at her, held up a finger to her—*hold on*—then walked away from the living room, out onto the alfresco.

When he returned, he saw Eli staring at a photo of him and Jake, the one he had left on the living room shelf. "All okay?" she asked.

He nodded.

And then the unexpected: "Jake really hates me, doesn't he?"

"What? What makes you say that?" he asked dumbly. As if it never had occurred to him.

He saw her finger trace along the top edge of the wooden frame. "Just a hunch."

"Eli, Jake's not what I would call a champion when it comes to people skills. He's got problems. Hell, half the time even I don't get him. And we're best friends," he said and willed her to leave it at that.

She did.

With a smile, she turned to him. "How about I make you scrambled eggs on toast?"

"Cool. See you in a bit." He took two steps, a random thought hit him, then he stopped. "Care to join me? I could wash your back. Or any other parts you'll let me."

She blushed then dropped her gaze. When she lifted her eyes again, he saw them gleam with memories of last night. That, and the hot pink cheeks were a dead giveaway.

"Rain check?" Her voice was a soft murmur.

He grinned, covered the distance between them, angled his head, and kissed her. Hard, deep, until she turned into putty in his arms. His hand closed around one rounded breast, but then he remembered his slashed tires, the call he should have made to Chief Chalker. He stopped. "I'll hold you to that promise."

He was whistling when the water hit his head and sluiced down his body.

⁓⁓⁓

After Max left, Eli made herbal tea then carried it to Max's home office. She had been doing her research on the laptop he had left for her use, hitting one dead end after another. Still, it wasn't all wasted efforts. So far, she'd come up with three names—three possible persons on police missing-persons lists. Now if she could connect those names to the evidence in her hand, then maybe she would have a slim chance of success.

She hated lying to Max, especially now that they were on intimate terms. But it was for his own good. The less he knew, the better. That was the least she could do for the man she loved.

Loved? Yes, loved.

Lie to everyone, Eli, but never to yourself. Her mom used to say that. So, she was admitting it to herself. She was in love with Max. Probably had been forever. Not that she could do squat about it. But it was the truth, and she might as well get used to it.

She had a moment of panic yesterday when Max stumbled upon her trawling through the Facebook account of *Natasha Palmer.* She'd set up the account after the agent she contacted insisted that she needed some means to reach Eli. She'd uploaded a photo she found online.

One of a female model with gangly red hair and a nose piercing. Thank God, there was no law that insisted your profile picture had to be your own. So when Max asked, she had concocted some lie about the girl in the photo. A long-lost friend. Someone she had met at uni and lost touch with.

Her Facebook messenger pinged with a message from the agent. Nerves strung tight as violin strings, she clicked on the icon.

I've tracked down Sam Wilson & family. They moved

to Yanchep in June and run a B&B. Sunshine B&B on Capricorn Esplanade. I hope this helps—Erin

PS: I don't think I can keep doing this. Supervisor has started asking questions. Maybe it's time to let go.

Elena sighed and shut the laptop. It was decided then. Time for her to say goodbye to Max.

Most of her things were packed and ready to go. If she was lucky, she could catch a bus out to Glengarry and, from there, the first train to Yanchep. The question was, if this lead turned out to be a dead end, what then?

❧❧❧

Jake Sinclair was having a crappy day. First, his coffeemaker quit on him. Second, he found that he had lost his wallet.

Exhausted after turning his house upside down looking for the damn thing, he plopped his ass on the dining chair and dragged a hand through his hair. Someone must have lifted it while he was at the bar last night, plastered as usual. He sat up straight as a snippet of memory flashed through his hard drive. Hang on. Someone had felt him up. Fire engine red nail polish. A brunette. Green eyes. Jiggling tits. *Annnnnd—*a restroom cubicle. *Shit!*

A call to the bar didn't help much. Cherry, the head waitress at Paddy's, the one he had fucked and dumped a year ago, answered the phone. "Sure, Jakey, I'll keep an eye out for it." In Cherry-speak, that really meant, "You can go to hell, asshole."

He never carried much cash around. And he used a debit card with an eight-hundred-dollar withdrawal limit. But since he habitually forgot his passwords and keycodes, he had made up a list specifically for that purpose and stored it in the inner pocket of his wallet, along with his driver's license. Worry drove him to ring up the bank to cancel his cards, and his security system people to change his passwords. Shuttling from one automated answering system to another, it took him nearly an hour before he managed to get everything sorted, change his passwords, and override his security system.

Next stop—Transport office. Hopefully, there wouldn't be as many dramas there as he had with the idiots who handled his money.

As he opened his front door, a cold June wind struck his face with a force that had him cursing. The sky looked a murky gray. Too dark to put on sunglasses. Shielding his eyes against the wind, Jake got into his battered Holden, backed out of the driveway of his small unit, and shifted his gear to drive. The engine sputtered and coughed as he hit the accelerator, before settling into a smooth purr. Damn the cold weather. The last thing he wanted was his car to give up on him.

"You hang in there, buddy. I promise I'll get you serviced, ASAP."

He turned the corner to Barden street. Signals turned red as he approached the intersection to the busy Wanneroo Road. The car ahead of him, a white pickup stopped. Jake stamped on his brake pedal. Instead of coming to a smooth halt as he had hoped, his car sailed through, and he realized that the pedal underfoot had shot forward to hit the floor. *What the fuck?* He pumped the pedal again. Fucking hell. He had no brakes.

He had a moment of shock, then reality kicked in. He swerved to the right to avoid hitting the pickup and careened straight into the two lanes of traffic.

He knew he was about to be hit big time. As a last-ditch effort, he grabbed the handbrake and yanked it up.

Bad move!

Wheels locked, his Holden went into a crazy spin.

He saw a flash of red before an oncoming car rammed into his passenger door. The momentum spun him to his right. Grimly, he fought for control. His front end fish-tailed wildly, before clipping the rear bumper of a fast-moving black sedan. Time slowed to a crawl then froze altogether a moment before impact.

His seat belt caught him hard across his chest. The airbag deployed, smacking into his nose. He had a split-moment to see the driver of the other car. A blonde. Pale face. Then his head was reeling.

Smoke was billowing out from under his Holden's hood, which incidentally looked like a crumpled soda can. A quick mental inventory told him his face was numb, so was the rest of his body. When darkness started clouding his vision, he struggled to bring up the faces of all those were important to him. First his long-dead mom, then Max, and finally Sarah.

So, this is how it's all going to end.

He had wanted a second chance, but it looked as if the bitchy fates weren't about to grant him his wish.

That was his last sickening thought before his lights went out.

CHAPTER 15

Max ran through the foyer of Sir Charles hospital, guilt a dead weight in his gut, his phone conversation with hospital staff still playing through his head.

"Are you Max Logan? Jake Sinclair's business partner?" the woman with the thick Scottish accent had asked.

"Yes. That's me. Why?"

"Mr. Logan, Jake has been in a car accident. Before you ask, his condition is stable for now. But the doctors want to keep him under observation for a couple of days."

"Ah...okay."

"We need you come and sign a few papers if that's all right."

Max told himself that they had it all wrong. Hospital staff, they're notorious for blowing things out of proportion. That had to be it.

He took the lift to the third floor and asked the nice Asian lady behind the semi-circle desk to point him to Jake Sinclair's room. There was a moment of confusion when the receptionist couldn't find Jake's name in the system. Max was damn near ready to push the woman out of the way and browse through the hospital records himself when someone, an elderly male volunteer, suggested that Jake could very well be up in fourth floor ITU. Intensive therapy unit. Max didn't wait to hear the rest. Not having the patience for the lift to arrive, he yanked open the fire exit door and took three steps a time to reach the fourth floor, his heart beating like wild drum inside his ribcage.

ITU…ITU…Where the hell was the ITU?

In the end, Max found Jake in the high dependency unit on the hospital's second floor. He was ushered into a stark, white room, where three frail people lay sleeping on electric beds, shriveled up like scraps of humanity, hooked up to some seriously intimidating machines. He found Jake on the last bed, the one pushed closer to the wall, sleeping in a white hospital gown. He looked pale, nose swollen red, deep purple bruises on his hands from IV fluids. Max didn't even bother to count the white gauze bandages decorating the guy's face and upper body. There were far too many.

Max called his name, saw Jake stir. Slowly, he opened his eyes, glanced over, saw him. Jake's eyes widened, and a teardrop leaked out of the corner of his eye.

Clearly, he recognized Max.

He tried to speak, but all that came out was a croak. Frustration flickered in Jake's eyes as he moved his arm, but it was difficult with all the wires.

Max tamped down the urge to scream and touched the small square patch of skin on Jake's forearm. Then he leaned forward. "You're going to be okay, buddy." Tears clogged his throat, but he managed to say that much.

He saw Jake's throat work on a swallow. He opened his mouth, but once again, all Max could hear were a few garbled words.

"Do you want to tell me something, mate?"

One blink.

"What is it?"

Someone moved in his peripheral vision. A woman in green scrubs. A nurse, with a disapproving look that sat at odds on her porcelain doll face. "I'm sorry, but you'll have to go. He is getting very agitated."

Max looked at Jake. Then he nodded at the nurse. "I'll be back."

She gave him a curt nod. "If all goes well, he'll be moved to the ward this afternoon."

"Thank you."

He turned to leave.

There it was again. The same croaky sound.

Max looked at the nurse. "What is he saying? Is he in pain?"

She shook her head. "No. But he has been saying the same thing ever since he came around. I may be wrong, but does he know someone named Elena?"

Max looked sharply at Jake. He blinked.

Despite himself, Max felt the first tug of uneasiness. "Maybe. Why?"

"I think that's what he is trying to say. Her name."

"Oh, I see." No. He didn't know what was going on. He couldn't figure out why Jake was mumbling Elena's name. As far as he knew, Jake disapproved of their relationship. Unless Jake, himself, had a monster crush on her. Why else would he think of her while lying broken on this hospital bed?

If anyone's, he should be saying Sarah's name. She used to be the love of his life.

The nurse looked at him with bright blue eyes, waiting. Max gave her a helpless shrug. "She is a friend of ours."

The nurse nodded then turned to adjust the drip flow. "Oh, he was also saying something about car brakes. Don't know what that's all about."

Max gave Jake a last puzzled look. But he was already slipping back to sleep.

ভ৹৫৩

When Eli left Yanchep on the last bus, it was already getting dark. As she got off, the wind and rain made it damn near impossible to walk, let alone see. Large gusts of wind shook off dead leaves from nearby trees straight onto her face. Once or twice, her sneakers sank into the glinting dark puddles on the pavements. She didn't care. She simply walked, past the lit-up houses, past the row of shops toward Max's house.

She didn't want to go home. Not to face Max's watchful eyes. But he cared for her, and he would worry. She really had thought today was the day. The gnawing, clenching sensation inside her had been near absent all day, and she'd been aware just how giddy with anticipation she felt, how truly happy. First, the orgasm Max gave her, then the positive news from her agent. For once she had thought things were looking up for her. All gone. Hopes shredded like confetti. Worries were closing in on her again, fear rising up to swamp her. She didn't know what to do about them anymore.

She had seen Justin again. Quite by chance on her way to work. He was waiting in an unmarked car a few yards down the street from the fish and chip shop where she worked. His unblinking cold blue eyes as he scanned the entrance to the shop had told her how pissed off he was. There was no use in pretending there was any reason other than the truth. At this stage of the game, both players knew where they were at, how they rated on the scoreboard. Her time was running out. One more week. So far Justin hadn't made any attempts to reach her at Max's place. So she had to assume that he hadn't figured out where she lived. Yet. He would, though. There was no hiding from a man like him. She was just prolonging the inevitable. Her mind rebelled at what was being planned for her at the end of her allotted week. She had witnessed Justin peel back enough layers of himself to know who he really was, what he was capable of.

Oh, well, that was thought for another time, another day.

The wind hit her full on her face as she opened the gate and rushed to Max's front door. When she used the key he had made for her, to let herself in, he was pouring over some documents at his dining table.

"Eli! Where were you?"

For a moment, she had this insane urge to push her hands into pockets of her coat and walk on as if she hadn't heard him. "Out." Her tone was so abrupt that Max raised his eyebrows at her.

He unfolded from his seat. "Bad day?"

She shrugged and gave him a smile that she knew wouldn't reach her eyes. He watched as she toed off her sneakers, removed her parka, and left them both on the doormat. She would deal with them later. "No. Just felt like a walk."

Max crossed his arms over his chest, the movement stretching the old Perth Zoo t-shirt over his shoulders. His expression said he wasn't completely relaxed as he wanted her to believe. "You went for a walk with your backpack? In this pouring rain?"

There was a long pause. She could hear the beat of her heart. Taste the foul taste of lie on her tongue.

"Eli?"

"Sorry."

"You're miles away. What's going on in your head?"

She hated it when people asked her that. Dr. Stevens used to do the same. "Nothing. Everything's cool. I'm fine. I just felt like a walk and thought, damn, I better take my stuff with me in case someone broke in again." Lies. All lies. Her eyes twitched. She felt brittle and on edge. She didn't want to have this conversation now. She hated lying to Max.

He nodded, then walked to the linen closet, found her a towel and brought it back to her. She reached for it, but he shook his head, motioned her to turn around. She did. It felt good, standing there, letting him towel dry her hair. After, he led her to the couch, where she curled up like a contented cat. He left her there to putter around the kitchen and got her a glass of warm milk. He had the heater on high, heat blasting down through the air vents. The milk, combined with the heat made her feel warm, sleepy.

"This is nice," she said, a yawn working its way through her mouth.

He chuckled. "You better hit the bed, sleepy head. Or I'll have to carry you myself. Not that I mind, but I think I pulled a muscle on my back last night. Just how much do you weigh, Princess?"

She laughed, stood to leave. "Ha, ha, very funny."

Grinning, he put his hand over her wrist. "Do you want some dinner? I didn't feel like cooking, so I've ordered a pizza."

She shook her head. "No. But thanks for asking."

"Goodnight, Max." On an impulse, she reached out and ruffled his hair. Before she could straighten, he caught her face in both hands and pressed a toe-curling kiss on her lips.

"That's the way it's done, Princess."

She caught herself from blushing, then settled for a snort. "I'll keep that in mind, *Sensei.*"

She had walked two steps when his voice followed her. "Eli, when did I tell you about the break-in?"

She froze then slowly turned. "What?"

"The break-in, how did you know about that?"

She wasn't feeling warm and sleepy anymore. She was cold, and very sober. "What are you getting at, Max?"

He turned his face away from her, looking both confused and irritated at being confused. Then he looked back at her with an intensity that unnerved her. "Nothing—it's just that I don't remember telling you about that stuff."

She gave him a nervous laugh, her voice cool and bitter. "Of course, you did. The other day when we were playing chess. I asked you about the security alarm, and you said it was necessary after the way someone broke in here a few weeks ago."

His expression softened, then he gave her a sheepish smile. "Oh, did I? Sorry. Must have slipped out of my mind. Too much has been going on lately." He dragged a hand over his face, smothering a yawn. "Did I tell you about Jake?"

She shook her head.

"He's been in a car accident this morning."

"Oh? Is he okay?"

"Yeah. Just banged up pretty bad. They moved him to a private room this afternoon. He should be there for another two days."

"That's okay then, isn't it?"

He nodded, suddenly looking tired, his pretty eyes ringed with dark circles of fatigue.

"You should get some sleep too, Max. You look really tired."

He yawned on cue. "Yeah. It's been a long day." He looked at his watch, then at her. "Where's that damn pizza?"

The doorbell chimed announcing the arrival of his much-awaited pizza. "There's your pizza now."

"You sure you don't want a bite? It's pulled beef. Your favorite."

"Maybe tomorrow." A part of her wanted to ask him more about Jake's so-called accident, but it felt too complicated. Besides, it was better to leave sleeping dogs alone. So she faked a yawn, tapped her fingers against her open mouth. "I'm really tired. Goodnight, Max. Enjoy your pizza."

She was well aware of his eyes following her as she walked to her room and shut the door behind her.

Far out! That was a close call.

CHAPTER 16

Max worked through his karate routine in the dim light of his covered alfresco, sweat running down his face and chest. He trained every day, kept his body in top condition, knowing how close he had come to ruining it with street drugs and cheap booze. The routine also helped him feel centered, keep a level head. He had been working out for an hour now. He should stop, hit the shower, then get some sleep. But he was too tense, his thoughts circling around the woman sleeping in his spare bed.

He shifted his mind to the dojo, boring accounts that lay in wait for him, and it boomeranged back to Eli. *Again.* He really should stop thinking about her so much.

Damned if he knew how.

So when his phone rang, his first reaction was gratitude.

"Mr. Logan?"

He froze, mentally swore.

"Hello, Adams." He walked to the alfresco with the phone and eased himself into the wooden chair by the barbeque that, in the summer, he made use of every weekend. Now that it was easing into winter, and the temperature was dropping, the sky a perpetual steel gray, it stood under the waterproof cover. "Thanks for wrecking my car, asshole."

There was a pause. "Your car?"

"Yeah, yeah. Real original, Sherlock. Slashing my tires. What are you fifteen? Can't you fight like a man?"

"Mr. Logan. I can assure you I had nothing to do with your car. But there is someone there with you who knows quite a bit about vehicles."

"And who would that someone be?"

"Elizabeth, of course. Didn't you know that she got a diploma in automotive mechanics from TAFE? That's how we met. My car had a flat tire, and she helped me change it on the side of Kwinana freeway. Didn't she tell you?"

That had Max's eyebrows snapping together. "Adams, I don't have time for this shit. What the hell do you want?"

"I…ah…I heard about your friend."

An uneasy feeling skittered down Max's spine. "How?"

"My partner was in the area. He was called to the scene of the accident. He filled me in."

"Right. So?"

"Nothing. I just—How's Elizabeth?"

"Fine." Max paused. "This is getting damn awkward, Adams. You need to let this go. Get a life, dude. Stop being so fixated on her."

On the other end, Justin laughed softly. "Take care of her, Max. She needs her meds. Without that, she will prove to be a real handful." He hung up.

❧❧❧

Fractured arm. Hairline crack on to his jaw. No wonder Jake felt so bad. The airbag had done a fantastic job of smashing the bridge of his nose and two upper front teeth. His car was a write-off, a donation to the scrapyard. The nurses had said Jake had been lucky to come out of the accident alive, but Max doubted if his mate would agree with their conclusion.

According to the doctor who treated him, and the few nurses who changed his dressing, half his problems could be solved if he had a better attitude. Max wanted to tell them not to hold their breaths. Jake was who he was. He didn't take well to injuries, illness, or pretty much anything that incapacitated him. Except alcohol.

Hmmm…they would have to have a chat about his little drinking problem at some point. Serious chat. Maybe an intervention. Or even rehab. That wasn't such a bad idea.

Since Jake had his eyes closed, Max took a moment to watch his buddy. Thanks to the cuts and bruises, he still looked like shit. But his skin had lost its pale, ghostly look. And his nose didn't look so swollen anymore. Someone—Paddy probably—had drawn some lewd pictures and suggestive cracks on the white cast on his right arm.

Memories surged, and Max smiled as he recalled a different place, a different bed. Max had been a patient then—pneumonia, the doctors had claimed. Jake had been his nursemaid then. Boy, he'd sucked at that shit. His MO had been to bully Max into taking medication. That failed, he used to threaten. In the end, it had gotten the job done.

"If you are thinking about what to say in my eulogy, I got some ideas. I'm not dead yet." Jake didn't bother to open his eyes as he made that statement.

Max chuckled as he walked over to Jake's bed, he took the seat closer to his right arm. "Actually, I was thinking about what to do with your Star Wars collection.

There should be a few collector's items, aren't there? I could make a fortune."

Jake opened one eye, gave him a mean glare, then shut it back again. "In your dreams, fucker."

Max laughed and took his right hand. "It's good to have you back, Jake."

Jake's eyes peeked open again. "Oh, God. I'm dead, aren't I? I was sure I saw a white light. Fuck. I was so young."

Max shook his head. "No. You're not dead, you crazy asshole."

"Then what's with your sappy line?"

Max dropped his hand, then leaned back against the backrest. His gaze fell on the white lilies. "What's with the flowers?"

Jake looked away. "Ah…Sarah sent them."

That gave him a pause. "Sarah? Your Sarah?"

Jake looked at him, irritation firmly back in place. "She is not my Sarah. We're divorced, remember?"

A loud knock alerted them both, and, a second later, a nurse peeked past the green curtains. "Time to check the vitals, Mr. Sinclair."

"I'll be waiting outside." Max stood and made room for the nurse to pass through.

He went outside and wandered around the corridor. At some point, he rang Eli and checked if everything was okay with her. She sounded tired, but otherwise fine.

"You can go in now." The nurse reappeared, armed with a tray of medicine and BP apparatus.

He gave her a smile and slipped back into the room.

Jake had his eyes glued to the TV.

"Can you believe this soap opera shit? The damn thing is so addictive. I can't seem to stop. He—" Jake pointed to the guy on the mini screen. "—believes his wife is pregnant with their first child, but she is totally faking it. And she—"

"Ah, man. Don't reel me into it. I don't wanna know. Let me be a man and enjoy my football and rugby."

Jake gave a long-suffering sigh and turned off the TV.

For long moments, neither spoke.

Then Max had to blurt what was at the tip of his tongue. "So…Sarah, huh?"

"Yup."

"That's it? You're not gonna say anything more?"

"Nope."

Max snickered.

Changing the subject, Jake leaned toward Max. "Where was Elena on the day of my accident?"

That threw him off a bit. "Eli? What do you mean?" He had a vision of her returning home like a drowned rat that night, and the first twinge of uneasiness ran up his spine.

"Elena. Where was she on the day of my accident? Was she with you?"

Max shook his head, then explained, sticking to partial truths, "No. I was at the workshop, my car needed some work, then I had something to do at the dojo. She was home all day. Why?"

"Because I think she was responsible for my accident."

That made him smile. "Good one, mate," he said before he realized Jake wasn't laughing. "Shit, are you fucking serious?"

Jake nodded.

Max pushed back his chair and stood. "What the fuck have you got against Eli? This has to stop, man." He wasn't a naturally violent man, but Jake was provoking him into unnecessary violence.

Max still held out hope that Jake would smile and re-call his bluff.

Jake paled, then he licked his dry, cracked lips. "Nothing. I've got nothing against her. But there are a few things that happened in the last two weeks, and I've been lying here all day thinking, hoping, that I'm wrong about everything."

Max did a crisp about turn and walked to the single window in the room. Outside, gusts of wind blew dead leaves and twigs along the pavement. "What things? What the fuck made you think Eli would be responsible for such a thing? The day your accident happened, you were drunk, mate. The nurses told me that your blood al-cohol level was point seven percent. That's borderline, you idiot."

Jake shook his head, then winced. His hand flew up to cup the side of his head. "I know I had a drink that morning. But I definitely wasn't drunk as you think. And I definitely am not drunk now, because I'm telling you, Max, someone had deliberately cut my brake lines."

Like a sucker punch, the words knocked the air out of him. Max swallowed loudly. "What?"

Jake glanced around. Cautiously, he struggled to sit straighter before he began. He explained about his stalk-er, the long blonde hair, missing red bag from his home, the terror he had felt when he knew he had no brakes, and the flash of a blonde in the car that had hit him on the two-way lane.

Max sat through it all, frozen to the core, his brain scrambling to compute the input overload. At this point, he wasn't sure who or what to believe. But he hadn't wanted to doubt Eli, and knowing she was safe in his house made it easier for him breathe.

Max made an aggressive move forward. "Still. You don't know for sure. All you have are assumptions."

Jake nodded. "Yes. If that's what you like to call them."

Sickness burned in his gut. Justin's words came slamming into his head.

She has a diploma in automotive mechanics from TAFE.

Added to that were images in his head. So, damn many of them.

Lies? Were they all lies?

Drawing a deep breath, he shook his head. "Know what? I think the drinks have messed up your head."

For a small moment, Jake just looked at him. Then he nodded sadly. "Mate, I'm not making any of this up."

Max took a step back.

Air. He needed some air.

Max couldn't picture it in his head. Eli deliberately hurting Jake. Sneaking out to cut his brake lines. How many women even knew where the damned brake wires were under a car?

"Sorry, man. I didn't say this to—"

"I'll see you later."

"Max!"

But he was already running down the corridor, running because he had to do something. Numbness was setting in. Eli had been lying to him? He knew she had plenty of secrets. But this…could she be that callous? A double-faced bitch?

Could Justin be right about her all along? What about Jake's car? Could Justin have tampered with them?

Later. Max would deal with all that later.

Right now, he needed some answers. And he knew just the right person for that.

In his mind, he saw Chief Chalker—a big, beefy man with a round belly, bushy eyebrows, and a kind heart. His pale blue eyes always held a world-weariness, as if he'd reached his limit of bullshit the world had to offer him. He supposed a lifetime in the police force, dealing with the scum of scums, might do that to any man. The first time he had seen the chief was all those years ago in the Bayswater Police Station. Terrence Chalker had been a senior sergeant back then. Max still remembered the way the chief had scared the crap out of him that night. Caught for selling crack to teenagers at the age of nineteen, Max had known his future was bleak. He was destined to rot in a Casuarina prison cell. If it hadn't been for Chief Chalker, he would still be there.

Time to pull out the big guns.

CHAPTER 17

Chief Chalker lived in a Victorian style townhouse, in a neighborhood where people kept to themselves and lived at the mercy of state-of-the-art surveillance systems. Night stretched cold and dark over the city, fighting back the rain, cloudless sky spilling like a dark blanket overhead. Max pushed open the heavy front door and went into a long corridor that led him to a room cluttered with antique furniture and brass knick-knacks. The smell of burnt meat and rich tomato sauce permeated the air, along with the familiar scents of stale beer and Cuban Cigars Chief favored.

"Take a seat," Chief said, dressed in black sweats and a Cancer Council apron tied around his ample waistline as he manned the cooktop. His accent was pure rural Aussie, a lingering evidence of a childhood spent on his father's farm in Chidlow. The wooden spatula looked like a toy drumstick in his meaty palms as he stirred the pot vigorously.

Max looked around. It was clearly the home of a very disorganized single man. Coffee table buried under newspapers. Kitchen sink filled with coffee mugs, cabinets filled with useless junk Chief had picked up at garage sales. Wasn't he a bit old for this?

"Hi, mate."

Max heard the vaguely familiar voice and turned around. Justin Adams stood there, arms crossed, eyes wary.

Uneasiness crackled through him, like a bushfire. He turned to Chief. "What the hell is he doing here?"

"Justin came to me this morning about a little domestic problem. When you told me you were coming over, I asked Justin to join us so we could get it all out in the open."

"But—"

"Beer?"

The sudden change of topic threw him off. "Yeah, sure."

Chief grabbed two beers from the fridge and plonked them on the kitchen counter behind him. He then motioned Max and Justin to take a barstool behind the counter.

Max sat, twisted open the bottle, and took a slow chug. "So…are you gonna to tell me what this crazy bastard has told you?"

"Sorry, man. I had no other choice. I had to tell him the truth," Justin mumbled, as if he was frightened by the line of inquiry.

Max's pulse tripped. He placed the bottle on the counter and stared at his friend Chief.

Justin was rolling the bottle between his palms, his expression troubled, his gaze hooded by the hair falling over his eyebrows. Max stared from him to Chief then back again.

"Tell him about what?"

Justin hesitated a moment, then he shrugged. "Elizabeth. My wife. I thought he should know."

Max jerked to his feet, feeling a burn that had nothing to do with the toasty room heater. "You—"

"I had to," mumbled Justin, leaning forward, shoulders hunched. "You are not thinking straight where she is concerned. She is my wife, Mr. Logan." His lips wobbled.

Shit! Is the asshole gonna cry?

Justin took a deep breath, shuddering on an exhale, as he tried to compose himself. "I know she doesn't want anything to do with me anymore."

Max felt his spine grow stiffer. "Exactly. It's her life, her business. Stay away from it."

Justin looked up, met his gaze. Caught off guard by the pain he witnessed in other man's eyes, Max searched his face for signs the psycho was messing with him. All he found was sincerity. "Please, Mr. Logan."

Is this guy for real? Max had to stay in the moment, hold onto the anger.

"I just want to help her. I knew you would listen if it came from Chief," Justin said desperately.

"And how exactly did you come to that conclusion?"

For a moment, Justin didn't speak. Then he sighed. "I am a cop. I am not completely without resources. I checked up on you."

"I don't know what you're trying to achieve here," Max said frostily, implications of Justin's words bringing his mind to a shuddering halt. Still, he plowed on. "Eli is with me, and that's where she will be staying."

For a few awful seconds, they stared at each other. Then Justin dropped his gaze.

"I love her. And I told you before, Elizabeth is sick. She needs help."

An hour ago, Max would have vehemently denied such an accusation. But now, all he could do was stare at Justin's pleading face. *What if this bastard was right?* Then he remembered Eli's terror-stricken eyes, her incoherent pleas, the nightmare she lived through day and night. *No. Justin was lying.* Max had to believe that.

"You are fucking unbelievable. I'm sorry I wasted your time, Chief." His voice high, he pushed back the chair and turned to leave.

Chief's voice followed him. "Max, wait."

He kept walking.

"Max Logan, you walk away, and I'll haul your ass to jail so fast you won't know what hit you." That tone meant business. It was a voice that could make grown men with guns quake in their uniforms.

Teeth clenched, Max jerked to a halt then slowly turned. Chief was watching him, his hard cop gaze assessing. Too furious with Justin and embarrassed to stand still, Max thrust both hands through his hair and rocked back on his heels. "What do you want from me?" His voice had lost some of its defiance. He lifted his arm toward Justin then dropped it back to his side. "Obviously, you're on his side. Or he wouldn't be here."

Chief Chalker stepped out of his open kitchen, plopped the pot of fragrant sauce on the eight-seater dining table, and looked up at him. "Have dinner with us. And while you eat, you both can tell me all about this girl who has you two by the balls."

CHAPTER 18

There was silence when Max finished bringing Chief up-to-date. He didn't move. His face remained expressionless, giving nothing away. Next to him, Justin sat quietly, playing with the golden band on his left ring finger, twisting the ring this way and that. Once, he held it up so the light could reflect on it. His hands looked all girly, thought Max with irritation. All smooth and pink.

"Chief?"

When he finally spoke, it was in a tone of deep trouble. "Max. This is quite an accusation you're making against an officer."

Max gave a snort of disgust. "Didn't you hear a word I said?" He tipped his chin at Justin. "That guy's a psycho."

Chief met his gaze, held it, seeming to measure the emotion behind them. Then he turned to Justin. "Why didn't I know about this before?"

Justin shrugged. "I honestly thought she would move back once she—" He stopped, flushed crimson. "I mean, I didn't think her attraction would last this long. But when I came to know about Jake Sinclair's accident, I realized things were getting out of hand."

Feeling an irritation that went beyond lack of sleep, Max fixed Justin a pointed glare. "You're still on about that? There is nothing wrong with Eli. You—you must have messed with Jake's car brakes."

Chief held up his hand. "That's enough boys." He turned to Justin. "I've heard both sides of your stories. Obviously, we have an issue here, Officer Adams."

Justin nodded. "I understand, sir. But Elizabeth, my wife, she really needs help. I hope you'll see to it that she gets help before it's too late."

Max half rose from his chair, his stance aggressive. Listening to Justin drone on about Eli as if she was his was like closing a door on a raging storm. In this instance, the storm was inside his head. There was only so much crap you could take, and next thing you know, wind rushes through, and the door has blown off the hinges. "Let me make something clear, Adams. Elizabeth is not your wife. She never has been." Each word was spat out with so much vehemence, even the Chief quirked brow.

Justin sighed. "Getting aggressive is not going to change the facts, Mr. Logan. My marriage to Elizabeth is registered with WA marriage registry on third March two thousand and ten. I've got the records if you want to cross check. As for Elizabeth being sick, if you don't believe me, you can speak to Dr. Stevens at Graceland hospital. She'll attest to it. She has all her medical records."

Max snorted then sat back in his chair. "You really gonna take his word on this, Chief? I wouldn't. I bet this crazy asshole has the foc in his pockets. You and me both know how easy it is to forge documents these days. For a thousand bucks, there are people out there who will make you genuine, real-deal stuff. Hell, I could get myself a visa to Mars if I want to."

Chief waited a couple of seconds, an eyebrow raised

in question, then turned slightly to face Max. "What do you think we should do now, Max?"

Max drummed his fingers on the table and blew out a sigh through his lips. "I don't know. Book this bastard for stalking? Order a search warrant for his place? Go through his records?"

The old cop gave him a stubborn nod. Then he sighed. "I can't send a team of officers to search a fellow officer's house just based on your suspicions."

Bloody bureaucratic red tape. His powerlessness enraged Max. "You're gonna let this guy go free?"

"You do realize that you don't have enough to make a case here, Max. It's your word against Officer Adam's. And from what I've heard so far, I'm not convinced Ms. Campbell is completely innocent in this whole mess. Who knows, maybe she is acting out based on a previous grudge. Women are known to play hardball with the guys who pissed them off," Chief said finally.

"So that's it, then? You're going to let this psycho get away with it?" Max said quietly.

Chief spread his hands in a gesture of helpless innocence. "I'm a cop, Max. I'll follow where the evidence leads me, and this case, in my opinion, is not so black and white."

Max locked his eyes with Justin's for a moment. The guy looked unflappable. The tension in Max's shoulders quadrupled. "Well, if that's the way you want to deal with it, then fine." Max heard his own voice, cool and hard-edged. He stood up. "I don't think Eli is making any of this up. I'm going to stand by her, no matter what. And I'm not going to let this bastard lay a hand on her."

"Max!" Chief rested his hand on Max's forearm, attempting to block him.

Max knocked the hand away. "Night, Chief." He turned to leave.

"Fuck, Max. Sit back down. Give me a minute to think about all this."

Hope bloomed in his chest. He turned to face Chief, crossed his arms over his chest. "You'll do it?"

Chief laced his fingers, tapped them against his lower lip. "You do realize you're putting me in a very awkward situation?"

Laying on guilt. Chief was good at that. Max had forgotten just how good. "Sorry, Chief."

Max got a glimpse of tired blue eyes. He was used to seeing Chief like this, but now he felt an odd pang, that he was persuading a man he considered equal to his dad into doing something against his ethics. It didn't matter that he was really desperate. Guilt was guilt.

"All right then, I'll see what I can do."

"You'll start a case?"

Chief quirked a brow. "Let me make one thing clear, Max," he said, with a stab of annoyance. "From this point on, you're not directing this show. I am."

"But—"

He softened his voice and said, "The answer is no."

"So, what are you going to do now?"

"I will assign an officer to look into the facts. He or she will check with the marriage registry, Graceland hospital, Elizabeth's old apartment building. I'll also get someone to look into Jake Sinclair's accident. But it will all take a few days to actually get the records to us. I'll try and speed things up, but you know how it is, Officer Adams."

Justin nodded, again, his face gave nothing away. Either the guy was an Oscar-worthy actor, or he really had nothing to hide. "Yes, sir."

Chief turned to Max. "In the meanwhile, I want you to bring Ms. Campbell to the station on Wednesday morning ten a.m. sharp."

Wednesday morning. That gave him one more day with Eli. A day where he would have to watch her like a hawk.

"Don't tell her what you're planning to do, or there's always a chance she might bolt. And Officer Adams—" He turned to Justin. "I want you there as well. We need to wrap up this drama before it gets out of hand. Or before someone else gets hurt."

There was a gleam of satisfaction in Justin's blue eyes that stuck in Max's throat like a barb. "Sure."

"I know how frustrating this must be for both of you. But I promise I'll look into this matter in detail. Until then, Max, keep this woman away from trouble. And officer Adams, hang in there for a few more days," Chief said in his serious cop voice.

Afterward, Chief walked Max to his car. "Just how involved are you with this girl?"

"I—" Max cleared his throat. "I love her, if that's what you're wondering."

Chief swore. "Even knowing she might be a fruit-cake?"

Max shrugged. Love was love, there were no conditions attached to it.

"Somehow I'm not really surprised. I did a bit of digging before you got here, you know. This girl, she is the reason you got into trouble in the first place, isn't it?"

He nodded. Apart from Jake, Chief was the only person who knew about his past.

"Fucking hell, son, this is a clusterfuck."

"I guess."

"I want you to hear this loud and clear, Max. All my career, I've seen innocent-looking people do terrible, horrific crimes. I'm saying this because there's a chance your girl is guilty. Or sick. I can if I want to, take her into protective custody. But I'm trusting you to do the right thing. You might be all tempted to protect her. Don't make me regret my decision."

Max swallowed then nodded. "Sure. I won't let you down." He turned to leave then stopped. "You really believe that guy, Chief?"

Now it was Chief Chalker's turn to shrug. "I've known him for a while now. He is hardworking, reliable, and his records are spotless." Chief gave Max a reassuring smile. "And you know what they say: Innocent until proven otherwise. I have to give him a fair chance, Max."

Max snorted.

Chief sighed. "Look. This is a police officer you're accusing. All officers have to go through some pretty intense mental health checks and psych evals from time to time. Do you honestly believe that officer Adams would have slipped through every goddamn screening and test? If he is a psychopath as you believe, then he should have shown some signs before, Max."

Max exchanged a dispirited glance with Chief, then bid him good night.

"Max?"

"Yeah?"

"For Christ's sake, take care of yourself, son."

"It's not me you should worry about," he said boldly.

Chief came closer to him. "I'll do what I can, okay? I know you're worried about this girl. For your peace of mind, I'll make some unofficial inquiries into this case. In the meanwhile, I'm afraid officer Adams hasn't done anything that we can use against him as evidence." He rubbed his chin, looking thoughtful.

"But—"

"Tell you what? Just to be on the safe side, I'll ask my team to put an alert on your home address and phone numbers. If you, or anyone else, calls in from those numbers, it will be treated as an emergency. I'll also assign a patrol unit in your area. Other than that, there's not much we can do at this stage."

Max hesitated. "So, you do think he's dangerous."

Chief shook his head. "No. I believe in being prepared. Good night, Max."

Max looked back at Chief's house. Justin stood there, still as a tombstone, watching. As Max got into his car and drove back home, he felt he had seen something and hadn't seen it properly. As if he knew something about Justin but didn't know what it was.

Shit. His life was getting blurrier and blurrier.

&ε&

She woke up suddenly, going from deep sleep to wide awake in a blink, heart galloping, mouth dry as sawdust. For a moment, she had no idea where she was. Then she remembered she was still in Max's spare bed, and it was dark. No sound except the small alarm clock ticking away. She listened, straining to hear what had woken her.

The door to her room opened partially. The shock of it made her freeze. In the next instant, a shape materialized at the doorway, illuminated in the soft light that streamed in through the crack between the half-open door and the wall. Max! He stood there for a long moment, watching her, a guardian angel watching over her, then he closed the door after him and left.

She sat up, feet still tucked under the thick quilt, her nerves stretched tight. From beyond the wall, she heard a soft rattle, the sound of the fridge door opening. Footfalls. Muted chatter from the TV. More footfalls. Creak of shower screen door, then the soft patter as water hit the tiles. He was settling in for the night.

Then she remembered about Jake, how stressed Max

had sounded earlier, and before she could talk herself out of it, she was out her bedroom door.

He'd just made it to his door, a dark blue towel wrapped around his lean hips.

"God, Eli," he muttered, dragging a hand through his wet hair when she moved into his line of vision. "You scared the shit out of me." He took a step forward, gave her a quick once over, taking in her sleep shirt and bare legs, then paused. "What are you doing out of your bed? Did I wake you? Or was it another nightmare?"

She stared at him for a moment, the way water droplets clung to his chest hair to be precise, words forgotten in her head. For some crazy, stupid, bizarre reason, her heart began thudding, her breathing fast.

"Eli?"

The atmosphere between them shifted suddenly. The tension in the room multiplied, became thick as congealed soup, until she wondered why he wasn't making some smart-ass comment about it.

"I—" Her gaze fell on the neat row of cans she'd aligned at the foot of the window earlier. "I came to check if you'd locked the door properly."

She felt him give her another look, but she kept her eyes fixed on those cans.

At last, he said, "Yes. Of course."

"Okay, then." Now what? She couldn't very well stand there and just stare at those stupid cans forever. She had to do something. "I'll…I'll just get a drink of water."

He didn't move.

All the way to the kitchen then as she pulled open the fridge and stared at the two bottles of water on the side shelf, she felt him watching her.

For a moment, she wondered if this was some kind of test. Justin used to do that. Only with him, she never knew what to expect. Most often things ended with her on the floor, bleeding from all pores. With Max—

Her heart nearly jumped out of her ribcage when he came up behind her and slipped his arms around her waist. She knew she should be fucking terrified, but she wasn't. It felt right. It felt as if she had waited long enough. He dipped his head, letting his warm breath caress her skin as he drew her hair away from her nape and placed a soft kiss where her spine began. He brought with him the scent of his spicy aftershave, the smell of security.

Slowly, it felt like hours, but it was probably only a few seconds, she turned. Her fingers were tingling. Her body was tingling all over.

"Eli." Just her name. Nothing more. Nothing less. But that was enough. His hands came up to bracket her shoulders, but he made no other move.

She knew he was waiting. The pause grew terrible with every moment. Inside her head, there was some sort of internal battle going on, one she wanted no part of.

But she knew which part had won when she reached up, touched his chin, withdrew, touched it again, until he caught her wrist and made her place her entire palm against his left cheek. They stood there, staring at each other. She thought she couldn't do it. And he was doing nothing to take the decision away from her. The ball was completely in her court. It seemed to take forever, but in the end, it was she who twined her arm behind his neck to bring his mouth closer for that kiss they both wanted.

The kiss started gently, but only for a heartbeat. Max took over from there. He kissed her with a quiet desperation. Now and then, he would pull away to look at her, worry in those pretty green eyes, then he would dive back in for more. His fingers were cool against her skin as they trailed over her throat, her breasts, her midriff, her back. He tasted faintly like beer and rich tomatoes. She felt her knees start to give, but he was there, hooking an arm under her thighs, then carrying her off to his bed.

His bedroom was dark, the only light coming in from the living room, but even then she saw the arousal gleaming in his eyes. The sight warmed her from the inside out. He placed her on the bed, tugged off her nightshirt and ran his hands over her. When he leaned over her with both arms braced on either side of her shoulders, the image of Justin flashed before her eyes, and she froze.

"I—I can't—"

Max gave her a puzzled look, but then he lifted her up against him, so that he was leaning against the headboard, and she was straddling his thighs. They sat there like that for a second, her body hyperaware of every delicious inch of him. Her skin was cold against his, but he warmed her quickly, with his tongue, and hands, and then his whole body. Somewhere along the way, he lost his towel, and she ended up sitting facing away from him, her feet planted on the bed, his cock trapped between their bodies. She felt his touch as they ran over the disfigured skin where Justin had carved his initials on her arms and outer thighs. Nerve damage had ensured she wouldn't have sensations in those sites, ever. But for some reason, when Max touched them, she felt it all the way through to her heart. He didn't make a big deal out of it, or it would have embarrassed her, he just skimmed over them and went searching for more exciting bits.

"Max, I—"

He cut her off by slipping one hand between her open thighs, then used his fingers to tease open her lips.

"I like you here," he whispered in her ear, playfully nipping her earlobe.

She began to move her hips in circles against his fingers, needing more friction, but hardly aware she was doing so. Behind her, his cock was a hard iron spike, twitching, trying its best to find its way into her. A shiver of fear slid through her as memories surged, but she was determined to surf, so she reached behind her and wrapped one hand around his cock.

At first, his breathing hitched, but he quickly smoothed it out, trying his best not to rush her as she learned the thick veins running along his cock and satiny smooth head which leaked ever so slightly.

"Tell me what you want, baby," he rasped against her throat before taking one nipple into his palm to roll.

Shy to articulate the words buzzing through her brain, she took his hand and placed them where she wanted it most. At her silent request, Max withdrew his hand then covered her hand with his instead and guided it back between her legs. He made her rub herself, first in small circles, then more firmly until she began panting and writhing. They both moaned as she rocked her body back and forth, the movement rubbing his trapped cock against the top swell of her ass. Behind her, his skin felt feverish, and the fine sheen of sweat covered his forearms as he curled his fingers into her thighs and moaned.

He was still peppering kisses on her back when she lifted herself up and shifted down, sliding herself on him.

His hand clamped down on her hips. "Shit. Condom."

She stilled. "If you're worried about getting me pregnant, then don't. It won't happen." For some reason, speaking into the dark, facing away from him, made it easier for the words to gurgle out.

She expected him to prod, question the unexpected crack. He didn't. He simply lay there, hands squeezed into fists against his side, his breathing erratic. He didn't push into her, didn't lose his shit and pound, she took him freely into herself. The pace, the depth, the rhythm—it was all hers to decide. She was in control. For some reason, that small act of kindness meant more to her than she realized. Max, what he had given her was a gift. One she would cherish till her last breath.

As she slid up and down him, she realized the position wasn't as comfortable as she hoped. He wasn't helping her, probably scared out of his mind that she would simply flip. After a few strokes, it just wasn't enough. So, she lifted herself off him completely, turned around, and crawled on top of him. Then much to his surprised look, she pushed him back onto the bed and slid herself onto him.

There. That was much better.

Then she began to move.

Fingers intertwined, breaths mingled. Her body moved as if it was made for this. Faster. Harder.

She came first, her throat letting loose a keening cry. Her body shuddered as tingles that began at her core raced along her nerves to spread the joy to each fucking nerve ending. He followed quickly. But unlike the men from her past, Max didn't slap her, choke her, or puke all over her. He simply flexed his fingers on her hips and groaned. A pure male sound of satisfaction.

This. This was how it was supposed to be. This was real.

When it was all over, and their breathing had returned to semi-normal, she cupped his cheeks in both palms reverently and dipped her head down to press a soft kiss on his lips. Then still straddling him, she rested her head on his shoulders. Only then did he begin stroking her.

Too much. It was simply too much.

That's why she cried.

CHAPTER 19

Max hated winters. The grayness, the cold, bare trees, the drizzle, wet streets. They were just weeks into winter, and he already had enough of it. Thankfully it never lasted long. One of the reasons he loved Perth. Seven out of twelve months in a year, he could enjoy yellow sunshine, electric blue sky, outdoor barbeques, and summer fun. He couldn't wait for the sun to resurface, so he could slap on sunscreen and go for a run at the beach, maybe book a cottage in Margaret River and take Eli down for a whole week. Maybe then she would feel safe and open up about things she had hidden too deep inside her head.

Eli! The thought spurred him to ditch the comfort of his bed, pull on a pair of sweatpants from his closet, and go searching for her. Where was she?

Jesus, he didn't spook her last night, did he? He knew every time they made love, gave each other out-of-the-world orgasms, they were silently confessing their feelings for each other, and their relationship tightened a bit more every time they came together, like knots made in shoelaces. It would only get worse from here on. The sharing, caring, simple everyday stuff, all adding up, until there would be nothing left to tie up again. But maybe the thought frightened her.

The house was dark and silent around him. Empty. He pressed his face to the windowpane and searched the small backyard with its neatly trimmed lawn and rotary clothes dryer. She wasn't in the house. The fuzzy feeling from the previous night was quickly morphing into ghastly dread.

He thought for a moment, and then went to her bedroom and began pulling open the drawers of the bedside table. There was nothing unexpected: notepad, charcoal pencils, a couple of pens, a small purse with loose coins, a paperback, and the bill from a supermarket. He replaced them in the order he'd taken them out and pulled open the door to the built-in wardrobe. He riffled through her meager collection of clothes. Then saw her backpack. He hesitated for a moment then quickly unzipped the main compartment.

He stuffed his hand in and pulled out a sheaf of papers. Then came the USB sticks, poster putty, markers, maps, bus timetables, knives. He had just opened what appeared to be a printout from a newspaper when he caught his reflection in the full-length wardrobe mirror. The man in the mirror looked at him with an acutely disappointed expression.

What the hell are you doing, mate?

Looking for clues. For something that would explain the mysteries shrouding the woman I love.

Then ask her, you asshole, don't go through your girl's stuff when she's not around. That's creepy.

Max swore, then replaced the stuff in the backpack in the order in which he took them. He wasn't particularly snooping, but it was suddenly there, the newspaper printout, open, and no matter what he ordered himself not to do, he looked.

It was an obituary printed in the *Geraldton Post*. From May 16, 2013. About one Mrs. Rosie Elderman,

Fifty-one years, beloved wife of Ivan Elderman. Eli's mom.

⚜

As Elena walked along Woodside Bridge, she pulled out the prepaid phone she had purchased the week before to reach Erin. The phone had been Erin's idea. Even though she had worried it might lead Justin to her, Elena had given in and bought one. But there was no point in keeping it. Erin would not be helping her anymore. Her agent had no more leads. No clues to supply. Her job was in jeopardy, she'd said.

Elena leaned over the bridge railing and opened her fingers. She stared at the small ripple in the river as the phone hit the water.

Inside, a voice was screaming at her to do something, run, find more leads. *Don't give up.* She knew that voice. It was the voice of her tired conscience, its last attempt to flicker before it died out of exhaustion.

She closed her eyes and saw Max, as in a picture shot in a LED photo frame. Max with his sexy smile, teaching her self-defense moves, him feeding her, watching stupid sitcoms with her, that last beautiful memory of him lying in bed after they made love. Suddenly she felt the urge to tell him everything. Share this awful burden. It would only take a few words. Let him be part of her search. But first, she needed to think this through. Form the words in her head. Rehearse. Present her story in the best light.

She turned and started to walk.

⚜

Gripped with confusion, Max walked down the hall,

stuffed his feet into sneakers, pulled on the windbreaker from the hook beside the front door and stepped outside, breathing in the chilly air into a rain-soaked garden.

The gate stood open.

He thought about Eli, sleeping next to him, one hand curled under her chin, her mouth slightly open. Where the hell was she? For the first time since she'd walked into his life, he felt curiously desperate and mad at her. They had done something immense last night, yet here he was, walking around in a daze, unanswered questions and half-truths bogging down his mind, and she had gone off to God knows where.

He heard frantic breathing and knew it must be coming from him. His feet hit the curb, and he skidded out into a run along the sidewalk. Trees, houses, people, they came in and out of his focus. He came over Woodside Bridge. The stream underneath ran sluggish, mist still hanging over like an eerie ghost. Joggers sprinted past him, some with pets, some looking bleary eyed. Wind hit his face as he got to the end of the bridge and turned into the small park where he'd taken Eli twice for a run.

The park didn't look like what a kid would have called a normal park. Not that he knew much about kids, other than the fact that he had a certificate which proved he was eligible to work with children, and occasionally he taught them how to stand up against bullies, he didn't have much to do with them. Still, he knew that he certainly wouldn't have enjoyed the place as a kid. For one, it was made as a dedication to Alice in Wonderland, someone he hated even as a kid. Pre-teen girl falling down a rabbit hole? Please!

But what weirded him out the most about the park was the giant mushroom shaped climbing poles, cubby house made to look like an enormous black goth shoe, and the ten-foot-tall gargoyle-faced rabbit with a hidden slide along its waistcoat. Like he thought, one hell of a spooky place.

He found Eli there, sitting on a park bench made to look like a deck of cards, throwing pebbles into the hourglass-shaped pond before her.

"Eli," he shouted above the noise of the wind.

She heard him and came back to where he stood, long coat flapping behind her. She didn't wait for him to speak. She caught his face between her palms and kissed him, her lips warm and tasting like salt. Had she been crying?

An old couple walked past, their skin all mottled and wrinkled, husband holding his wife's hand tight. They nodded their head in disapproval at the public display of affection and murmured under their breath.

He broke off the kiss and stared at her. Tears were running down her cheeks. He stroked back a loose strand of hair from her face. "What's the matter, baby?"

She didn't say anything for a moment, her chin buried in the collar of her coat. Then she tried to laugh. "Nothing. I'm just happy to see you."

She looked away, as if too afraid of making eye contact with him, so he looked at the pond, three ducks waddling along the bike path, not a single one heading for the pond.

"It's bloody freezing. Let's go home." He took her arm and kept on walking. They crossed the bridge together, the noise of early morning traffic increasing steadily.

Alison from next door walked toward them as they rounded the corner to his house, pushing a black buggy with little Declan in it. He was letting out an unhappy squeal, and she was trying her best to distract him by pointing toward the trees and buildings. The kid would have none of it. His voice got sharper and louder with each passing moment.

Max tried to just walk by, tried not to stare at Alison. She looked hassled, certainly not in a mood to chit-chat. But as they reached the buggy, Eli simply stopped. She first stared at Alison, gave her a wobbly smile, then squatted down on the sidewalk to touch little Declan's chubby arm. Declan paused then focused his big blue eyes on Eli's face. Slowly, his hand curved over her fingers. Eli opened her mouth, Max fully expected her to say something inane to Alison, like, *your baby is so cute* or some other nonsense clucky women always said when faced with pint-sized humans. Instead what came jabbering out of Eli's mouth was fluent baby talk, it gurgled out with ease, complete with sound effects. Much to Max's surprise, Declan started giggling.

"Hi," Alison smiled, giving Eli a speculative glance. She didn't seem to notice anything, her attention was fully centered on Declan.

"Hi, Alison, how is it going?" Max jumped in.

Alison gave him a shaky laugh. "Not so good. You should've seen him ten minutes ago, Max. He was such a monster." She went on and on about new-mum stress, how life was better when she ran her own business. All the while, her gaze strayed to Eli and a giggling Declan, speculating, calculating. Finally, she turned to him. "Your girlfriend certainly has the touch. Shall I borrow her for a couple of hours? I'll pay her good. Hell, I'll pay her Joe's one month's salary if that's what it takes to get my baby to sleep."

Max laughed, reached down, clamped his hands around Eli's forearms, and forced her to stand. She gave Alison a smile, and he saw something he had never seen in her eyes before. Envy.

Alison introduced herself, made some idle conversation about babysitting and weather and sleepless nights. Eli smiled through it all, vapid smile that never reached her eyes. When Alison wrapped up her chatter by asking if Eli had any kids, he saw the smile vanish. A cool detachment took its place. He saw the danger signs, and mentally prepared to barge in, although he had no clue what or who he was trying to save.

Eli shook her head back and forth. "No."

Alison smiled kindly and said it was Declan's nap time and they had to keep going.

Eli leaned over to Declan, gave his chubby hand a squeeze, and straightened. He giggled, then reached for her.

"You're so good with kids," Alison moaned.

Eli scoffed, "No, I'm not, Alison. I wish I was. My life would have been so much better if I knew how to take care of a baby."

Alison shot Max a look that said: *Is she nuts? Why else would she say such a strange thing?*

Max quickly wished Alison a good weekend, wrapped an arm around Eli and pulled her along. "Do you want to get some breakfast before we head back?"

She shook her head and cuddled closer. "No. I just want to go home."

Something about the tone of her voice didn't sit well with him. He caught her under her chin with his thumb and tipped her face up. "Everything okay, baby?"

For a long moment, she didn't say anything. Then she smiled and covered his wrist with her hand. "I love you, Max. I don't know why I never said this before. But I want you to know. I really do love you."

His heart soared at her admission, of course, it did. He had been waiting nearly sixteen years for those words.

But there was something else. He couldn't shake the feeling that she had been about to tell him something else, and, at the last moment, she had changed her mind.

He opened his front door, and she followed him. He

expected her to disappear into the safety of her room. She surprised him by stripping in his corridor. First the shoes, then her jacket, then the sweatpants and T-shirt. Underneath them all, she was naked.

"Eli, what—"

"I want you. Here. Now." She wrapped her arms around his neck and kissed him, deep and hard. He cupped her ass, lifted her, and she angled her head to deepen the kiss. They didn't make it to the bedroom. The thick area rug was good enough. After the first time, they baptized his granite kitchen benchtop, and again his shower.

Hours later, when it was dark, and the rain started lashing against the windows, he turned to her and saw the tears in her eyes. He pulled her close, adjusted her in the crook of his arm so that she lay with her head pressed against his chest. Her fingers played with his chest hair gently. He spent a few moments agonizing over the question in his mind, flipping it this way and that, until he could no longer stand the presence of those words inside his head.

"I know there's more to your story, Eli," he spoke into the night, rubbing her silky hair between his fingers.

He sensed it, the sudden tension in her. He fully expected her to bolt out of bed and make a run for it. But she surprised him by relaxing against him. "You're right. There's more. A lot more." It came out as a whisper.

His hand curled around hers. "Will you tell me about it?"

She gave him a little squeeze. "Soon."

CHAPTER 20

Max woke up next morning to the loud and obnoxious chime of his cell phone. He pried open one eye with much effort, then the other, and surveyed the room. He had to lift his head to get a good look at the alarm clock on his nightstand. Ten to eight! Who got a bug up their ass this early and why were they bothering him?

He looked to his right and noted that Eli was already up. The sound of running water from the bathroom confirmed his thoughts.

He picked up his phone and saw the missed call icon on the screen. With a few touches, he brought up the call log.

Chief Chalker? This early? He was supposed to meet Eli at ten. Had something changed?

Max flung the covers from his legs, stretched, and finding that he was buck naked, quickly grabbed a pair of boxer shorts from the closet and pulled it over his hips before returning Chief's call.

"Max?"

"Good Morning Chief. I wasn't expecting your call."

"Yes. About that—I want to talk to you. It's important."

Max frowned at his unmade bed. Outside, the bathroom door opened, and Eli walked out, humming a tuneless rendition of "Black or white."

"I can come to your place," he said quickly.

"Actually, I'm closer to your place. How about we meet at the Coffee Club around the corner from your block, like in ten minutes?"

Like a train speeding down a tunnel, his thoughts gathered momentum and raced inside his head. "Is there a problem?" He whispered into the phone.

"Meet me. ASAP. Alone."

The determination he heard in Chief's voice filled Max with a new, cold confusion, like an icy wind blasting through his guts. It was as if he had, for those few seconds, feared for his own life. Which didn't make any sense, because he was not the one in trouble, it was Eli. Unless Chief had unearthed some information that pointed toward Justin's plans.

"Chief." Max said before he hung up. "If this is about Justin—"

Chief interrupted. "No," he said. "This is about her." He didn't specify the *her* in the question "And you need to hear this. It's important."

With that ominous crack hanging in the air between them, Chief hung up. Worry rushed through him, and he could hardly stand up straight.

Breathe in.
Find your calming center.
Breathe out.

What the fuck was going on here?

en en

Something had happened. She knew it the moment she stepped into the bedroom and found Max standing with his forehead pressed against the door jamb.

"Max? Is everything okay?"

Her stomach dropped as he turned. What the hell happened here? He looked pale. She watched as he yanked back his iron-composure from where he'd lost it and pasted a fake smile on his face. Thoughts moved through her head, like Ping-Pong balls, some with purpose, others stray. Was it Justin? She didn't know how long they stood staring at each other. In the end, it was she who broke the silence.

"Max, you're scaring me." She crossed the space separating them and placed a hand on his bare chest. Firm. Warm. "Talk to me, Max. Has something happened?"

Vaguely, she realized she was speaking with more emphasis, feeling braver than she had ever felt before, thanks to Max and the gift of his love.

Max exploded out of his thoughts. "No, baby." He hooked a thumb under her chin and lifted her face. "Jake was on the phone. He needs…ah…my help." He released his grip and rubbed his face. "I'll be heading out now. Will you be okay here, alone?"

She tilted her head to look at him, a thought hitting her like a ton of bricks. He was lying. She just knew it. As if he read her mind, he continued. "Jake is getting discharged today. I need to give him a ride back home, okay?" He looked away, his gaze busy, as if he'd suddenly taken up a contract to trace the floor tiles with them.

Definitely lying.

"Sure. Go help him, then. I'll be okay here," she heard herself say.

He exhaled as if relieved. "Good. I won't be long."

She watched him sprint to the shower, heard the shower running for all but a minute. Another two, he was out the door.

In the long silence that followed his departure, Elena

waited for her thoughts to reorganize to some semblance of order. But her brain was like a live-wire gone crazy.

Dammit. Nothing made sense. She tried deep breathing next, until she felt the room had run out of air supply. Well then. There was only one thing to do.

૭૩૯૭

Coffee Club was a new, swanky, place two blocks down from his place. Part coffee shop, part patisserie, the place attracted a good amount of early morning commuters in desperate need of caffeine boost.

Chief was already waiting inside at a table by the front window. What surprised him was to find Justin lounging next to Chief, sipping a steaming drink from a tall red mug. Wearing a plain blue Tee, his blond hair trimmed, sunglasses perched on top of his head, he looked different. Less nerdy and more like the IT guy-next-door.

Then his gaze moved on to the woman seated next to Justin. Early fiftyish, salt and pepper hair neatly arranged in a chin-length cut, frameless reading glasses. Everything about her screamed money.

Who the hell was this lady?

"Yes, Chief." Max prompted as he pulled out a chair and parked himself opposite the woman.

Chief looked at Justin. He shrugged and motioned with his chin to go ahead. Max felt his heart thump like drumroll inside his chest. It took all his willpower to keep his expression in the indifferent mode.

"Max. Meet Dr. Natalie Stevens."

Max tried, but his brain wasn't helping him connect any dots. "Okay."

Chief sighed. "Max, Dr. Stevens runs Graceland hospital in Bridgetown."

Max let his fingers claw around the table's edge, hoping the small grip would help him weather the bad news he knew was sailing his way.

Dr. Stevens leaned forward as she spoke, her voice measured, firm. Max could picture her in a sterile consulting room, prying secrets out of hapless patients. "Elizabeth was my patient for six months. She voluntarily committed to undergo treatment for dissociative identity disorder. A few months into the treatment, she was getting better, then she did a runner on us."

Cold wind shot across his nerves, freezing any further thoughts. "Hang on, Doc. No. Eli is not crazy. You've got it all wrong."

Dr. Stevens shook her head, her expression leaden, the kind doctors got on their faces when they delivered bad news. He knew that look. Dr. Morrison had that look on his face when he came up to tell Max that his dad was dead. "Listen, Mr. Logan, I know this is difficult for you to accept. Chief Chalker told me about the situation. I can assure you, this is not some elaborate scheme. Elizabeth is a very sick young lady. At times, she may appear normal. But she got this problem called dissociative identity disorder. That's shrink speak for multiple personalities. In Elizabeth's case, it manifests as serious delusions. Often, she may start believing that someone is after her, trying to abuse her, or hurt her." Dr. Stevens fingered a small scar on her temple, just above her right eyebrow. Her brow furrowed, more contemplative than contentious.

"Justin here brought Elizabeth to me three years ago. She wanted to commit herself, but she had a baby on the way, and I thought it best if we wait. The plan was to bring her back when the baby was few months old. But it didn't happen that way, did it?"

The question was aimed at Justin. He went beet-red.

"I got promoted. Then with the new baby and new house. I know they are excuses. But—I never thought—" He looked like he was about to cry.

Elena has a problem. Ignoring it isn't going to make it go away.

As Justin took a small pause, Max tried to get his brain to work. "She—she would've—she would've told me." Even as he said that he knew how stupid that sounded.

"Not if she can't remember any of it, Max. But dealing with troubled clients on a regular basis, I know problem cases when I treat one. And Elizabeth, I can guarantee you, needs help."

You're right, Max. There's more. Lot more.

As Chief's rough palm gently covered his wrist, Max frowned and looked down. He had his hand balled into a knuckle-popping fist. Without a single word, Chief pushed a glass of water into his hand. He downed the entire load in one long drag and slammed the glass down on the table with enough force to crack the stuff.

Justin and Dr. Stevens looked at each other, then back at him.

Don't you lose it, Max Logan, he told himself. *Don't you dare lose it.*

"How do—" He cleared his throat and looked at Chief. "How do I know they aren't making any of this up?"

Chief leveled him with his patented hard cop look. "Everything Justin said has checked out so far. The registry of marriage and death faxed a copy of their marriage license to me yesterday morning. I looked into the Jerry Sanders case you mentioned. There was no missing person case, Max. Elizabeth made it up. Jerry Sanders committed suicide. He was suffering from depression. Elena met him at TAFE and they went out for a while. He died three months after they broke up."

"What about Jake's car?"

"Jake Sinclair's case—his car was twenty years old, nearly a museum piece. The brake pads had worn thin. It practically didn't exist. There were no cut brake lines, Max. The guy who looked into it found some grease, but that could've been due to a failed oil seal, *or* someone may have tampered with it."

Finally, they were getting somewhere.

Chief stopped, as if to give Max time to take it all in, then continued. "The thing is, Officer Adams got a solid alibi for the day Jake's car crashed, and for the evening your car got wrecked. But Elizabeth on the other hand..." He drummed his fingers on the table once. "The CCTV cameras have picked up an image of her at Glengarry bus station, the one closer to Jake's home, about nine in the morning. Two hours before the accident."

Max dragged a hand through his hair. He was aware of Justin's gaze on him. "Fuck."

Chief waited a beat, then reached out and patted his hand. "I'm sorry things turned out this way, Max. But its better you know now before it's too late. Maybe with treatment, Elizabeth will get better. We all have her best interest at heart."

Max was vaguely aware of Chief and Dr. Stevens attempting to make conversation with him. But the buzzing in his ears wasn't helping.

Chief is wrong, he thought.
Justin is wrong.
I know my Eli.
Eli can't be....

A sudden movement caught the corner of his eyes and Max looked up. He saw a flash of blonde hair. Gray rain jacket.

Was it her? Had she been watching them? His gaze searched the crowd, carefully going over each face. Whoever she was, she had melted into the background.

"Max? Are you okay? Jesus, you look like you saw a ghost." Chief reached out to him. Something must have alerted him, because he looked out the window, and quickly whipped his head back to Max. He saw Justin and Dr. Stevens do the same.

"What is it?"

Even as a chill skittered up his spine, Max forced his face to relax and his mouth to utter the words. "Nothing. I thought I saw someone from work."

All around him, people chattered. Someone spilled coffee on the counter. A harried young mum tried to entertain her irritable twins. Max continued to stare at a spot, the small scratch on the dark wood surface that gleamed under the overhead light. Was there an ounce of truth in Justin's words? For all he knew, he could have staged this entire thing with Dr. Stevens. Was this lady a real doctor? His hand trembled as he shifted it uncomfortably on the table. But Christ, what if they were right? Fucking hell. What if they were right?

Even as he thought this, the other part of him chided him, the part which unconditionally loved the girl in pigtails who had relentlessly annoyed him in his childhood. No. There had to be some mistake.

"I—I've gotta go." He stood abruptly.

Dr. Stevens surged up. For a fifty-something lady, she sure could move fast. "Mr. Logan, we need to get Elizabeth to the hospital. I've got an ambulance on standby. We'll go with you."

What he wanted to say was: *Fuck off, lady.* But what he said instead was: "I—I need some time with her. Then I'll bring her to the hospital myself."

Chief caught his shoulder. "Do you think that's wise?"

"She has been out of the hospital for months, Chief. Another couple of hours isn't going to make any difference, is it?"

Chief trained his eyes first on Justin, then on Max. With a shake of his head, he backed off. "I suppose not."

"I just—I just want to talk to her." He had to see her, explain. Plead. Beg. Whatever. He couldn't let her go without an explanation.

He expected Justin to take issue with the hard glare he leveled at the man. But Justin didn't react, he didn't even blink. The man certainly was a cop, good in crisis situations. He tipped his head in acknowledgment then extended his arm for a handshake. Max took his soft, pansy hands, pumped it once. Deal sealed the gentlemanly way.

"I wouldn't advise you telling Elizabeth about this meeting, Mr. Logan. You don't how she will react. Call us if you need back up," Dr. Steven said to his back as Max hurried to the door and slipped out into the street market mayhem.

Anger, hot and thick expanded from the center of his chest, threatening to scorch him from inside out. This was not how this meeting was supposed to go down. Chief was supposed to tell him Justin was indeed a psycho. Eli was supposed to win. His hand curled into fists. For a moment, he wondered if the whole thing was a setup, staged by Justin. Maybe Chief was on Justin's side, a puppet dancing to his strings. Then Max rejected the idea. Chief was Justin's boss, he may even be biased to save the police department from a media uproar, but he took crime seriously.

Max looked up, saw the darkened sky, then dragged a hand through his hair.

God had some cruel sense of humor.

の

She purposely kept the goodbye note short and to the point. There was no need pouring her heart out when she knew he wouldn't appreciate it. Just as he never appreciated her.

She wondered how long Max had known Justin. If she'd been thinking clearly, with her brain, instead of her hormones, she would have seen the signs. She hadn't even thought about the possibility of Justin turning Max against her, so she guessed that made her the biggest idiot alive.

She had seen the look in Max's eyes as he sat with her enemies, knew what he had been thinking in those moments. The sense of betrayal hurt. She'd given everything she could to him. Still, she didn't want to be angry with Max. He should have trusted her. His lack of trust was almost as painful as the years she spent with Justin. She had brought this on herself. She had trusted Max, let him in. And he had betrayed her in the worst possible way. He tangled up her insides, just as he messed up her carefully planned life. Now she was right where she started six months ago.

As she placed the memory stick, and the instructions to retrieve the rest of the evidence in a zip lock bag from Max's kitchen drawer, she thought about the irony of her life. First Mark, then Justin, now Max. She really had no luck when it came to men, did she?

With a shake of her head, she walked to Max's office, got a prepaid envelope from his desk drawer, then quickly wrote her agent's name at the front. Carefully, she inserted the Ziplock bag into the envelope. She had to believe that Erin would do the right thing.

'You can run, Elizabeth, but you can't ever win.'
The memory sent a tremor along her jaw.
You're wrong, asshole. I'm going to win this game.
Even if I wind up dead.

Armed with a purpose, she stalked to the spare bedroom and took the long sleeved blue jumper she had
bought from a thrift shop in Hillarys. The hem was slightly frayed, and it was one size too big, but it had pockets,
and that was a plus.

She deliberately left the lights off and the curtains
closed as she yanked the cami and sweatpants off and
pulled on the jeans and jumper. Next came the heavy-
duty boots. All the while she kept her gaze fixed on the
floor. No reason to meet her own eyes in the full-length
wardrobe mirror. She wasn't proud of what she was going to do next.

Backpack? Check. Envelope? Check. Hunting knife?
Check.

Moving quickly, she ran down the corridor but
paused before stepping out the front door. Something
prompted her to twitch the blinds in the living room to
make a small gap to see through. Outside, on the road,
was an unmarked gray van. Something about the van
struck her as odd. On impulse, she went to Max's study,
took out the iPad, opened the camera app and zoomed in
on the vehicle. Outside, the cold wind continued to blow,
stirring up dead leaves, inside, her gut churned with tension. The angle wasn't right, the hibiscus blocked her
from getting a good view, but it was enough for her to get
a glimpse of the driver of the van. Fair skin, thick ginger
beard, fingers tapping on the steering wheel.

Tap, tap, tap on her cheeks. *'Come on Elizabeth,*
take the meds.'

Tap, tap, tap on her bare calves. *'Pity, you're a cop's*
wife. I would've loved to fuck you.'

It was him—one of the orderlies from Graceland hospital.

Fuck. Don't panic.

A familiar sense of dread barged into her, squeezing her chest, making it difficult to breathe. Yet she did not give into tears. There were a million why-mes, and please-God's, clamoring inside her brain. She was well aware of her grief beginning to collide with anger, then the two-combined having a field day inside her brain. But she would not give into tears. Not today.

Slowly, her breathing returned to normal. Dreadful inevitability enveloped her, lending her a strange sense of calm.

Plan B.

Backdoor. Grab the ladder. Go over the fence. Exit through Alison's unit.

That's it.

Goodbye Max.

&∽&∽

He didn't go home straight away. He needed time to think, to regroup. His thoughts were driving him crazy, forcing him into a black hole tailspin. In the end, he walked to the nearest library, grabbed a book on Feng Shui, and plopped his ass on a stuffed chair in one far corner, away from prying eyes. He didn't see the words or the images. His head was full of Eli, her laughter, the soft sounds she made as she came, the panicked look she got in her eyes whenever the home phone rang. There was something else. Something he couldn't put his finger on.

Minutes passed, the small increments adding up to an hour, then two. Max forced his head straight and opened his lids.

Fuck it.

He headed home. Time to face the demons head on.

The first drop splattered Max across his right shoulder as he stepped outside. Another hit his nose. He caught the third in his palm. Thunder rolled, pushing clouds along the sky. As he stood there on the busy sidewalk, staring at the drop of water in his palm, with the wind tugging at his hair, it hit him.

Bloody hell!

Now he knew what he'd been missing all along.

CHAPTER 21

Elena wasn't sure what woke her. She felt a pain down the right side of her body and tried to figure out how she got hurt in the first place. Her eyelids felt weighted down as she tried to open them.

Have I been drinking?

The side of her face pressed into something hard and metallic. The scent was familiar. Before she could figure that out, a bump sent her sliding backward until her tailbone hit against something with a loud thud. *Dammit. That hurt.*

Only a primitive protective instinct urged her not to let the groan escape from her throat.

Concentrating on every breath of air, she lay there for a few minutes. What the hell just happened? She needed to think. She really had to figure it out. It seemed too important.

She considered waking Max up, he would help, but that wasn't fair. He worked too hard. He needed the sleep. Maybe if she lay still, listening, she could figure out what had gotten her into such panic state in the first place.

Bump!

Her entire body jolted, and her limbs flailed.

Oh, shit, I'm going to black out.

Then the world was cold and dark and silent.

c⁄ɔc⁄ɔ

Where the hell was she? He tried frantically to recall his last conversation with Eli. He had told her he was going to see Jake. Had she said anything about leaving the house? He pulled out his phone, brought up Chief's number. His fingers hovered over the call button, then he changed his mind and put the phone back in the inner pocket of his jacket. Not yet.

Another possibility occurred to him. The flash of blonde in the crowd. What if she had been following him and had seen him with Justin and the shrink? He felt almost feverish with worry and had to force himself to calm down.

She had no phone, no money, no friends that he knew of. Where could she have gone? On an impulse, he went to the spare bedroom. Her clothes were left untouched. But the backpack that she carried around like a joey in Kangaroo's pouch was missing. Worry bumped up a notch and began running through him in quick pulses. He looked around the room as if the walls could tell him something.

Then he saw it, a torn-off piece of paper, left on the side table beside her bed. It was weighted down by the black alarm clock.

Emotions played salsa in his chest when the implications of the note sank in. Hand trembling, he picked it up, saw her writing scribbled on it.

Thank you for everything, Max. I won't be your problem anymore.
It's about time I stopped running.
Elizabeth.

That was all. He didn't need to think about it. He knew what she planned to do. She thought he betrayed her, and, in many ways, he did. But he would get to that later. Once he found her safe and alive. First, he had to find her.

Suddenly he remembered. The GPS tracker. That was it, that should help. He ran to his office, fired up his laptop, then jabbed in the password with trembling fingers. Then he was running, as if the devil itself was at his heels.

He picked up the key to his rental, his phone, and was out of the door in a few seconds, banging it shut behind him. Wind howled against his face, thoughts inside his skull.

Stay safe, Eli.

৩৩৩

Humming woke her, the tune painfully familiar. Celine Dion's "My heart will go on." She shifted her head, felt the piercing pain. Better not try that again. Her eyes opened, a narrow slit of wavering light.

The humming stopped.

A flash of black, blurred in the closeness. Shoes? She tried to twist her neck, but she couldn't. Flecks of light danced across her vision, flickering, pulsing.

"Good, you're up. I was beginning to worry if Nat had given you too much."

The voice, the possibility, forced her to pry her eyelids open. Still, it took her a few precious seconds to focus. When it did, fear came riding on a giant wave, sweeping away all confused and jumbled thoughts.

Goodbye note. Dropping the envelope off at Erin's office. Boarding a bus to Kalamunda to see Justin. Pain, ending in black.

She wondered how long she had been out for. Hours? Days? Not that it mattered anymore.

Justin came into view. He walked to the long steel cabinet, took a key from his pocket and unlocked the second draw. He pulled out a pair of handcuffs, the same one he had used multiple times in the past to contain her.

"Justin. I don't think this is a good idea."

Elena couldn't see the owner of the pommy accent but knew who it was. The good old doc. Yipeee.

"Thank you for everything you've done, Dr. Stevens. But now you need to leave. I need some private time with my wife."

Elena heard arguments. No, argument implied a two-sided conversation. Only the doc was speaking in this instance as if she'd had a sudden case of conscience. She tried to talk sense into Justin, in that ever-fucking-calming voice of hers. To Elena, the shrink's voice always felt like sandpaper against a raw wound. As she spoke, the doc would scribble in her notepad. Scribble. Scribble. Scribble. Then she would stop and give her patient a look. It always meant one thing: *You're so fucked.*

Justin kept humming, that damned song. Over and over. He sounded calm, controlled. He was at his worst when he was in this mood.

Pop. Pop. Pop.

Three shots. He wouldn't have missed any. He trained with the best, and he never missed.

Natalie Stevens hit the floor with a loud thud accompanied by a wet plop. Ah, head wounds. That must be the sound of her brain leaking out. Despite the gravity of the situation, Elena smiled to herself. So that was it for the doctor then. Used up, thrown out.

Minutes dragged by. Elena was aware of him moving around. The door opened. She could see the first scattering of diluted orange clouds among dense, rain clouds.

She considered crawling on her belly across the floor to the open door, to find her way into the woods, and hide. Then she thought, why bother? She had tried that in the past, every time his fucking Pitbull had located her. Time was her ally. For now, she would listen to her captor, then when the time came, she would make her last move.

The old tarpaulin, faded gray with rusty patches of dried up blood across the fabric came into view. Justin grunted as he rolled the body onto the tarpaulin and dragged it across the carpeted floor. The dog barked. Twice. Then it growled. It wanted to play. With Dr. Stevens.

"Not now, Champ," she heard Justin say.

Some Champ. The bloody dog was more like a vamp.

In a few minutes, Natalie Stevens would be under six-foot of soil. Justin would have already dug the grave. He never left anything for last minute.

When he'd finished, he came back. She didn't even bother to sob when she heard the sound of his zipper being lowered. Seconds later, the warm, wet jets of his semen splashed over her face and chest. Some people got off watching porn. Justin got off on murder and burial. Once he moved away, she shifted, rubbing her face against the dirty red carpet. It still smelled like shit. Once or twice, the dog came up to her and sniffed her face. Once it licked her entire cheek with its rough tongue. Fucked up man and his fucked-up dog.

She felt him pulling at her hair. Hard. "Get to work, Elizabeth."

He grabbed her under her arm and hauled her to her feet. Pain shot up, but years of practice ensured that no sound came out of her mouth. The room swam. She could see now. Her wrist, swollen. Fresh blood started to trickle down her elbow. The scars on her upper arm had reopened, as if he had entertained himself by carving over it again.

A tear escaped her lashes, which seemed to amuse him. He brushed it back from her cheek with a wink. "Why the tears? This is a day for celebration." His voice was soft, almost tender.

Right.

"I knew you couldn't stay away for long, Elizabeth. You need me, just as I need you. Now everything's going to be okay, you'll see."

She opened her mouth, shaping the words "Fuck off" but her vocal cords refused to participate. So, she staggered to her feet, tried to straighten, then grimaced when her knees jerked. Had he raped her while she was out? It wouldn't be the first time. Then she saw she was still wearing all her clothes. Well, maybe he had spared her from rape, but not for long. So much for endurance training and plans to take him out with her Karate chops. Still, all hopes to escape hadn't gone, really. Unlike before, she didn't feel the need to embrace the horror and darkness inside her anymore. She wasn't yet ready to accept the inevitability of what was coming for her. Even knowing her world was once again going to be as unreal as a nightmare, she was prepared to fight. For her child.

Like a geriatric old woman, she shuffled to the adjoining bathroom. She knew the drill. Find the plastic bucket from under the sink. He would have poured bleach into it already. Fill it up with water. There would be no mop. Nothing solid for her to use as a weapon. Just an old rag and a dirty yellow sponge. He never left anything to chance. Everything in the cabin was padded, padlocked, or bolted down. Crockery and cutlery were handpicked plastic. There was no stove, he had taken it out after she tried to set herself on fire. The induction stove he got after that incident was always kept locked up in a drawer underneath the kitchenette sink. There was no shower screen rod, no heavy toilet cistern, no mirrors that she could shatter. Nothing lethal she could use against him. It was a shrine, a safe haven he had built especially for her.

It took a long time. By the end, her hands were raw, and the bleach stung her wounds. Somehow she had managed to turn the red trail on the carpet into a faded brown stain.

He came back, stood, and stared at her handiwork. Then he stomped toward her, lips curled into a snarl. Despite her determination, she cringed. He grabbed her by her chin, crushing until her teeth ground together. Inch by inch, his face came closer. She lost her balance and grabbed his forearm for support. He forced her head forward, until it was inches away from the smelly carpet. She struggled to move her head away, but he pressed her face forward so hard she thought he broke her nose.

"You missed a spot," he said, his voice vibrating with rage.

"Sorry," she managed to gurgle past the blood pooling in her mouth.

He let her go.

She fell on her face and stayed there for a moment, catching her breath.

He didn't come back for another hour.

Five hours. She had been gone for five fucking hours.

It was nearly four in the evening now, and drizzling. Soon it would be night, the visibility poor. The road ahead was a long ribbon, hemmed with gray-green of the eucalyptus. Occasionally a car rushed past him, or flashed its headlights as they came toward him. Where was she?

he wondered. The spot on his phone screen hadn't moved for the past two hours. That could mean many things. Too many bad things.

He hit the gas, and shot forward, overtaking a holiday caravan ambling along at sixty in a hundred zone. Worry plagued his thoughts, so did unwanted fear of the unknown. His chest was painfully tight. Eli was beyond his reach. Anything could happen to her. He clutched the steering wheel tighter, until his fingertips started tingling.

Fuck.

At last, he turned off the main road and down a narrow one then from there into a long, winding mud road. The steering wheel fought as the car rocked and jerked. His headlight illuminated thick trunks of cypress. He slowed the car, stared at his phone. He was on the right track.

"Christ, I'm so fucking scared," he admitted aloud, maneuvering the rental into a sharp hairpin bend.

Hang in there, Eli. Just a few more minutes.

୧༚୧

She spent a while sobbing, but not much. Her head spun, and she had to throw up twice. Obviously, that meant more cleaning up. Then she started searching. She looked for something, anything she could use as a weapon. He may have left something here while she was away, overlooked some little detail. She found her backpack stuffed into the gap between the dining table and the wall. It was empty. Her fingers felt like jelly as she fiddled around the kitchen drawers, hoping to pull out at least a splinter out of them. By the end, she felt so sick and so tired she wished he would just come back and finish this shit for once and for all. As she slumped down on the floor, resting her back against the wall, she saw it. It was something silver and blue. Whimpering, she crawled to it. It was a pen. She recognized it immediately. It belonged to the doc. Her dad gave it to her when she graduated as a shrink, she'd once told Elena during their sessions. It wasn't useful as a machete or a ten-inch blade, but it was something. She shoved the pen into the pocket of her jumper and once again resumed her post at the door.

That was her spot, a circle marked on the carpet using a permanent marker. He'd drawn it the day he kidnapped her and brought her here.

The seriousness of her situation hit her like a brick between her eyes. How could she have been so stupid? She had been sure of her skills, was sure she could make him confess, yet with one blow he had turned the game upside down.

Don't think about it. Think about staying alive. You need to be alive to find your baby.

Her right hip was killing her, meaning, she had been in this position for a while. And she knew she would be here until the bastard felt good and ready to come for her. She didn't think for a minute he would keep her alive for long. She was a liability now, a loose cannon, an exposed lead into his secret life. No, he won't be keeping her. She had a fairly good idea where he would be taking her to finish her off. Inglehope. His favorite hunting ground, two miles away from the house. Inglehope wasn't exactly an ideal place for camping or bushwalking. She doubted if it would even come up on a map. But the land, with its abundance of eucalyptus and gum trees, was perfect for a man like Justin to bury his used-up toys. She had spent nearly five years here, amongst the ghost of his victims, she should know.

For no particular reason, a memory decided to show up that moment. The first time Justin took her, his dog, and a poor hooker he had enticed off the streets promising an hourly rate for a kinky threesome into the bushes. Elena was seven months into her pregnancy then. There had been no threesome, thank heavens for that. All Justin did was drive them all over to the camp he had set up the night before, handcuff her to his truck and set the dog on the poor hooker.

Elena had known all along he had been planning something vicious. It was a lesson for her disobedience. But she had never, in a million years, imagined someone else would have had to pay for her crime. So she had sat there, numb with terror and watched the dog chase the woman. Justin had given the woman a five-minute head start then he and his dog had tracked her through the bush.

Elena could still smell the sour tang of the other woman's vomit and blood, still hear her shrieks and sobs. Elena's heart had started to beat faster, and she had wished for the earth to swallow up her whole. Sensing her distress, her baby had moved restlessly in her belly.

Earth hadn't moved. No one had come to their rescue.

One hole between the woman's eyes. That was all it had taken Justin to finish off his prey. Then had come the dismemberment.

Once he had done it, he had wanted to do it all again. He had never taken Elena back there, but he had come home, bragging about his hunts. He had given her lengthy, details recaps of his victim's terror and the thrill he had felt during such hunts. Now the son of a bitch was going to do the same to her.

Memories receded as pain pushed its way through to forefront. Elena knew now was the time she should make a plan. If she wanted to come out of this alive, she should use her wits to outwit him, use her skills to out-skill him.

She turned ideas in her head but wasn't sure what

exactly would help her outsmart Justin. Plus, if he brought that damned dog with him, as he always did on trips out to Inglehope, then it would be doubly hard for her. Incapacitating the dog wouldn't be easy. The brute dog would easily bring her down and contain her. Probably rip out her jugular.

Maybe there was something she could say or do that would make him trust her. For Justin, it was all about power. Offering sex was out of the question. After Max—no way in hell. She would rather he popped her one right through her chest. Maybe she could pretend she wanted to be with him, that she realized he was her true love and not Max. *Aargh*—No. She couldn't do it. There was dignity in death, even premature death. She would not ever get to see her baby. But she would die knowing she had tried till her last breath. But she wouldn't bargain with a maniac like Justin.

One thing was certain. One way or another, this would all come to an end today. She had to consider—

Fuck.

The door opened.

☙☙☙

Max cut off his ignition and sat staring into the dark. He had come to a dead end. There was no through road from here on. All around him, there was nothing but miles and miles of bush and the inky black blanket of night. A derelict, no-mans land. His heart sank a bit farther down in his chest cavity, and he could hear himself breathing hard.

Where are you, baby?

He picked up the penlight from the glovebox and the gun—he'd bought years ago but never used—then got out of the car, trying to avoid making even the smallest noise.

The air was cold, saturated with rain droplets, and the smell of eucalyptus hit him in the face. His chest tightened with the suddenness of it. He tried to check out the surroundings as far as the thin beam of light would allow. Up ahead, he could make out nothing but massed shapes in the darkness.

He squinted through the tangled branches, wondering what direction to take. Then he saw the flattened fronds of damp bracken and the patch of earth where the rotting leaves looked as if they had been disturbed. Someone or something had used this path before. Max began to walk. The low hanging branch of a small mountain tree scraped at his shoulder, another at his hair. Thorns snagged at his jeans. He walked for a long while, stopped, and pushed aside a long branch of Tea tree. *Just keep going?* He pulled his phone out, frowned at the screen, and resumed walking.

About twenty minutes into his trek, the pristine silence of the wilderness was suddenly pierced by the sound of a dog barking. Max drew to a halt, switched the penlight off, and dropped it into the pocket of his jacket. The dog barked again as Max hid behind a tree. Was it Justin's dog? Was it possible it had spotted Max and was waiting for his master? No, the bark hadn't sounded like an alert, more like a bored whine.

Max stood still, expecting the dog to appear at his feet. There was no sign of any movement. But the wind was picking up, it wouldn't be long before the dog caught his scent and came sniffing this way. Max looked around. Nothing but blackness.

He would have to continue and risk the dog. After letting his eyes adjust, Max crouched and crept through the shadows toward the barking dog.

೧೦೩

She was lying on the thin bed, fully clothed, legs spread out. Her brain, what was left of it inside her skull, felt like an egg she'd once put into a microwave. Everything was sore, even her eyelids. She wiggled her toes. Her boots were gone, and her ankles had ropes around them. Justin knelt at the foot of the bed, anchoring her legs to the bedpost. A part of her was grateful that he'd let her keep her clothes, another part worried what that might mean for her. Nothing good.

"Before you kill me, I need to know something," she said, her tongue parched and leathery, her voice barely there.

Justin stilled, looked at her, then smiled. "What makes you think I'm going to kill you?"

"Aren't you?" she asked, feeling her heart sink to the floor. If he killed her, at least this mess would be over, and she could move on. If he wasn't planning on killing her, then what the fuck was he going to do to her?

He cocked his head to one side, then looked at her curiously. "You sound disappointed, Elizabeth. Does that mean you want me to kill you?"

Despite the ugliness, despite the horror he inflicted, his child-like curiosity and open wonder made her smile. "Yes, Justin. I would really appreciate it if you would kill me."

He was quiet for a moment, then he said, "Why would I do that? You're my wife. I love you. I always love you. Even when you behave like a slut."

Ha! Finally. She was wondering when he would get around to that whole *behave like a slut* issue.

He carefully tightened the rope around her other leg, gave it a tug, then stood staring at her. For a moment, she stared back at him, really seeing him, this fucked up man, this monster. "Why are you doing this?"

He was directly above her now. His hair was greasy,

a thin sheen of sweat on his forehead, the light from the candles throwing shadows across his cheek. Her question seemed to startle him. A look of panic came to his face, then he composed it back to the familiar blank canvas.

"Why, Justin?"

She stared at him, waiting for something to happen. She didn't know what she was expecting. A breakthrough?

He looked away, but not before she saw the tears in his eyes. Those tears used to give her hope, back when she was still an optimist, now they made her feel sick.

"You've made me really sad, Elizabeth. We were apart for three months. Three months when you were out there in the filthy world, mixing with dirty bastards like Max, letting him touch you, fuck you, getting yourself filthy. Why, baby, why do you insist on doing this to yourself?"

Wistfulness, almost real, tumbled out with his words.

Back to where they started.

This was no good. She should've known there was no point encouraging him to talk. In the five years she had lived with him, ate with him, and slept with him, she hadn't figured out what made him tick, what would make him forget about this obsession he had on her. It wasn't going to happen today.

So, she closed her eyes and tried to find that stupid calming center she knew she had somewhere inside her. She thought about the dojo, lessons she'd learned. As ever, her thoughts circled back to Max. His green eyes. Killer smile. The power he projected when he taught the class. It had made her, and everyone gathered, feel alive, believe in themselves. *'The best way to gain self-confidence is to simply do what you're most afraid to do.'*

'Inhale Confidence, Eli, exhale all your doubts.'

The first blow came to the left side of her face, the

second caught her on her breast. Her eyes popped open, and she gasped.

"Elizabeth," Justin said, his voice calm. "Never look away from me when I speak."

Tears flowed freely, trailing from the corner of her eyes, down her cheeks. She looked up at him. But her left eye wouldn't focus. So, she swallowed, once again donning the subservient posture that had become second nature to her. "Yes."

"Huh?"

Elena fisted her palm on the mattress below. "Yes, sir."

He sighed heavily. "Good." He stroked her cheek then bent over and placed a soft kiss on her lips. "Now, what is it that you wanted to ask me?"

Her left eye kept drooping shut, but she tried to keep it open as she voiced her question. "Where is my baby?"

He bit his lower lip then shook his head. She saw the evil glint in his blue eyes before his entire face broke into a smile. "Elizabeth. Elizabeth. Elizabeth." He sat down beside her, stroked back her hair from her face. "You're so stupid. You know that? This is why you need someone like me to keep you safe. Because you're so fucking dumb."

She let that slide. At least there was a grain of truth in his words. She was stupid.

Body and voice trembling, she said, "Sir, please. I'm begging you. I just—I just want to know if my baby is okay. I don't even know his name. Please."

His eyebrows rose, and in his eyes, she saw a gleam of mad pride. Then he sighed. She watched him saunter over to one of the barstools. But he didn't sit. He came back, blurring in and out of her vision. "Your baby? Dog food, you mean?"

Her blood ran cold at his words, at the easiness with

which he had delivered the blow. Something vile churned in her gut. "What are you saying?"

"Oh, yes. If I remember right, Champ really loved that treat." Justin continued with words that sickened. He wasn't showing too much expression, but he was staring intently into her eyes. "Our baby, the poor critter only lived for five hours. I thought about burying him. Maybe put a headstone. Put some flowers. You know, do the right thing. Being a good dad. But the little shit had this bloody slime on his body, and soon it started to stink. I didn't want to touch him then, so I let Champ do all the work."

Hot bile rose. She pressed her palms into the mattress as her world continued to spin. Was this monster telling the truth? Her pain-fogged brain struggled to remember the events of that horrible day. She had passed out in her struggle to get the baby out of her body. Even though it had been her second labor, it hadn't been easy. The pain had been intense. She didn't remember pushing out the after birth, or her baby's first cry. When she resurfaced, he had told her she had given birth to a boy, and that they were better off without him. He made her believe that he had given up the baby for adoption.

"But the adoption agent. I saw the papers," she whispered around horror clawing up her throat.

He laughed at that. Then put his face close to her and slowly said, "You mean the papers Erin forged for me?"

She opened her mouth, but no sound came out.

A smile appeared on his face. "Involving Erin, leaving the papers around for you to find. That was a neat trick, wasn't it? And you fell for that. Hook, line, and sinker. Dumb bitch."

It wasn't just his words that made her scream, but the smugness of his voice when he said them. So, it was true. There was no baby. No hope. He had deliberately set her up on a wild goose chase. She gulped, breath after breath, her throat convulsing.

Shaking his head, he sat beside her hip. "You know what it took to get Erin to make up those papers for me, Elizabeth? One phone call, one flash of my badge. She fell for it. The stupid woman thought she was doing a great service to the nation, by helping the cops catch a serial offender," he spoke slowly, taking pleasure in it.

Despite the plummeting sense of misery in her gut, she got the words out: "You set this up. This sick game. You were playing with me. Why?"

He smirked. "Why do you think, Elizabeth?"

Thoughts gathered momentum, converged, thickened. Sickness buried deeper into her gut, wily worms with needle-like teeth. She remembered the night she had taken off from Graceland. The orderly had 'forgotten' to lock her door. Was it deliberate? *Think, Eli, think.* A week after her escape, Justin had found her in a homeless shelter. She'd expected the worst. But all he did was smile and tell her that they were going to play a game. He gave her three months to find her baby. If she found the baby, she would get to keep him. But she had to find him first. In the meanwhile, Justin would do everything possible to thwart her attempts. Like an obstacles course in a video game, he'd said. If he caught her, the game was over. And if she failed, at the end of the three months, she should voluntarily return to him. Or else, he would track down the baby himself and kill him. Desperate, she had agreed to his terms. But now as she looked at him, she knew the truth. "You deliberately set me free that night. You wanted me to escape from Graceland. This was your plan all along."

"Yep. Now you're getting somewhere. I was worried all that fucking had toasted your brain cells." He smiled, eyes oddly bright. To her horror, he started kissing her.

Soft kisses, butterfly light, all over her face and breasts. "And do you know why I did it, Elizabeth?"

She stared at the ceiling as he started to pull at her neckline to expose her breasts. "Do you, Elizabeth?"

Silence.

Sharp pain on her breasts. The fucking bastard was pinching her nipples.

"N—No, sir."

His fingers stilled. "To teach you a valuable lesson."

She stared at him, almost wanting to laugh, at the sick fuck who leaned over her, looking smug. Of all the things, she'd thought he would say, that certainly wasn't it.

"Teach me a lesson?"

He leaped out of her bed, smiled, and let out a sigh of contentment. He walked to the kitchenette, had a drink of water, then came back, smiling. "Oh, yes, where was I? Ah, the reason—" He cricked his neck, rolled his shoulders once. Then he took off his T-shirt. "You, my darling, needed to learn something." He started to work on the buckle of his jeans. "I brought you here, gave you a safe house, all the luxuries you deserved, hoping we could build a life here. Away from the sick world. But were you happy here?"

What the hell was she supposed to say to that?

His eyebrows rose. "No. Even after we had Alex, you were fucking miserable. We could've been a real family, Elizabeth."

She gave a strangled, angry sob. "You killed him, you bastard. You killed my Alex. You drowned your own kid in the bathtub. What kind of monster does that?"

She watched as he stretched, then lifted one leg, then another to remove his boots and socks. "Someone who loves his wife more than anything in the world."

Her chest constricted with pain and she made a mewling sound.

He stared at her then shrugged. "The kid was okay, I suppose. But he was starting to get in the way, Elizabeth. Always wanting your attention. Sucking from your breasts. Whining through the night. I'm sorry. But he had to go. You understand that, don't you?"

She hadn't realized she was shaking until he bent over to kiss her lips. The pain in her chest was so intense she wondered if her heart was failing.

"Alex was one. My son was only one. An innocent baby. And you killed him. Just like you killed my other baby."

He straightened and shrugged again, as if the murder of an innocent, young child was no big deal for him. She raised her head to stare at him, wanting to hear the rest of his fucking explanation, wanting to see how far he would take this game. He was enjoying it. The erection that leaped free from within the confines of his boxers confirmed just how much. "You always thought if you got away from here, you'd be free, didn't you? You thought you'd be happy." He stepped out of his jeans. "And were you happy, Elizabeth? Living in shitholes, being with your childhood sweetheart, fucking him, telling him you loved him—did that make you happy?"

She didn't bother to ask how he knew she had told Max that she loved him. Certain questions were best left unasked.

He removed his watch and placed it on the floor. That done, he climbed on to the bed and sat astride her chest. His hand began to mold her breasts, squeezing, pinching. He loved to leave his marks. "Do you know how lucky you are? You're one lucky girl."

Lucky? This was her at her lucky best? God, she'd hate to be unlucky then.

"You belong to me, Elizabeth. Me. No one would love you as much as me. Certainly not your Max. You know why he fucked you? Because he felt sorry for you." He leaned down and rubbed his nose on her breasts. "Yes, Elizabeth. It was a pity fuck. How does that make you feel?"

A soft bite.

"Here I was, prepared to give you the world, and you still ran away, to be with him. And what exactly did you achieve? Did he give you happily ever after? No. He wouldn't. Your happily ever after is with me, Elizabeth. With me."

He began stroking her face, his smooth fingers shaping her eyebrows, her nose, her lips. It always began like this. Soft, gentle, sweet. Then he would go stir crazy. She thought of pummeling his chest, punching his junk, but it wouldn't bother him in the least. He loved her resistance. All she could do was make him mad, force him to lose his shit, expedite her death.

If you've nothing to lose, you can try everything, Eli.

So, she looked at him in his eyes, showing a lifetime of contempt. "You're a sick fuck, Justin. A sick fuck."

He just smiled.

"Look at you. Look how pathetic you are. You have to tie up a girl to get her to have sex with you. That's beyond sick."

His smile grew.

"Do you know what else I feel for you, Justin? Hate. No one can hate you as much as me. No one despises you or prays for your death every second of every day like me."

He laughed, as if she had said something funny.

"I hate you, Justin. I hate you with every cell in my body," she said slowly, never taking her gaze off his, emphasizing each word.

The blow caught her across her cheek. Something rattled inside her mouth. A tooth maybe. Then he was wrapping his hands around her neck and choking her. Still, her eyes stared straight into his eyes.

"Take that back," he rasped, moving his face closer, his breath fanning her nose. His fingers tightened, aiming to send her into blackness and eternal rest.

Pain jogged her memory. Her last hope, her lifeline.

Once chance. She only had one chance.

Instead of going for his arms, she went for the pen she'd hidden in her pocket. Yes.

She lifted the pen as his grip tightened, aimed the sharpened edge at his head.

Up and in.

She rammed it into the side of his neck.

It made the oddest sound.

She saw the shock and fear in his eyes. Saw his hands reach for the pen.

"You bitch," he said. "You've—" He didn't speak anymore.

There was a gurgling sound, and then blood started spurting like a fountain. The sticky redness gave her no comfort. Two things happened simultaneously. Justin's mouth twisted in a scream, his whole body jerking. Then someone grabbed him from behind, and he was off of her. She heard him crumple to the floor with a loud thud.

All the walls closed in. Sobs tore out of her throat, but she couldn't breathe past them, so they got trapped in her chest, strangling her. When she tried to sit up, the world tilted. Someone was beside her, touching her, gathering her into warmth. Familiar scent. Familiar hands. The smooth voice was talking, soothing, asking if she was okay. She wanted to scream that she wasn't okay. She was never going to be okay.

That someone left her. Cold. So, fucking cold.

"I need an ambulance," she heard the male voice say into the silence.

Once again, darkness enveloped her, this time she welcomed it with both arms.

EPILOGUE

Two months later…

J ake rang the doorbell on the unfamiliar door. He heard it ring somewhere deep inside the house. He waited for a few moments. No sound. He pushed the bell again, then for added measure he rapped on the door with his knuckles several times. Where was she? The manager at Hilton had told him she had called in sick. He stepped back from the door and looked at the window. Sunblock curtains, all pulled shut. He was just about to leave when he heard the sound of key turning, and then the door opened.

Sarah stood there, looking puzzled and confused. She was dressed in a pair of grubby sweatpants and an over-sized Star Wars T-shirt with brown stains over her chest. *His* Star Wars T-shirt. From where he stood, he could smell sweat and…ice cream? She had clearly spent a night or two indulging in a pity-party, keeping chocolate ice-cream company.

"What the hell are you doing here?" she asked.

"Good morning to you too, sunshine," Jake said.

"You shouldn't have come here," Sarah said.

"Well, I'm here now. Can I come in?"

"Better not." She started to shut the door in his face.

He pushed his way past her and stood, staring at the mess in front of him in shock. Retching would be impolite, so he didn't, but the urge was there. Wherever he looked, he saw the wreckage of empty pizza boxes, coke cans, empty ice cream tubs and take away containers with long-forgotten Chinese food in them. Sarah had never been a good housekeeper. Her excuse had always been, *We can't all be Martha Stewarts.* But this? Good lord.

"If I had known you were coming, I'd have straightened up," she said defiantly from behind. "I've been unwell."

Jake felt an impulse to scream at her. But he couldn't do it. He had come here with a purpose in mind. He would go through with it and then leave her.

"You sent me flowers. And there was that fucking get well card. Why?"

She glanced at him. "Felt like it."

"Thought you would be happy to see me dead."

The atmosphere chilled for a moment. "Why am I not surprised?" she asked. "You always had such low opinion of me. Glad to know that hasn't changed one bit."

"What the hell happened to you, Sarah?" The question was out before he could reel it back.

She stood, staring at him for a second. He saw tears filling up her eyes. But she blinked them away. "Feeling pity now, Jake? Don't. I know I am a mess. You don't need to point that out. I know what you're going to say: You brought this on yourself, Sarah. Yes, I did. But it's my life, I'll live it the way I want. So, you can shove your compassion up your ass and get the hell out of my house."

One minute he was staring at her, and the next, he was clenching and unclenching his fists. "I will. After I ask you a few things."

She turned away. "I'm going to put the kettle on. Do you want coffee?"

He shook his head.

"Suit yourself."

He followed her as she walked to the kitchen and put on the kettle. He saw the way the sweatpants stretched across her ass as she fiddled around with teabags and felt the familiar flicker of desire.

To take his mind off the woman before him, he took inventory of the mess covering the small breakfast table. Unopened mail, community newspapers, plastic shopping bags. And—

"That's the bag you left at my place."

The red leather bag he'd been looking for was laid out open amidst the mess, its contents slopping out in a heap. Lacy edge of a pink satin nightie, red velvet covered jeweler's box. An empty CD cover.

Sarah leaned back against the Formica benchtop and lifted the yellow mug to her lips and took a gulp. "Yes."

For a second, he couldn't move. His skin went hot. There was a heaving inside his chest and head. "Y— You!" he finally sputtered. "You broke into my place." He looked speculatively at Sarah, who didn't seem embarrassed at all.

"In my defense, I didn't exactly break in. You left the spare key under that loose brick next to your front door. The exact same place where we used to leave the spare key when we were together."

More dots connected in his brain. "Were you the blonde who followed me outside Paddy's place?"

She shrugged and took another sip. "Yup. Got the wig from Annabel. She bought it for a Halloween party. Thought it would give me an edge." She touched her red highlights. "I always wanted to be a blonde."

"Jesus, Sarah." He jammed fingers of both hands into his hair and thrust back. "Why? Why the fuck were you stalking me?"

She looked up, met his gaze. In her eyes, he saw something fierce. "I wouldn't call it stalking. I was—" He saw her take a deep breath. "I had to know what I did so wrong that made you throw me out of your life one fine morning. I was looking for clues."

For one long, tense moment, they stared at each other, a battle of wills. Then she dropped her gaze and turned away to plonk her mug on the table behind her. He saw her hands tremble as she wiped her mouth.

"Why the hell do you care? We're not together anymore." His voice sounded bitter even to his own ears.

His eyes must have revealed something, though, because she started crying. "We had a solid marriage, Jake. I thought we were happy. How could you do that to me? I came back from work to see my bags packed and waiting at the front door. You changed the bloody locks. You wouldn't pick up your phone. Before I could process everything, your lawyer slapped me with a divorce notice."

Not one of his best moves. But he had done what he had thought was right. He had to protect himself. So, he had played the offense.

Her eyes blinked desperately to hold back tears. "And that floozy bimbo, did you really sleep with her?"

Her eyes pleaded with him to explain it to her, but he couldn't. How dare she, after all she put him through, how dare she question him?

A pulse throbbed in the side of his neck. He took a deep breath and made himself speak quietly. "Maybe I did. Is that why you were stalking me, to take notes?"

There was a fierce glow on Sarah's face. "No, that's not why I was stalking you, you jerk. I did that because I had to know what the hell I did so wrong to deserve such treatment from you. I wanted answers."

At that moment, he had to control his emotions. Choking his ex-wife, yelling at her, would make an already tense situation worse. "That's funny, coming from you," he said with an exaggerated calm.

She looked puzzled. The funny furrow which popped up between her brows when she was confused reappeared. "What's that supposed to mean?"

"You want to know why our marriage broke up, Sarah?" Voice vibrating with rage, he went toward her. She stood her ground. She had never been one to back down from a fight. Gripping her by shoulders, he jerked her. Once. "Because you cheated on me."

He saw her face pale. "Wh—what?" she asked, voice low and trembling.

His heart slammed against his ribcage, but surprisingly, anger left his body as he stared at her. All that was left was acute disappointment. "That's right, sunshine. I know all about it. Every Wednesday, two p.m. You left your car at work then took the ninety-eight bus to Galleria. Then you would walk half a mile to Collier Road. From there you would go to that dark and dingy Chinese therapeutic center, and disappear for an hour. I know it because I followed you. Several times. Word around the street is that place is a massage parlor that caters to all kinds of creeps."

There was the sour-sweet reek of chocolate and coffee on her breath as he brought his face toward her. "Was it the Asian masseur, Sarah? The one with long, black hair? Or was it the buffed-up owner guy?"

He was still looking into her eyes, willing her to drop her gaze when her hand shot out and slapped his cheek so hard he felt his teeth rattle inside his mouth.

"Bastard!" she screamed, pummeling his chest.

He caught her wrists, brought them together. As he stared at her in confusion, her face changed, twisted, and crumpled. He let go of her and watched in dismay as she slumped to the floor and broke down in tears. All life was gone from her.

"Sarah." He reached for her, but she leaped off the floor and ran out of the kitchen. Soon he heard some drawers opening and closing from somewhere inside the house.

What the hell just happened here?

Guilt? Anger at getting caught out?

She came back, armed with a stack of papers. Bills, he noticed as she came closer. "There. Take it. Read it, you moron." In a dramatic flourish, she threw the papers at his face.

He caught one as they floated to the Lino covered floor.

Ming Health Clinic.

Seventy dollars charged for an hour of F and D treatment.

"What the hell is this?"

Her body tensed against his side. "Bills. For the acupuncture and Chinese herbs, they were giving me to help me get pregnant."

For a few seconds that felt like hours, the only sound in the kitchen was the drone of the refrigerator.

"Pregnant?"

She nodded. "We'd been trying for months, Jake. And I knew how disappointed you felt every month when I had my periods. You wouldn't say anything, but you would get this look in your eyes. It used to kill me. So, when someone from the office told me about this Chinese medicine thing, I thought I might try it out. I didn't tell you because I didn't want to get your hopes up. But if I had known this shit was going through your head—" She sniffled then sucked in her breath. "Fuck, Jake, why didn't you just ask me?"

Her eyes dared him to say anything. There was an intense pain in them he hadn't noticed before. Confusion turned to horror as he lifted the paper up and reread the words.

God.

Fucking hell.

No.

Snap out of it. Say something. She's watching you, moron. Snap out of it.

He lifted his palm to touch her, but unsure of her response, slowly dropped it back down to his side.

Shit, how the hell was he going to fix this?

His mouth struggled to form words. "You—are you saying—" But he was asking the air because she'd already left the room. She slammed the door behind her, leaving him to sort out the spectacular mess he'd made of his life. He wished he could break down and scream until his throat was raw.

He stood there for a few minutes, then, knowing she wasn't going to come back, he left the house. Besides, he didn't have enough strength to convince her just yet.

ↇↈↇ

The last time Max saw Elizabeth, she'd been a screaming mess tied to a stretcher, and paramedics were fussing over her. Now, two months after that crazy night, as he fidgeted in the plastic seat at the Midland Police Headquarters, Elena sat beside him—straight-backed, calm, composed.

Beyond the four walls of the interview room, the station was at its busiest. Across the oval-shaped glass table that separated them sat Chief Chalker, flanked on either side by two senior sergeants.

Assistant Commissioner Simon Hopkins was present, a slim-built man in his mid-sixties. He wore a poorly cut gray suit and a pale blue tie that appeared as if he'd nicked it from a garage sale. Everything about him, everything except his dark brown eyes, appeared dull. Those eyes were shrewd, and when they got down to business and Eli started talking, they got downright fierce.

Someone coughed, the sound pulling Max out of his thoughts and back to the meeting. He looked up to see Chief Chalker watching Eli, his expression grave. He clearly felt guilty about what had almost happened to her under his watch.

The male sergeant to Chief's left picked up his notepad and brought it very close to the tip of his nose, as if he was severely short-sighted. "So, you're stating that Officer Adams persuaded Dr. Stevens to perform a hysterectomy on you, even when there was no need to do so?"

Max clenched his fists on the table. How could they ask stupid questions at a time like this? He realized these were the questions that needed to be asked. But they had done all that before. So why this gruesome recap?

He saw Eli flinch as if the sergeant had backhanded her, but then she nodded. "I can't say that for sure. But my second labor had some complications. Something to do with bits of placenta left behind. I ended up with a nasty fever. Added to that, I wasn't breastfeeding, so I also had a bad case of…" She paused as if searching for the right word.

"Mastitis," her attorney, Anne Bartlett said, speaking for the first time.

"Yes, mastitis. That's the word. I was really sick. I guess Justin must've thought I was dying. He wouldn't have taken me to Dr. Stevens if that wasn't the case."

The guy gave Eli a thoughtful look. "So doctor Stevens did a hysterectomy on you, even though she was a psychiatrist, and then when you recovered, you were committed as her patient."

Max gritted his teeth. Why the fuck were they putting her through this again? Hadn't they taken her statement and collected the evidence while she was at the hospital?

"No." Eli shook her head. "Look, I told you, Justin had me committed to Graceland even before that."

"Do you know why?"

She paused, took a deep breath, then looked at the commissioner. Her hand clenched into a fist, then she relaxed it, but not before he heard her knuckles crack. Max itched to hold that hand, gather her to him. But she hadn't looked at him even once throughout the hour-and-a-half meeting. He wondered if she even knew he was here.

"I was pretty hysterical after I lost Alex. Justin convinced Dr. Stevens to commit me to help me with my...issues. I think his plan all along was to establish me as a nutcase."

The other sergeant, an Asian woman in her late forties, with pin-straight dark hair arranged in a sleek bob, leaned forward. "Why do you think Dr. Stevens assisted Officer Adams in committing such a horrific crime, Elizabeth? If the news had leaked, she would have lost her license. She had a reputation to uphold, not to mention she was running a very lucrative business."

Eli crossed her fingers on the table then uncrossed them. She was getting agitated. Max cleared his throat, prepared to intervene, but she beat him to it. "I once heard Justin threaten Dr. Stevens about some evidence he had against her. From their conversation, I got the impression that Dr. Stevens once had a well-off patient. He committed suicide while he was at Graceland. But Dr. Stevens kept charging his family for expenses. Somehow the news got out, and the cops were called. Justin got involved in the case, and he negotiated with the family to drop the charges. I think he got Dr. Stevens to co-operate by blackmailing her using that story."

The female sergeant narrowed her gaze. "Let's get back to the story of you in that cabin. In the statement that you gave us on April twentieth, you said that Officer Adams used to force you to have sex with different men. And later he murdered them all. Do you—"

Max stood. Fuck them. He would be damned if he'd sit there and listen to them put his woman through hoops again. "I don't think you should be questioning her anymore. Can't you see she has reached her limit?" His voice came out louder than he intended.

The female sergeant rose to her feet as well. She now had a pinched look on her face. "Look, Mr. Logan, this is a police officer we're trying to convict. I'm just verifying the facts, so we don't look like fools before the jury. We need to cover all bases, get the story straight."

He glared at her. "For the love of God, just how much more do you want from her?"

Anne Bartlett gazed first at Max then at the sergeant before rising from her seat. "Mr. Logan is right. I don't think you should put my client through this again."

The assistant commissioner gave a grunt then placed both hands on the table, palms down. "All right, Officer Heng. I guess that's enough for today."

Officer Heng looked at Commissioner Hopkins, face flushed crimson, then she sat down heavily.

The commissioner turned to Eli. "So, Mrs. Ad—"

"Ms. Campbell," Eli corrected him, her voice firm. She looked good today, in a smart suit, her hair back to dark brown. A month in the hospital and another in the respite center had done her good.

"Yes, of course." Assistant Commissioner Hopkins nodded, cleared his throat. "So, Ms. Campbell, Dr. Tran from RPH assures me that Justin Adams has recovered enough to face the court. Since you're ready to testify before the court, we'll proceed as we decided."

Elena smiled, a slight smile. A deep breath. "Okay."

When she stood up to shake her hands with the officers, her hand was steady. She was ready, or as ready as she would ever be. And she had done it all by herself.

He watched her smile at Chief in goodbye. The fucking sergeants who grilled her mercilessly received a vague nod. But what the hell did she give him?

Zilch. Nada. A big fat nothing.

When he realized she was leaving the room without so much as a smile or goodbye, he knew he had reached his limit. For two months, he had told himself that she needed space. He had pretended to be okay when she refused to see him, had pretended that he respected her decision. But fuck that. Not anymore. He wanted to know if they stood a chance. He wouldn't fault her for protecting herself. But he had to know, if it was time for him to let her go, little by little, every day, just so that he could build up his defenses again and free himself.

He ran after her, pushing open the glass door, past a group of school kids out on their field trip, then past a crowded reception area. She stood there, chatting to her attorney and the commissioner.

"Eli!"

She looked up at him at long last. His heart rate kicked up.

One shot. He could do this. He had to do this right.

A pause.

She turned to the commissioner. After a few quick words with him and her attorney, she walked up to him.

"We need to talk, and you're going to listen to me." His voice came out raspy, his normally laid-back Irish voice razor sharp.

An even longer pause.

As moments ticked past, for the first time in his life, faced with a cold inevitability of a life without Eli in it, Max understood Jake's pain. Found some sense in his friend's inability to part ways with Vodka.

Eli wrapped her arms under her breasts then looked past the automatic sliding doors to the small paved courtyard. Two three-seater timber chairs stood under a triangular shade sail. "How about we sit over there?"

Thank you, Sweet Jesus.

They were silent as they walked outside and sat. She scooted to the far end of the chair to make room for him. Her hands clasped in her lap, her handbag taking up the space between them, she took every precaution to avoid physical contact. Maybe she felt it was easier to keep him away than to take a sledgehammer and break down all those walls she'd built around herself. She'd once told him that she often felt put-together inside. Maybe she felt he would never be able to love her broken pieces. Funny thing was, he loved her vulnerable, broken pieces more than her shinier whole ones. Those jagged, irregular, glued-together pieces were what made her unique. He loved her, no conditions attached.

The wind was down, cold spring air blasting them in their face. Max glanced at her, watched her face compose into the blank mask as she prepared for his interrogation. Despite his best intentions, his gaze strayed to the pulse beating at her throat, to the creamy swell of her breasts. Even knowing she didn't want him didn't stop the ache in his chest.

Dammit, Logan, Focus.

"Thank you," she blurted, cutting off his next line of thought.

"For what?"

"Inside. For standing up for me. Officer Heng is a

hardass. I had it handled, but it was sweet of you to intervene."

He waved a hand dismissively. "Never liked that woman. And the word you're looking for is insensitive bitch, not hardass."

Her lips curved a fraction.

Silence reigned for a few beats, in which he could hear himself breathe hoarsely. He smoothed a hand over his thigh and saw that his jeans had a small tear, just above the knee, though he couldn't remember how it'd happened. He waited.

Frustration and anger chased through him. Fuck this. "I can't keep going like this. I want you back."

At last, she looked at him, big gray eyes wary, so fucking gorgeous.

He grabbed her hand closest to him, holding it firmly in his palm. Their gazes clashed. He saw the devastation in them. "You pushed me away. I'm so fucking mad at you, Eli."

Her lashes dropped, veiled her eyes. "I know." A soft whisper. A husky sniffle. "I was mad at you too. For a while. But not anymore."

He stared, that small flicker of hope flaring within him.

Her fingers curled inside his palm. She sighed. "I'm sorry I didn't tell you the full story about Justin. I wanted to. God, Max, I did. I won't lie to you. But I was ashamed. What man would want to be with a woman with a shitty past like mine? I knew you would look at me differently. So, I thought I would wait for the right time, but there was never really a right time for it. By the time, I got the nerve to open up, you had already met Justin." Her voice broke at the last word and tears started tracking down her cheeks. "You believed him. I told you I loved you, and you still believed him."

Every spark of rage faded. He moved. In a heartbeat, he knelt at her feet, caging her between his body and the timber chair. They stared at each other, breathing ragged. "Fucking hell, baby. It wasn't like that. You wouldn't tell me anything. And I—"

He stopped abruptly when a grimace of anger flashed across her tear-stained face. It was his own damn fault. The words were coming out wrong, all tangled up.

He reached out to wipe her cheeks, but she pulled away, as if she couldn't bear his touch.

Dammit. He had to get this right. "Eli, baby, I—I'm so sorry."

Tears chased each other down her cheeks. "You hurt me."

"I know," he said desperately. "I messed up. When I met Justin, heard his version of the story, I didn't know what to think, who to trust. I was a fucking mess. But I came back. I swear to you, honey, I came back to talk to you. I wanted to get everything out in the open, tell you that I trusted you, but you were gone."

She looked past him. "I always wondered. What made you come after me? I thought you'd be happy to see me go." The bitterness in her voice was clear as daylight.

He didn't answer at first, wondering how to tell her in a way that wouldn't make him look like a fool. Then he decided to go for it. "It was his fucking hands."

She frowned. "Huh?"

"I always thought there was something wrong with his hands. Too soft. After I left him at that coffee shop, it finally clicked in my head. The bastard had smooth fingers. Baby soft fingers. As if he'd burned off the skin on his hands. Then I started thinking why someone would do that. Unless he had been in a fire, the only other option that came to me was that he didn't want to leave any fin-gerprints."

"Oh. Wow. That's—you should've been a cop, Max." She paused then stared at him, her expression ear-nest. "But how did you know where to find me that night? I know Justin wouldn't have told you. He was—" She stopped, biting her lip.

"GPS tracker. I had one installed in your backpack." He lifted both arms in surrender when she opened her mouth. "Before you get all worked up, I only did it be-cause I wanted to reach you in a worst-case scenario. You wouldn't tell me anything. You wouldn't share so much as that fucker's name with me. I had to—" He licked his sandpaper lips. "Fucking hell, Eli. I had no other choice. You're my girl, and I wanted to keep you safe."

A faintly ironic smile appeared on her face. "I get it." She paused as two cops walked past them to get in their cars. After they were gone, she stared at his forearm, at the still healing wounds, with a pained expression.

"Chief Chalker told me you were attacked by the dog that night. How did you—how did you get past that fuck-ing monster?"

"Oh, that." He gave her a sheepish smile. "I once saw a TV show where a guy pulled the front legs of the dog apart when it tried to bite him. I guess the idea is to collapse its ribcage. It took a while for me to work up the nerve, but it finally did the job." He lifted his arm up and glanced at the marks. He still saw that fucking dog in his sleep, charging at him, saliva dripping from its open jaws. He could still feel its canines clamping down and tearing chunks out of his flesh.

"Fuck, Max. I'm so sorry." She reached forward, seized him by his shoulders, then froze, as if having sec-ond thoughts.

Her action seemed to take both of them by surprise

so that they stared at each other for a few seconds before she threw her arms around his neck and hugged him hard.

"I've missed you, Max." There were tears in her eyes when she pulled back.

"Christ, baby, I've missed you, too. Like crazy."

He lifted himself off the ground, snaked an arm around her waist, and crushed his mouth to hers in a deep, possessive kiss. And dammit all, she kissed him back without reservation, with a searing passion that poured warmth into him. Love. Home. Wrapped in her arms, he truly felt he was home.

With a soft gasp, she broke the kiss, keeping her lips against his as she sucked in breaths.

"Max, I—"

She didn't say anything for a long moment. Christ, if she expected to shock him, she succeeded. The bottom dropped out of his stomach as he waited for her to finish the sentence. He could feel her bracing herself. He half expected her to say: "I'm sorry, but I can't do this."

But she didn't.

"Nothing has changed, Max. I'm still a fucking mess."

His throat tightened at the pain in her voice. Every muscle in his body went hot with fury.

Fucking Justin asshole Adams.

Clasping the back of her neck, he kissed her softly on her lips. "But you're *my* fucking mess." He kissed the corner of her mouth and hugged her close. "I love you, Eli, and if you still love me," he breathed into her mouth, "if you think you can forgive me, then I'm keeping you, baby. Forever."

The End.

About the Author

Elvi Joy lives in Down Under Australia with four extraordinary men in her life. She began her career in community services, assisting women who had suffered from domestic violence, before shifting her focus to writing. She's best known for her paranormal romances, and her blog which she has aptly named, "Ramblings of a crazy author." *REDEEM ME* is her debut novel in thriller category.